D0132400

"An intriguing novel of suspense as well as an evocative portrayal of the inner workings of a mind tormented by terror."
—Jonathan Kellerman, *New York Times* bestselling author

"Aaron Elkins delivers a mind-bending, heart-pounding read. Count me as a lifetime member of his fan club. I'm in awe."
—Ridley Pearson, *New York Times* bestselling author of *In Harm's Way*

"This is the kind of novel that gives genre fiction a good name—thanks to its high energy, smart characters, classy writing, palpable suspense, and one whopper of a surprise ending . . . Elkins is a crime fiction veteran known mainly for his Gideon Oliver series, but this may well be his best book. It's a joy to read."
—*Booklist*

"A well-calculated change of pace for normally laid-back Elkins, with mounting thrills, a heavy emphasis on self-therapy, and a nice surprise at the end." —*Kirkus Reviews*

"It starts with a memory of a horrendous kidnapping at age five . . . Crippling panic attacks and claustrophobia for decades sent him to therapy. He had experienced 'The Worst Thing' he ever would—or had he? Elkins's riveting, intricate thriller, rich with psychological insights, should win him his second Edgar® Award."
—Elizabeth Loftus, distinguished professor, University of California, Irvine; past president, Association for Psychological Science; and coauthor of *Witness for the Defense*

continued . . .

Praise for Aaron Elkins's Edgar® Award–Winning Gideon Oliver Mysteries

"Breezy . . . Fascinating . . . [It] dazzles."
—*The New York Times Book Review*

"A series that never disappoints." —*The Philadelphia Inquirer*

"First rate! Elegant, ingenious, and beautifully crafted."
—Sue Grafton

"Elkins is a master." —*The Dallas Morning News*

"Witty and oh so clever." —*New York Daily News*

"Aaron Elkins is one of the best in the business and getting better all the time; when his new book arrives I let the cats go hungry and put my own work on hold until I've finished it."
—Elizabeth Peters

"Aaron Elkins always tells a story that keeps the reader turning pages." —*The Denver Post*

"[An] intriguing mixture of forensic anthropology and real skull-duggery." —*Los Angeles Daily News*

"Atmospheric . . . A suspenseful puzzle." —*Publishers Weekly*

"Grips the audience . . . Filled with foreboding and thick suspense." —*Midwest Book Review*

Elkins, Aaron J.
The worst thing /

2011.
~~33~~
cu   01/31/13

The Worst Thing

AARON ELKINS

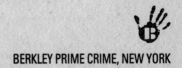

BERKLEY PRIME CRIME, NEW YORK

THE BERKLEY PUBLISHING GROUP
Published by the Penguin Group
Penguin Group (USA) Inc.
375 Hudson Street, New York, New York 10014, USA

Penguin Group (Canada), 90 Eglinton Avenue East, Suite 700, Toronto, Ontario M4P 2Y3, Canada (a division of Pearson Penguin Canada Inc.) • Penguin Books Ltd., 80 Strand, London WC2R 0RL, England • Penguin Group Ireland, 25 St. Stephen's Green, Dublin 2, Ireland (a division of Penguin Books Ltd.) • Penguin Group (Australia), 250 Camberwell Road, Camberwell, Victoria 3124, Australia (a division of Pearson Australia Group Pty. Ltd.) • Penguin Books India Pvt. Ltd., 11 Community Centre, Panchsheel Park, New Delhi—110 017, India • Penguin Group (NZ), 67 Apollo Drive, Rosedale, North Shore 0632, New Zealand (a division of Pearson New Zealand Ltd.) • Penguin Books (South Africa) (Pty.) Ltd., 24 Sturdee Avenue, Rosebank, Johannesburg 2196, South Africa

Penguin Books Ltd., Registered Offices: 80 Strand, London WC2R 0RL, England

This is a work of fiction. Names, characters, places, and incidents either are the product of the author's imagination or are used fictitiously, and any resemblance to actual persons, living or dead, business establishments, events, or locales is entirely coincidental. The publisher does not have any control over and does not assume any responsibility for author or third-party websites or their content.

THE WORST THING

A Berkley Prime Crime Book / published by arrangement with the author

PUBLISHING HISTORY
Berkley Prime Crime hardcover edition / May 2011
Berkley Prime Crime mass-market edition / August 2012

Copyright © 2011 by Aaron Elkins.
The Edgar® name is a registered service mark of the Mystery Writers of America, Inc.
Cover photos: *Eyeglasses and Blood on the Ice* © Image Souce; *Paved Road* by Ethan Welty/Aurora; *Road to Vatnajökull Icecap, Iceland* by Gavin Hellier/Robert World Imagery.
Cover design and image composite by Diana Kolsky.
Interior text design by Laura K. Corless.

All rights reserved.
No part of this book may be reproduced, scanned, or distributed in any printed or electronic form without permission. Please do not participate in or encourage piracy of copyrighted materials in violation of the author's rights. Purchase only authorized editions. For information, address: The Berkley Publishing Group,
a division of Penguin Group (USA) Inc.,
375 Hudson Street, New York, New York 10014.

ISBN: 978-0-425-25144-7

BERKLEY® PRIME CRIME
Berkley Prime Crime Books are published by The Berkley Publishing Group,
a division of Penguin Group (USA) Inc.,
375 Hudson Street, New York, New York 10014.
BERKLEY® PRIME CRIME and the PRIME CRIME logo are trademarks of
Penguin Group (USA) Inc.

PRINTED IN THE UNITED STATES OF AMERICA

10 9 8 7 6 5 4 3 2 1

If you purchased this book without a cover, you should be aware that this book is stolen property. It was reported as "unsold and destroyed" to the publisher, and neither the author nor the publisher has received any payment for this "stripped book."

ALWAYS LEARNING   **PEARSON**

Acknowledgments

It is a pleasure to acknowledge my debt to two eminent psychologists:

- The groundbreaking research of Dr. Elizabeth F. Loftus (Distinguished Professor of Social Ecology, and Professor of Law and Cognitive Science, University of California, Irvine) was the basis for key elements in the story. In addition, Dr. Loftus kindly reviewed and critiqued sections of the manuscript.

- Dr. John E. Carr (Professor Emeritus, Psychiatry and Behavioral Sciences and Psychology, University of Washington) helped me through problems of my own that were similar to (but not nearly as exciting as) the ones that Bryan Bennett runs into in the following pages, and provided many insights into the nature of panic.

In Iceland, Chief Superintendent Hördur Johannesson of the Reykjavik Police Department generously took the time to explain many aspects of Icelandic police procedure.

I also owe a good deal to the experiences and expertise of others as described in a number of books, chief among them:

- *Kidnap, Hijack, and Extortion*, by Richard Clutterbuck

- *Terrorism and Personal Protection*, edited by Brian Jenkins

- *Surviving the Long Night*, by Geoffrey Jackson

- *Winter of Fire*, by Richard Oliver Collen and Gordon L. Freedman

In addition, the members of tAPir (the Anxiety Panic internet resource group) helped me to explore the question: How do you think you would react if you were actually confronted with the situation that terrifies you more than any other—The Worst Thing you can imagine? Thanks for all the scary insights!

Chapter 1

The food had been wonderful, the wines had been excellent, and the crème brûlée was slipping down our throats like nectar from Valhalla. Wally, Lori, and I were all feeling relaxed, happy, and expansive. I knew it couldn't last, and it didn't.

Wally slid his unfinished dessert to one side and leaned earnestly forward. "Bryan, I have a proposition for you that I think you're going to love—that you're both going to love."

Well, that was when the alarm bells really started jangling. Actually, they'd been jingling quietly in the background ever since he'd offhandedly invited Lori and me to dinner at Café Campagne at Seattle's Pike Place Market. The ostensible reason was to celebrate our tenth wedding anniversary, February 23, 2010, but I knew Wally well enough to know that very little that he ever did was offhanded. There was always something behind it, and that's what had me worried.

It's not that I don't trust him, you understand. I do trust him. Sort of. Most of the time. I even like him most of the time. He's intelligent, quick-witted, and fun to joust with. That said, this is a guy you have to watch your step with.

"Somehow, I doubt it," I said.

"Now you just let me speak my piece before you say no," Wally said, reaching out to squeeze my shoulder encouragingly. The alarm bells got louder. "Just hear me out, that's all I ask."

"That sounds fair," I agreed, getting back to my crème brûlée. "Okay, I'll hear you out. *Then* I'll say no."

Wally laughed and winked at Lori. "Listen to him. You'd think I wanted something from him instead of offering him an assignment that anybody else would kill for."

Now, there was Wally in a nutshell, going out of his way to pretend that he was conning the hell out of you in order—he thought—to disguise the fact that he was in fact conning the hell out of you. You'd think it wouldn't work, but apparently it did. Wallace North, executive director of the Odysseus Institute for Crisis Management and Executive Security, had been a great success in doing what the board had hired him to do, which was to bring in more outside income. Wally is also my boss; I've been a research fellow at the institute for over nine years now, hard as that is to believe sometimes.

For seven of those nine years, the director had been the estimable Laura Hyzy, she of the unpronounceable name, a woman whose approach to life was very much in sync with my own. She'd been a social psychologist, a quiet, modest scholar, constitutionally averse to artifice and publicity. Her replacement, Wally, who had come out of the public relations department of a giant media conglomerate, lived for such things. I understood that Odysseus was in dire need of someone with Wally's skills, but I was having a hard time getting used to his style.

"How," he said, subjecting us to his most engaging and confident grin, "would the two of you like to spend a week in Iceland? The best hotel in Reykjavik?"

It was spoken in the same tone in which he might have said, "How would you like to spend a month in the South of France?" and it made me burst out laughing.

"A week in *Iceland*? In *February*? That's a deal that anyone would kill for?"

"In March, actually."

"Oh, in March, well, that's different. We'll be sure to pack our bathing suits and suntan lotion. Thanks all the same, Wally, but—"

But Lori was intrigued. "Why Iceland," she asked, "of all places?"

The check had come, and Wally paused to fish out a credit card and hand it to the waiter before he answered. "Because that's where GlobalSeas is, and they specifically asked for Bryan. Demanded him."

"GlobalSeas," Lori echoed, frowning. "Do you mean the fisheries company? The one that does all that research?"

"That's them. They're all over the world, of course, but their headquarters are in Reykjavik."

"And they specifically want Bryan?"

"Demanded him. The CEO himself, Baldursson. Bryan or no one. You're the deal-breaker, kid," he said to me.

"Demanded me for what?" Okay, I was curious; no harm in that. I wanted to know. Not that there was a ghost of a chance that I would take him up on it. I wasn't flying to Iceland. I wasn't flying anywhere.

"They want our corporate-level kidnapping and extortion seminar," Wally said.

"Well, then, how about Sandy Sechrest? She knows it inside out. She's done it a dozen times."

"Yes, but—"

"And Sandy's a terrific trainer. People connect with her. Don't let the gray hair fool you; she's a little dynamo."

"Yes, I know, but—"

"And she's from Wisconsin. She'll be right at home in Iceland."

Wally sighed. "I am aware of all that, Bryan, but, you see, she didn't write the program, you did. The thing is, GlobalSeas has had a little trouble in the past, and they want the expert himself, the man who *created* it. Face it, Bryan, you're our heavy hitter in this field."

"Well, that's flattering, but it's not in my job description. Creating programs is what I do. I don't put them on. Read my contract."

"I know that, Bryan. I'm asking you as a favor. A relationship with a company like this would mean a lot to us. Fisheries are a huge industry nowadays, and we don't have one single client in the business. Besides, these folks are counting on us—on you."

"Wally, honestly, I'm sorry to disappoint you, but it's out of the question. Forget it. I'm not going. No. N-O. Period." I laid my napkin on the table. "Look, thanks for a great dinner. This was—"

"Tell me, Lori," Wally said. "Why is it so hard to get a straight answer out of this man? Why won't he just up and say what he thinks? Is he always this mealymouthed, even at home?"

Lori laughed, hesitated, and said: "How come I got invited to go along? That seems a bit extravagant."

Wally saw what he thought was an opening and pounced. "That's the result of my famed negotiating prowess.

No, look, the truth is, they *really* want Bryan, they *need* Bryan, but they realize Iceland isn't exactly everybody's cup of tea—"

"Really?" I said. "I was under the impression people would kill for it. I may have been misinformed."

"—so they've been very generous with their offer. Not only would you get to go with him, sweetie, but they'd fly the two of you first class, put you up in a posh suite at the Hilton, give you a car to tool around in and, of course, a no-holds-barred expense account. And Bryan would be training only five days, Monday through Friday—four-and-a-half, really, since it starts with lunch Monday—and we'll throw in the weekend after, assuming you want it, for him to rest up from his mighty labors. Hell, we'll throw in the weekend before too. Lots to see there, they tell me—glaciers, waterfalls, geysers, huge thermal baths. And Reykjavik's supposed to be a great town. Great restaurants, great night-life. You'll have *fun!*" He finally took a breath. "Now somebody tell me, what am I missing? Is there something not to like here?"

Lori's warm, hazel eyes flickered down to the table. "Well, I was just asking. If Bryan's not going, there's really no point in talking about it."

"Bryan's not going," I said.

Wally shrugged in apparently affable defeat. The credit card bill had been placed before him and he signed without a glance, with his usual flourish. (This was on the institute, of course, and he was as good at spending their money as bringing it in.) "Well, I did my best. Look, Bryan, if you can possibly see your way to changing your mind, it'd really get me out of a bind. Think it over."

"Sorry, Wally."

A final no-hard-feelings shoulder clasp for me and a

friendly, smiling shrug to Lori. "Hope I haven't created any discord between my two favorite people."

"LIKE hell he does," I grumbled, flicking on the headlights and starting the car out of the parking garage and on its way to the I-5. I got the windshield wipers going too, almost automatically; standard practice on a February night in Seattle.

"Bryan, he doesn't know about—you know . . ." Lori placed her hand gently on my thigh. "And it doesn't matter anyway. Really."

But there was a resignation in the way she said it, an unvoiced sigh that burned my heart. Besides, I hadn't failed to notice her expression earlier, when she'd told Wally, "I was just asking." I covered her hand with mine. "He knows," I said, after a long, silent interval. "He may not know about the . . . the worst of it . . . but hell, he knows how I feel about actually *doing* training. He knows how I am about flying. God."

"But he doesn't know why," she said softly.

The windshield wipers whished back and forth—*beat, beat*—before I answered. "No, he doesn't know why."

"Anyway," she said, "there's not much point in talking about it, is there? It doesn't matter." This time the sigh was audible. She stared out the window into the wet night.

"But he does know you'd love the chance to see some of what GlobalSeas is doing up there," I said after a few more strokes of the wiper blades. "Why else do you think he waited for tonight, when you were with me, to bring it up?"

She looked at me. "Why would he be so sure I'd be interested in GlobalSeas?"

"Because he knows you're a marine ecologist. He knows you're a consultant to the aquarium; he knows you've written about aquaculture and sustainable marine harvesting and that kind of thing."

"How would he know that? I never—"

"Trust me, he knows. He also knows you've got a couple of weeks' vacation coming. Wally does his research on things like that."

"Well, even so, it doesn't necessarily mean I'm dying to see GlobalSeas."

We were on the Woodinville-Redmond Road now, on the other side of Lake Washington, out in the sticks well east of Seattle, heading south toward home. "Aren't you?" I asked.

There was a long moment's silence. "Not dying, no."

"But you'd like to see it."

Another pause. "Well, naturally, but so what? There are a lot of things I'd like to do. Ah, well." She gave me a big smile, took her hand from my thigh and went back to looking out into the darkness. "Bryan, honestly, it doesn't matter."

But I was unable to let it alone. "There's nothing stopping you from going by yourself, babe. I wouldn't mind, you know that. We can afford it."

"I don't want to go by myself. I want to go with my husband." She turned suddenly toward me. "Oh, Bryan, I want the fun of . . . of . . ."

"Lori . . . honey . . . if I could do something about it I would, believe me."

I barely heard her murmured reply, delivered to the dark windshield beside her. "Would you?"

Chapter 2

W^{ould I?}

Even at the best of times I'm not much of a sleeper, and when something is worrying at me I'll toss for hours until restlessness, discontent, or plain boredom drives me from bed into my study to read or to work, or, if the weather isn't too bad, out onto the back deck of the house, where the fresh scents and the hollow, hooting night sounds from the lake—geese, ducks, an occasional owl on its midnight hunt—generally soothe me back to sleepiness, or at least makes being awake tolerable.

We had bought the house off West Lake Sammamish Parkway (or W L*k* S*amm* P*kwy*, as the cost-efficient street signs put it) in 2000, when we were married. Redmond had still been a relatively sleepy little town then, well away from the influence of booming Seattle. The house was about sixty years old, a simple, gray-shingled structure on a pleasant grassy acre that sloped down to the lake, probably built originally as a weekend retreat, one of a row of similar places that lined the shore. In the ten years since we'd moved in, Redmond had come into its own as a super-hot place to live; being headquarters for Microsoft hadn't hurt property values. Many of the longtime owners had sold, and the buyers—newly rich Microsofties, usually—had promptly torn down the old, perfectly serviceable weekend houses and put up huge new mansions complete with gorgeous docks, sailboats, cruisers, and boathouses.

As a result, our house, once about average, now comprised the low-rent district of the neighborhood. Moored to our dock, instead of the usual handsome, tethered sailboat or cruiser, were a couple of battered plastic Necky kayaks.

But the ducks and the geese and the soft lapping of the water in the dark were as lovely as they'd always been. At a quarter past two, unable to make my brain quit churning, I'd given up on sleep, gotten quietly out of bed so as not to disturb Lori, slipped a parka on over my pajamas, gone out onto the deck, and turned on the light. The rain was still misting down, but I found a dry lounge chair under the roof overhang, pulled it within the small, friendly circle of illumination, and sank into it. Annoyed by my presence, a flock of mallards sleeping on the shore below clacked and squabbled for a few minutes but soon resettled themselves. I lay in the chair, my parka zipped up to the neck, fingering a thin file folder and thinking.

Would I?

I had a belief, not formed from books but from personal experience, that each life has a defining moment, an episode that shapes and colors, for good or ill, all that follows. It might come early or relatively late. It could be calamitous or outwardly trivial: an unjust punishment in grade school, a parent's death, involvement in a war, a disastrous prom date, a lost love, a failed business. Sometimes the person recognizes it for what it is but it will do its work just as well without being identified or understood.

About my own defining moment I had no doubt. It had come early—more than thirty years ago, when I was five years old—and it had been calamitous. Almost everything that I was, the good and the bad, derived from it. Could I indeed go back now, after so many years, and somehow "do something about it," reprogram myself into someone else?

If so, it wouldn't be the first time I'd tried. Fifteen years ago, when I'd hit one of my lowest points, I had gone to a highly reputed psychiatrist but had quit after three sessions, finding the psychiatric theories and explanations either wildly baroque or naively simplistic. The one useful thing that had come out of them had been the narrative of the incident that the psychiatrist, Sky Benson, had asked me to write. The idea, Dr. Benson explained, was that the act of setting it down on paper might enable me to separate myself from the experience and so move on with my life. That hadn't come close to working, but I'd kept my essay and had read it many times since, sometimes with a perverse gratification, basking in the fascination of bygone horrors, but most often for the reassurance of knowing that I had indeed lived through it, that I had come through alive and whole—or at least relatively whole—and if I could survive that, what couldn't I survive? It was that narrative that was in the folder on my lap now.

I looked up at the thin, luminescent clouds and at the hazy, shimmering moon sailing behind them, took a breath, opened the folder, and began to read.

In the winter of 1978, when I was five years old, I was kidnapped from the children's play area behind the Pera Palace Hotel in Istanbul. I had been playing with my seven-year-old brother, Richard, under the eye of a guard from my father's company, when four gunmen burst onto the scene, pulling me from the slide, brushing Richard aside, and shooting our guard to death. A chloroformed rag was clamped over my face, and I was thrown into a waiting car. At the outskirts of the city, semiconscious and hysterical, I was stuffed into a potato sack and transferred to a farm truck in which, under a load of manure, I was taken to an isolated house in a remote farming village near the Bulgarian border.

My kidnappers demanded a $5-million ransom from my father's employer, Driscoll Construction Enterprises, a Los Angeles–based company then engaged in repairing and extending the military runways at the Istanbul Ataturk Airport. Despite the frantic pleas of my parents, the firm's board of directors held back, and in the end the kidnappers accepted a ransom of $250,000, $75,000 of which was personally raised by my father, the project's on-site engineering superintendent.

For this they waited fifty-eight days and nights, during which time I was kept in an unheated, six-by-six-foot underground cell, the rough stone walls of which streamed with moisture and glistened with cockroaches. The furnishings, from beginning to end, consisted of a plank bed bolted to the wall, two blankets, a gallon jug of water sporadically refilled, and a plastic bucket.

My largely silent captors, with their frightening, eye-slitted black hoods, seemingly had but one English phrase: "Shut up." And even that they rarely used. My food needs were handled by means of a tray placed in the six-inch-high space at the bottom of the heavy wire-mesh door, so that I had to go down on my hands and knees to get it, and I generally wolfed it down on the concrete floor, except for the many, many times when I was too ill or too sick at heart to eat. The menu consisted

*of porridge, rice, root vegetables, and various uniden-
tifiable soups, with an occasional gobbet of chicken or
something like chicken. No utensils, no napkins. And
always bananas, so that by the time I was freed all I had
to do to throw up was to look at one. How often they fed
me, or how regularly, I never knew. Because there were
no windows and the light was left on twenty-four hours
a day, I had no way of distinguishing day from night, let
alone one hour from another.*

*Elimination needs were taken care of by the plastic
bucket, which was sometimes emptied in the morning,
and sometimes not. When it overflowed or got too smelly
the guard on duty, who naturally would have preferred
leaving it for the next shift, usually got angry about it
and I quickly learned to scuttle under the bed whenever
the door was swung open, so that cuffing me around
required more trouble than it was worth.*

*When I was "bad" I was screamed at, threatened,
slapped around a little, and shackled to my bed, sometimes with a chain around my ankle and sometimes by
a metal collar locked around my neck.*

The need for bathing wasn't handled at all.

*As proof that they had me and that they meant busi-
ness, the little toe of my left foot was mailed to my parents about a week after they got me. Thank God, I have
no memory of their actually doing it, so probably I was
chloroformed again. I hope so.*

*When I was released on the fifty-ninth day, still in
what was left of the clothes I'd been wearing when they
took me, doctors found two dozen ulcerating sores on my
body as a result of malnutrition and poor hygiene. I had
lost nine pounds—more than twenty percent of my body
weight—I had gum abscesses, infections in both eyes,
and a raging case of dysentery. I was too weak to walk.*

It was the day before my sixth birthday.

Dr. Benson had wanted me to write more, setting down my recollections of the aftermath, but by then I had lost confidence in the whole thing. Besides, my memories of the next few months were jumbled and blurry, too confused to put on paper in a coherent way. There were dimly recalled doctors and a hospital stay during which the rough-and-ready surgery that the kidnappers had done on my foot was repaired to the extent that anything could be done. My parents refused to openly discuss the abduction in my presence (although, like any kid, I picked up plenty of inferences in their conversations that they assumed I couldn't possibly decipher) and slowly, slowly, the terrible memories had been laid to rest and covered over.

It was the agitated honking of a flight of low-flying Canadian geese that woke me; that and the welcome, unexpected warmth of the sun clearing the firs on the far shore of the lake and glinting off the water and into my eyes. The file lay beside me on the wet deck. It was about seven-thirty a.m., I judged; I'd fallen asleep and been outside for more than five hours, and although my hair was dewy and my face and my bare feet chilled, I was otherwise cozy and relaxed in my parka, not yet ready to move, and still inclined to reflection.

Laid to rest and covered over; was that the way I'd put it to myself during the night? Not quite, I thought now, closing my eyes again for the pleasure of feeling the sun on my eyelids. Covered over, yes. Laid to rest, well, not exactly. The bodily lesions had healed with no ill effect beyond a slight hitch in my stride, unnoticeable except when I was tired, but the mental wounds were a different story.

Now thirty-seven, I still suffered from sporadic nighttime panic attacks. Always the same: I would wake up with a strangled yell, thinking that I was back in that Turkish dungeon with that chain around my neck. That would start the whole megillah: heart racing, overwhelming, indescribable terror, and all the rotten rest of it. For these, always at the ready in my bedside table there was a bottle of Xanax, which brought me back to sanity inside of three or four minutes. Without them, the panic could go on for an hour or more before it wore itself (and me) out.

I even had a small vial that I carried with me when I was away from home. My motto, I sometimes joked with the very few people who knew about it, was "Don't leave home without it."

I also had a continuing horror of being trapped in confined places, one of the effects of which was that it was impossible to get me onto an airplane without drugging me up to my eyeballs. And even then you'd have to fight me. Getting me onto a train or a boat was possible (but not easy) because there was at least the hypothetical possibility that one could leap from a moving train or boat if necessary and hope to live. Cars were much the same, although when I was at the wheel there was no problem at all; I was able to tell myself that I was in control, so that if things got to be too much for me I could always switch off the engine and get out.

There were other, more trivial things. Nobody loves cockroaches, but I positively loathed them. If an Orkin commercial came on the TV, I got up and left the room. About bananas I was better than I used to be. Being in the same room with one no longer bothered me, but if someone started to peel one in my presence, I found an excuse to go and do something somewhere else. The smell of burlap made my stomach tense up, and my routes to and from work were chosen to avoid as much as possible the smell of manure from local farms.

Oh, I almost forgot. I also lived with the conviction, the certain conviction, that somehow, somewhere, I was going to get myself kidnapped again. It was simply in the cards, that's all. The gods had it in for me, and there was nothing I could do about it. For a while I even carried a gun to fight my attackers off. But, finally, having read and reread the statistical probability of being kidnapped for ransom in the United States (one in one-and-a-half million), I convinced myself to stop carrying it on the grounds that doing so was paranoid, and I wasn't paranoid.

Besides, if it was in the cards, what good was a gun supposed to do me?

Despite these little, ahem, idiosyncrasies, I considered myself a reasonably sane, reasonably capable human being, even brave where physical courage or endurance were required, and generally able to cope with daily life pretty much as well as anyone else. Long ago I had come up with a mental process in which I could usually put my various mental quirks into an imaginary box, close the lid, shove the box in a drawer, and slam the drawer shut. They were there, all right, and never very far away, but they were a separate, walled-off part of my life. "That's the nutcase part," I'd once explained to Lori. "That's the ten percent of me that's certifiable. But the other ninety percent is one hundred percent functional."

I believed it too. With a little care, after all, how hard was it to keep clear of manure and bananas? And as long as I didn't leave the United States, there wasn't anywhere I couldn't get by means of a train or a car. As for the occasional unavoidable crisis or those nighttime screaming meemies, there was always the Xanax.

Certainly, I had as active a social life as did most men in their thirties, plus a few close friends. I'd been married to Lori, joyfully so, for a decade. And I successfully held down not one but two steady, responsible jobs. I was a senior research fellow at the Odysseus Institute, at which I specialized in issues relating to kidnapping and extortion. I was also a one-course-a-year adjunct professor of management at the University of Washington, where my specialty was the development of corporate crisis management and security policies.

Which, on the face of it, posed the great paradox of my life: How could anybody with the mental hang-ups I had, especially someone with my particular history, choose to continue to have anything to do with extortionists and kidnappers? Why in heaven's name would I want to? Even I couldn't say for certain, but Lori's theory was that my abduction had left me with some extremely heavy baggage to lug around, but also with a compulsive interest in, or perhaps even an obsession (her term) with, kidnapping, extortion, and captivity. That is, I was scared to death of anything to do with them, but fascinated at the same time.

It made sense to me. My work at the university and the institute was a way to satisfy the fascination and avoid the fear. I wrote policy papers, I did research, I prepared course lectures and training materials; but it was all from a theoretical, safely removed vantage point. What I could not do, would not even try to bring myself to do, was to participate directly in hostage negotiations, victim-counseling, or anything else that required actually dealing with kidnappers, hostage-takers, or their victims. That would have been getting too close; a lesson I'd learned the hard way. Even *talking* about the subject—as opposed to writing about it, which was more removed, more abstract—was something I stayed clear of. Hence, my running screaming from putting on that training program, even though I'd written it myself.

Well, I said it made sense to me. I didn't say it would make sense to you.

"Hiya, Shep, how's it going this morning, buddy?" I said,

offering my hand for nuzzling when the elderly golden lab came slowly through the dog door from the kitchen and made his arthritic way across the deck. He was having hip problems now, and his back legs weren't working as well as they once did. The silvered muzzle nestled in my palm for a few moments before he settled stiffly down on the deck with an aged sigh. I stroked the soft ears and let my hand hang down over the side of the chair so he could lay his snout on it the way he liked to when he dozed off. After his rough tongue scoured my palm a couple of times, he settled his jaw securely into its hollow, snuffled like the ancient he was, and went peacefully to sleep beside his master.

I'd been collecting myself to get up and brew some coffee, but now dropped the idea, unwilling to disturb Shep's repose by moving my hand. Amazing, when you thought about it. Here I was, a grown man—with a PhD, no less— who was yearning for a cup of coffee, but who, rather than going to get it, sat there motionless instead, with his hand lying somewhat uncomfortably on the deck, palm up, so that he wouldn't disturb the dog who was resting his snout on it. Now *that* was really crazy. After a while I must have dropped off again, because it seemed to me that Lori had materialized out of nowhere to stand by my chair.

"Oh, Bryan, you haven't been out here all night, have you?"

"I guess I have, honey; most of it. I must have fallen asleep without meaning to."

"Is everything all right? Nothing's the matter, is it?"

"Everything's fine. I just couldn't turn my mind off, that's all. Just one of those nights."

"You're sure you're okay?" I hated to hear the concern in her voice. Did I really seem skittish enough that last night's session with Wally might have set me off on a nighttime "episode" of some kind? Maybe I was more of a nutcase than I thought.

"I'm sure. In fact, I could hardly be more comfortable. It's beautiful out here this morning, isn't it? Feel that sun."

"Mmm. It's wonderful after all that rain. Coffee?"

"Please. How would you feel about brewing up a pot and coming out here and having it with me? It's Saturday, no jobs to run off to."

"You're on. Come on, Shep. Morning biscuit time for you."

The magic word got the old guy on his feet and off he shuffled after her. Shep was coming to the end of his years now. It was going to be hard when the time came, when the pain in those corroded old joints got to be too much for him and for us, and we had to put him down. I hated thinking about that day. He'd been with us such a long while; with *me* right from the beginning.

In a few minutes Lori was back with the coffeepot and a couple of mugs on a tray and with Shep trailing along behind her, one end of a bone-shaped biscuit sticking out each side of his mouth. She handed one of the mugs to me and looked around for another chair.

I shifted my legs off the lounge chair, sat up, and moved to one side to make room for her, and she sat down and poured our coffees. Shep, who liked to be close to us when he ate, sank grunting to the deck at our feet. His once-mighty jaws clamped on the biscuit and the two ends broke off and fell onto the deck. Unconcerned, knowing they were safe, he chewed placidly on the middle part. Lori stretched with a sigh, her eyes closed, her lovely face turned up to the sun. Just looking at the graceful curve of her throat and chin made the day a good one already.

I looked at her with affection. *I love you*, I thought. *Ten*

*years. We are actually getting to be an old married couple,
the way we used to say we would, and it's not so bad, is it?*

She opened her eyes. "You're looking at me."

"Why shouldn't I look at you? You're beautiful."

"Because a gentleman would wait until a lady has had a
chance to put on some makeup and do something about her
hair before he looks at her."

"You look terrific," I told her sincerely.

She smiled. "You're prejudiced."

"Damn right. Listen, I've been thinking."

"Oh?"

"Well, it occurs to me—" But the words stuck in my
throat. It took more effort than I'd expected to force them
out. "It . . . it occurs to me that that Iceland assignment
might be fun after all. What the hell, what do you say we
go ahead and do it?"

She was so astonished, it made me laugh. "I mean, what's
the big deal anyway?" I said.

"But—are you sure? The flight . . ."

I shrugged. "I'll take a couple of Xanax. Or maybe a
sleeping pill so I'm zonked out the whole time."

"All things considered," she said. "I think a sleeping pill
might be better." She squeezed my hand. Her eyes were
shining. "Bryan—thank you."

I squeezed back. Deep inside my chest, something
glowed.

THERE had been a time, long ago, back when Shep had
been a furry little ball of a puppy tripping over his too-big
feet, when it wouldn't have taken all this ridiculously agoniz-
ing dithering to come to a decision like this. *You want to go
to Iceland?* I'd have said. *Great, sounds like fun, let's go.*

Back then, I'd come to think that I could face my demons more directly than one does from a university classroom or a think-tank desk. I was twenty-seven years old, with a newly minted PhD, eager to do good in the world and under the impression that the horrors of my childhood captivity were safely buried at last. Freshly armed with that doctorate in labor relations and crisis management, I had joined the Crisis Intervention Center at the University of Southern California as a consultant, and there I became a much-sought-after hostage negotiator, and even something of a celebrity, taking part in seven incidents and bringing about the release of more than a dozen hostages with only a single loss of life—that of a hostage-taker, bent on suicide from the start, who had more or less forced the police to gun him down.

I was the one who secured the release of Leslie Goldwin, the fifteen-year-old grandson of Linda Smith Rutledge, the dynamic president of Le Sport Cosmetics. I was even the one who came up with the plan that resulted in the recovery of all but four hundred dollars of the $1.25 million ransom money, and the capture of the three kidnappers. Two of them could hardly wait to turn state's evidence against the supposed "mastermind," a part-time teacher at the boy's private school, who was convicted after a two-day trial and a single hour's deliberation.

That had been the high point of my career, or at least the most celebrated. The low point, the debacle of the Houghey twins, had followed close on its heels, less than a month later.

Chapter 3

Irwin Houghey had been a Hollywood television producer known for a couple of long-running police series on NBC. Among insiders, he was also known as one autocratic, nit-picking sonofabitch. A year or so earlier, in one of his on-set tantrums, he had humiliated and fired on the spot a middle-aged assistant director who had neglected to pencil in five needed extras on the morning call for a complex shoot that had taken most of the night to set up.

The fired assistant director, Stanley Auerbach, had been unable to find other TV work and had spiraled into an alcohol-fueled decline, spending two terms in jail, almost back-to-back, first on a drunk-driving charge coupled with resisting arrest, and then for threatening his girlfriend and her baby daughter with a rifle, an episode that ended with a forty-minute police standoff. Not long after his second release, on a warm September morning twenty-two months after he'd been fired, he had walked into the Longworth School on Laurel Canyon Boulevard, unkempt and incoherent, with a Glock semiautomatic .40-caliber pistol in his left hand and a short-barreled, pump-action Mossberg shotgun cradled in the crook of his right arm. He had terrified the students, firing one pellet blast into the ceiling and using the butt of the revolver to smash the cheekbone of the assistant principal who'd confronted him. Inside of five minutes he had driven off with Casey and Corey Houghey, the nine-year-old twin daughters of Irwin Houghey, thrown screaming into the rear of his van.

The Los Angeles Police Department responded quickly. By two o'clock in the afternoon, laden with leads, they had caught up with him. He was holding the girls in an abandoned agricultural workers' shack, bereft of window panes and door, in an old celery field near the southeastern limits of the city, a few hundred yards from the Long Beach Freeway. I was brought in to assist.

I found the police surrounding the shack in efficient, by-the-book fashion. There was a manned outer perimeter about two hundred yards from the shack, through which only law enforcement people, other response personnel, and one or two informally approved media people were permitted. Then a sort of no-man's land where there was a lot of cigarette smoking and milling around, and finally, about ninety feet from the shack, the inner perimeter: a circle of a dozen uniformed, body-armored officers, some with rifles, hunkered down behind their cars. This was the tactical team—the sharpshooters and apprehension specialists who would make the assault, if an assault became necessary. Having satisfactorily identified myself to a guard at the outer perimeter, I was fitted out with a flak jacket and taken to the mobile command post, an air-conditioned RV-like truck that sat just beyond the inner perimeter, armored with steel plate and crammed with communication and scanning equipment.

Detective Lieutenant Ed Reese, a burly, red-faced man seated with a sergeant at a table that folded out from the wall, looked up from a roughly penciled diagram. "And you are?"

"I'm Bryan Bennett, Lieutenant. I'm—"

"Yeah, chief told us they called you in." He stood and offered a callused hand. "So, you going to give us some advice here, or what?"

"Advice, yes, if you want it, but actually, what I generally do is to more or less handle the negotiations part of it—if that's all right with you."

I was being properly deferential here. Police officers aren't known for tolerating civilian interference on their turf, and I was walking on eggshells. Ordinarily, the police used their own trained personnel for hostage negotiations, but LAPD was trying something new. I was there as part of an experimental—and controversial—program in which the police department had contracted with the USC Crisis Intervention Center to bring in people like me to deal with particularly sensitive situations. The idea behind it was to separate the negotiator from the police in the mind of the hostage-taker. Still, there was only one person in charge, and that was the designated incident commander, Lieutenant Ed Reese.

"Hell, yeah," he said. "We can use all the help we can get. Only there's nothing to negotiate. Creep hasn't asked for anything."

"Oh, there's always something to negotiate, it can just take a while. Fill me in on what's been happening, will you? Are the girls all right?"

"Yeah, we can hear them every now and then. They sound okay. I mean, they're weepy, but there's no sign he's hurting them."

"Good. He's not making threats?"

"Nope. He just sits in there. But he's armed. A shotgun and a handgun, a semiautomatic. He took a couple of wild shots at us a while back, but I don't know how serious he was. He's real spacey, lah-de-dah. Besides which, he's crazy to begin with. You know that, don't you?"

"So I hear. What about demands?"

"Nothing. We don't know what the hell he wants. I don't think he knows. We ask him and he yells back to shut up, he's trying to think. So I figure the best thing is to wait him out. If we get any sense he's hurting the kids we'll rush him, but so far they seem okay."

"Good, that makes sense. How are you communicating with him?"

Reese laughed. "Who's communicating? But we've been trying with a bullhorn. You want to give it a try?" He reached behind him to offer it.

"No, thanks." At this point the thing I needed to do was to build some rapport with Auerbach to get him talking. And if there was any way to establish rapport with a bullhorn, no one had yet figured it out. "How about a portable phone? Do you have one?"

"Oh yeah, take your choice. We got a throw phone right here. A thousand feet of wire and all the bells and whistles. We got an Army field—"

"The throw phone will be fine. You haven't tried to get it in to him?"

"Yeah, we tried. That's when he took his potshots."

"Hey, you cops!" It was Auerbach, his voice cracked and reedy, yelling from the shack. Everyone stiffened.

"This is something new," Reese said.

"It's damn hot in here," Auerbach yelled. "How about something cold to drink?"

"Do you have anything to give them?" I asked the lieutenant.

Reese gestured with his chin. "The fridge over there is full of stuff."

"Can't see him," one of the nearby cops said. "He's not at either of the windows. He can see us, though. Lots of cracks between the boards."

"Somebody better answer me!" Auerbach called. "I'm telling you."

"Let's go talk to him," I said. "Closer, where it's easier."

Reese shrugged, and he, the sergeant, and I all got out of the truck, keeping low to the ground, and dropped to our knees beside one of the police cars, where we could peer over the hood and see the shack.

"Okay if I answer him?" I asked Reese.

"Be my guest."

"Mr. Auerbach!" I yelled. "My name is Bryan Bennett. I'm not a policeman, sir, I'm a negotiator, and from now on I'll be the one you'll be talking to."

"Like I'm supposed to give a shit what your name is? Just get us something to drink in here."

The *us* could be a positive indicator, I thought. If it meant that Auerbach was concerned about the girls, thinking of them as something more than objects—as human beings—that was good, a really good sign.

Or it could mean absolutely nothing. "Well, here goes," I murmured.

I stood up slowly, in plain sight now, brushing the lieutenant's restraining hand from my sleeve. Over the years I'd developed a pretty good sense of when a situation was risky and when it wasn't. And this one wasn't, not yet. Auerbach hadn't shot anyone at the school, after all. In any case, I was wearing body armor, and the chances of Auerbach being able to hit me in the head, or anywhere else for that matter, with a handgun were remote. As for the shotgun, at this distance the pellet spread would be too thin to do me much damage, or so I hoped.

"Well, I understand that, sir," I called, "and I think we can arrange that."

"I don't believe this," I heard one of the cops mutter to his partner. I knew what was bothering him. I was being too polite with this dangerous psycho. But my agenda was different from the police's. I had to get on Auerbach's good side; they didn't.

"But you'll have to make a deal for it," I shouted. "That's the way we work things."

This brought on a hoarse laugh of disbelief. "I'm not making any deal. What are you, stupid? These kids die of thirst, it's on your head, man."

I had placed where his voice was coming from by now. Auerbach was to the right of the doorless entry, probably in the corner, low to the floor. Chances were he was peering between the loose boards down there. "Don't you want to hear what the deal is?"

"No. Fuck you. All you want to do is kill me, you think I don't know that?"

"That's not true, Mr. Auerbach, but if you're not in the mood for a deal now, let's forget it. We can talk about it later." I settled back down behind the car.

"Yeah, you can talk to yourself about it," Auerbach yelled.

"You know, those kids probably do need something to drink," Reese said. "What's the problem with giving them something? Why do we need to make a deal for that?"

"Don't worry, we'll get them their drinks. Look, Lieutenant, what we have to do is make him understand that anything he wants, he has to negotiate for. He doesn't get anything from us unless he gives us something in return. He has to work for everything he gets. Otherwise, he'll start feeling as if he's the one holding all the cards. And that's when things really get dangerous."

"Yeah, like they're not dangerous now. But what do we get from him in return? You think maybe he might let one of the girls go?"

"Too early for that, I think. But—"

"What kind of deal?" Auerbach shouted, and I stood up again, my hands held out from my sides so he could see that they were empty.

"Mr. Auerbach, nobody here wants to kill you. I'd really like to talk to you, just you and me, because I think we can work something out, but we can't do it this way. I'd like you to let us put a telephone in there. Then we can talk, just the two of us. My job here is to help you out if I can. Really, I think we might be able to work something out."

Auerbach hooted, *hee-hee, ho-ho*. He sounded crazy, all right. I got down behind the hood of the car again.

Auerbach was quick to take it as a sign of weakness. "Hey, old buddy, you don't need a telephone. Just come on right in and set right down. We can talk right here, just you and me."

"No, I'm not ready to do that yet. I'm trying to establish a little trust here. So, what do you say? We deliver a six-pack of ice-cold Cokes, and in return you let us put a portable phone in there."

There was no answer.

"What do you say?"

"Do you have Pepsi?" Auerbach asked.

"I'll be damned," the lieutenant said.

I looked at Reese, who looked at the sergeant, who shook his head. "Coke, root beer, and Dr Pepper."

"Sorry," I called. "Coke, root beer, or Dr Pepper."

"Okay, Coke." There was a pause. They could just hear the choky, complaining voices of the girls and a hissed "Shut up!" from Auerbach. Then: "And one Dr Pepper. Listen, what do they have to do to get this phone here? I'm not letting anybody inside."

"No, it's just a handset on a line—you know, pretty much like a regular telephone with a wire back to here. Whenever you feel like talking to me, you just pick it up, and I'll be on the other end. Tell you what. We'll put the drinks and the phone down right by the door and then back off. If you don't like the idea of getting them yourself, you can hold on to one of the girls and let her bring them in."

"How do I know there's no bomb in it, or gas, or something?"

"Do you think we'd risk hurting the kids?"

There was a pause. "Okay, you can bring the phone, but don't expect me to talk on it."

"Is that okay with you, Lieutenant?" I asked.

"What makes you think he won't start shooting again if somebody goes out there with it?"

"Because he wants the drinks, and he wants to trust me. I think it's safe. I'll be glad to take them to him."

Reese rolled his eyes. "Oh, right, that's all I need, getting a civilian killed. No, thanks. Pender here'll do it."

"Oh, hey, thanks a million, Lieutenant," the officer in question said.

Back in the truck, Reese got out the telephone set, a high-tech assemblage of equipment packed into its own fitted case, with headsets for me, himself, and one other person; a tape-recording device; and a hidden, voice-activated microphone in the ordinary-looking receiver that would go to Auerbach. Once it was inside they would be able to continuously monitor what was going on in the shack.

"I sure as hell hope you don't object to snooping on him," Reese said, getting the components out of the case. "Because if you do, then you and me might have a difference of opinion."

"No, I don't object. The more we know about what's happening in there the better."

"Remember, I'm watching you," Auerbach shouted. "You hear this kid crying? That's because she's got a gun stuck in her ear. Don't do anything stupid."

"Let's nobody do anything stupid," I called back.

Pender, slipping on a protective helmet and face piece in addition to his body armor, guardedly made his way toward the shack, a six-pack filled with five Cokes and one Dr Pepper in one hand and Auerbach's receiver, trailing wire from a spool in the truck, in the other. A cop—a sharpshooter with a telescopic-sight-equipped rifle, raised himself up slightly, the barrel of the rifle propped on a small tripod on the hood of a police car and trained on the doorway.

The delivery went without incident. The six-pack and the telephone were left in the doorway, the policeman retreated, and Auerbach, or perhaps one of the girls, used a jointed piece of pipe to drag them into the shack and out of sight. The sharpshooter hunkered down behind the car again.

"Nobody's saying anything," said the officer tuned to the microphone that was now in the shack. "The sound's not real good, but I can hear them popping the cans. "Wait . . . one of the kids says she has to pee. He's telling her: tough, he does too . . . she's starting to whimper . . . he says, 'Oh, for Christ's sake, do it in your pants.' Now she's bawling, and he's cussing."

"How do you make this thing ring in there?" I asked. I was at the table with Reese now, with one of the headsets clamped over my ears and the attached mike beside my lips.

"He just said he wouldn't talk," Reese said.

"They say all kinds of things. No harm in finding out."

Reese flicked something in the case and I heard a staccato

buzz in the headset. A second later Auerbach's voice was in my ears. "Hello?"

"Hi there, Mr. Auerbach, this is Bryan Bennett again. How are things in there?"

"Doing just fine, great. Couldn't be better. Happy little family."

"How are the Cokes? Cold enough?"

No answer.

"Look, do you mind if I call you Stanley? You can call me Bryan."

"What do you want?"

"Well, it occurred to me, maybe you might like a cold beer for yourself. I think I can probably arrange that too."

"Yeah, sure," said Auerbach. "You could also just arrange to put something in it to knock me out."

My estimation of him went up a notch. *Damn right I would*, I thought. Drugging drink or food was something that you didn't ordinarily do because the hostages might wind up consuming it. But would Auerbach be sharing his beer with a couple of nine-year-olds? I didn't think so. In any case, it wasn't an option now.

"Stanley, listen to me. I want you to know that everything is going to come out all right. You've done a great job of keeping things under control in there so far. You haven't hurt the kids, and that's going to make it a whole lot easier to wind this up without anybody *getting* hurt."

"Bullshit. You're going to kill me. I'm going to die right here in this shitty shack. But I'm not going out alone."

That was the second time Auerbach had talked about dying, and I didn't like it. I began to worry that I might have a suicide ritual under way, that what Auerbach might have in mind—maybe consciously, maybe not—was his own death at the hands of the police. And that presented a terrible danger to the girls.

"Stanley, you couldn't be more wrong. Believe me, I want you to come out of this in one piece. That's the only reason I'm here."

"Yeah, you, maybe," Auerbach said grudgingly. "But those damn cops . . ."

"I can take care of the cops, you don't have to worry about the cops. But you have to work with me, Stanley, you have to trust me. Believe me, everything's not as hopeless as it seems. Look, I know the way it feels when you're down—"

"What'd you say your name was?"

"Bryan."

"And you're what again?"

"I'm a negotiator. I work for the USC Crisis Intervention Center, not the police. I have only one job, and that's to work with you, to negotiate the best possible—"

"Yeah, well, listen, Bryan, I don't want to talk anymore right now. I'm pretty upset."

"I can understand that, Stanley, but if you tell me what the problem is, I bet there's something I can do about it. You'd be amazed—"

But Auerbach had hung up on me. I took off the headset and rubbed my ear where it had pinched. "I'm worried he might be suicidal," I said.

"Good, what can we do to help him along?" Reese answered.

"Well, I don't think—"

"I used to work in a town outside of Oklahoma City. You know what we did when some nut threatened to jump off a freeway overpass during rush hour? You think we stood around futzing with him? We put an inflatable mattress down underneath and pushed him off. Most of the time, they hit the mattress and we hauled their asses off. Sometimes they missed. Either way, traffic got moving again in a hurry."

I smiled in spite of myself. "Believe me, if we could manage something like that here, I'd go for it. But in this kind of thing we get a big leg up once he decides for good that he wants to live." I fitted the headset back on. "I'm going to try him again."

"Try what?" Reese said with some impatience. "What's the point? You can't do anything for the guy. It sounds like you're just dragging things out."

"I am dragging things out, Lieutenant. Time's on our side here. At this point he's not rational."

"Obviously, but what gives you the idea he's gonna *get* rational?"

"Maybe he won't, but right now he's scared too, and all pumped up. Let a few hours pass and that can change, especially if I can keep him on the line and get him to do some venting. He'll start wanting more stuff too—food, cigarettes, a fan, maybe; it's going to get hotter in there as the afternoon wears on. That all works in our favor. He'll get tired, he'll get sick of just sitting around."

"I guess so," Reese said rolling his head around to limber up his neck. "I know I'm sick of it—and we've got air-conditioning."

"And there's one other thing," I said. "As long as he's talking, we know he's not busy harming the kids."

"Point taken," said Reese. "Okay, what's happening now?" he asked the officer at the tape recorder.

The officer pressed the headset against his ear and fiddled with a dial. "Not much. He's mumbling to himself, the kids are sort of sniffling—you know, like how they cry themselves to sleep?"

Another telephone on the shelf beside the sergeant's head chirped. He snatched it up and listened for a few seconds. "Okay, I'll pass it on. Listen, tell him to stick around. We might need him later. But have him wait in his car, okay? I don't want him inside the perimeter, you understand? Under no circumstances is he to get through. Not until I say so."

He hung up. "That was one of my guys. The girls' father is out there being crazy. He says they're diabetic, and they have to get their insulin shots by bedtime. If they don't, they could die. That's what he says, anyway."

I sipped the Dr Pepper I'd gotten from the refrigerator. This was bad news. In a situation like this, time was on the side of the negotiator. The more time passed, the more intelligence you could gather, and the more likely that the hostage-taker would get tired and make mistakes. Time constraints worked in nobody's favor. "Well, bedtime's still a while off," I said. "We'll worry about that later."

Reese stared at me. "Yeah, but shouldn't we tell Auerbach? To get things moving? I don't think he really wants those kids' deaths on his conscience."

"I don't think so either, but telling him about the girls' problem doesn't resolve *his* problem, and resolving his problem is the way we get everybody safely out of there and get to go home ourselves."

"Well, what the hell is his problem?"

"I don't know. Listen, Lieutenant—I'm not sure it's a good idea to have Houghey sitting out there in his car. He's not just the father of the girls, he's the guy who fired Auerbach in the first place and got this whole thing going. Obviously Auerbach isn't the most stable guy in the world. Seeing Houghey might send him over the edge."

"I'm aware of that," Reese said sharply. "That's why he's out there and not in here." He was beginning to chafe under too much "help" from me.

"Look, I only mean to suggest that it might be better if you just sent him—"

"He's being kept in his car, out of sight, beyond the outer perimeter," Reese snapped. "They won't let him out. Does that meet with your approval?"

I backed off, raising my palms. "Okay, I'll let you worry about Houghey. Now I think we should try talking to Auerbach again. Okay?"

Reese nodded, and the call was placed.

This time it took a few seconds for the phone to be picked up. "Hey, I thought I said I didn't feel like talking anymore right now."

"Well, I know that, Stanley, but we do have this problem on our hands. Do you prefer 'Stan,' by the way?"

"You don't have any problem. I have a problem."

"I know you do. And if you tell me what it is, I'm betting I can figure out some way around it. I've done it a lot of times before, Stanley."

"Yeah, right."

"All, right, you tell me, then, Stanley, what—"

"It's 'Stan,' for Christ's sake."

"You tell me then, Stan, what would it take to solve your problem? Come on, try me."

"Well—" Auerbach must have heard something because he turned suddenly wary. "Wait a minute, the cops are listening in on us, right? You're taking everything down on tape!"

"Well . . . yes, Stan, that's true," I said. "I guess I thought you understood that. But if you want me to, I can—Stan, don't hang up. . . . Damn."

"Jesus Christ," Reese said, shaking his head in disbelief, "do you have to tell him the truth just because he asks a question?" Now Reese was really irritated, with angry red streaks showing at either side of his nose. "Couldn't you just say no, we're not tapping in? What, is it against your ethics to lie to this fucker?"

I was suddenly tired. It was my second case in a month, and the second in which children were involved—always the most emotionally exhausting cases. I felt drained, unable to muster an answer. No, it wasn't against my ethics to lie to Auerbach. If I believed it would save the children, I'd happily promise him he was going to get a reward, a medal, and a lifetime job from the governor. But one of the things I'd learned and learned well was that if you lied to a kidnapper about what was going on—even a little, innocent white lie, a lie that benefited everybody—the odds were that it would come back and bite you before it was over. The one thing that worked above all in a negotiator's favor was trust, and the one thing that would most surely destroy trust was lying. That is to say, being caught in a lie.

"Look, Lieutenant," I began wearily, but Auerbach had picked up the phone again. I hit the receive button.

"Stan, I'm sorry about that misunderstanding. I can have—"

"It doesn't matter." Auerbach sounded weary too. "Bryan, I really want to get out of here."

"Great, that's what we all want. How about this? You send the girls to the door and tell them to walk over to where I am, in this truck. You can see the truck, right?"

Reese, listening on his headset, was opening and closing his fist. "Good, good."

"Then, once they're safely here—" I went on.

"No, I can't do that," Auerbach said. "If I let them go, what'll stop the cops from killing me? They could shoot me, they could blow this place to bits. They got rockets and stuff."

"Stan, why would they want to do that? You haven't killed anybody, you're being cooperative—"

"*You* come," Auerbach said. "I'll walk out with you."

Reese silently shook his head no.

"Sure, I'll do that," I said. "We can walk out together. I'll come right along with you. First, you let the girls—"

"No, you come first. We all walk out together."

"Well . . ."

"Forget it then!" Auerbach suddenly shouted. "You think I don't know what you're doing? The hell with it! The hell with everybody!" In the background, I could hear the girls' wailing pick up in volume.

"Wait, wait!" I pleaded. "Don't hang up! Okay, Stan, I'll come, that's the deal. I walk over there—"

"By yourself."

"—by myself. Then you and I and the kids all walk out of there together. But you have to leave the guns in the shack. You can't come out with the guns. You understand why that is, don't you?"

"And you won't let them touch me?"

"They'll have to put handcuffs on you, but no one will hurt you, I promise. And I'll ride in with you, right in the same car. Is it a deal?"

"All right."

"I'll be right there. Take it easy now. This is all going to work out okay, Stan."

"Okay, hurry up." Auerbach's voice was breathy. "If anything happens, the kids are the first to go, I swear it on my mother's life. And then you."

"This is not a good idea," Reese said as I took off the headset and stood up.

I wasn't as confident as I might have been either. The turnaround on Auerbach's part had been faster than I would have liked, but I didn't see how I could pass up the opportunity. "I think it's all right, Lieutenant, but we have to be careful. We don't want to upset him. No redeployment of your men, no sharpshooters setting up, everybody just stays where they are. All right?"

Reese sighed and nodded. "I want you to put on a helmet and face piece."

"No, it'll make me look like a cop. The body armor is enough."

Reese made a clucking sound, tongue against teeth, and gave in. "Okay, I hope you know what you're doing."

"You and me both."

We shook hands, I took a deep breath, and I stepped slowly down from the truck and edged between two of the cars that formed the inner perimeter. "Good luck, pal," one of the crouching officers said.

Feeling very much naked and alone, I stood facing the shack for a moment, looking in spite of myself for the glint of a gun barrel at the door, or the windows, or the spaces between the boards, but there was nothing to see. The shack might have been deserted. I began to walk slowly toward it over the parched, furrowed ground, keeping my hands spread wide.

"Okay, Stan, I'm on my way," I called. "Everything's going to work—"

"Hey! What's *he* doing here?" It was Reese's voice, coming from behind me. Then, more urgently: "Get that crazy bastard out of there! He's got a gun! Who let him—?"

Confused, I spun around to see a lean, distraught, middle-aged figure, his long, thinning gray hair tied into a ponytail, who had made it into the inner perimeter after all. Houghey. He was screaming something toward the shack, his whole body shaking. And he was brandishing a revolver, literally waving it around his head in a circle like the Lone Ranger on his horse.

"Houghey!" Reese yelled. "Get out of there, lay down, put down the—"

There was a shot—from the shack, I thought—and then another, from where I couldn't tell, and then, *pop-pop-pop*, guns were going off all over the place. Instinctively I dropped flat on my face, hands covering my head, nose pressed into crumbly earth that still smelled of celery.

I stayed that way until the shooting and the shouting slowed and stopped, and I heard Reese's voice again, low and phlegmy with emotion. "You stupid, stupid bastard, what have you done?"

Houghey was on his knees in the dust, pressing both hands against his bloody shirt front just below the right collar. There was blood on his thigh too. His eyes were unfocused. He looked as if he were trying to figure out what was happening. Reese loomed over him, like God himself about to pronounce judgment. Other policemen stood uneasily nearby, darting glances at the shack.

I looked too. Auerbach was hanging weirdly from a window, caught only by the crook of one knee, with his head and shoulders on the ground, as if he'd tried to leap through it backward, the way a high-jumper rolls over the bar. There was blood all over him. The shotgun lay a few inches from his right hand. There was no sound from behind him in the shack.

Reese and I ran toward the shack at the same time, Reese a few feet behind, so that I was the one who found the two small, blood-soaked bodies crumpled in a corner, tied by their ankles to the radiator, with their arms around each other.

Chapter 4

W ho killed whom and exactly when was never satisfactorily established—there had been too many
.40-caliber slugs flying around—but it made little difference
to me. I knew who was ultimately responsible. Against my
own better judgment, I'd given in; I hadn't *insisted* that
Houghey be made to leave. I'd had the ability to have him
removed, and I hadn't done it. I'd made a terrible mistake,
and two innocent, beautiful little twin girls, their father
and mother's darlings, were dead.

Not only did that terrible affair kill LAPD's experimental
program using civilian negotiators, it damn near killed me.
The very next night the panic attacks started up again, and
all the rest of it soon followed. It was as if a dam had burst,
and all the long-stopped-up poisons had come boiling up
out of my brain, along with this awful new thing. My
hostage-negotiation career was over, and I came perilously
close to breaking down altogether.

One shaky year later, no longer as unflinchingly self-confident as I'd been, but with a clearer idea of my capabilities and my limitations, I'd moved out of California and accepted the fellowship at the institute, where I have toiled in welcome obscurity ever since, writing my training programs and policy guidelines and occasionally consulting with corporate clients. The part-time faculty position with the University of Washington came along shortly after.

That was when Lori and I met and got married too, with full disclosure on my part as to what it was going to be like living with me. How many times since then had I startled her from a sound sleep with howls straight out of hell? Dozens, surely. Hundreds, probably. And how many times had she let even a glimmer of irritation show? Maybe twice in all that time, and then only when it had happened two or three nights in a row, and she was as haggard and unsettled from it as I was.

It wasn't all one way, of course. Lori is the most consistently positive, upbeat person I know, but like anyone else she has her low moments (not many), and when they happened I was there for her. But, God knows, she gave more than she took. Still, we were a good team, each coming through for the other when needed, and as much in love as ever. Ten years now, and still I couldn't believe my luck in snaring this beautiful, sexy, witty woman all for myself. Just looking at that heart-shaped face in the morning, that easy-to-bring-forth smile, was enough to set me up for the whole day. And, although it was hard to comprehend why, I didn't have a doubt in the world that she was just as happy about it all as I was.

Except on one score. Lori was a natural-born world traveler. If she could, she'd have spent half her life tooling around Europe, or New Zealand, or the South Pacific. But with me for a husband, that wasn't to be, not unless she chose to do it without me, which indeed she'd done now and then: with a friend, with her sister, with colleagues on scuba-diving jaunts to various remote outer reefs and inner lagoons. I missed her like crazy when she was gone, but I had no real objection (how could I?), and until lately such trips had sufficed. But she hadn't been on one for a couple of years now, and recently I'd sensed a growing restiveness—not a dissatisfaction, I wouldn't go as far as that—but a gentle regret, a wish that things were different. Last year I'd turned down a chance for us to go to a weeklong conference in Buenos Aires. The year before that it was Sydney. And she hadn't said a word.

But last night, on the drive home, she'd finally let it come out. Or almost: "I don't want to go by myself. I want to go with my husband. . . . I want the fun of . . . of . . ."

It had squeezed my heart then, and it squeezed it again to think of it now. How difficult could that Iceland assignment be? The worst of it would be the two flights, but I intended to sleep through them. If necessary, I'd take tranqs for a couple of days before each one so I didn't get worked up worrying about them. It obviously meant a lot to her, and it had been a long time since I'd given something like that a shot. Who knows, maybe I was ready. And if not, well, the meds were always there if I needed them, although the worry of getting hooked was always at the back of my mind.

But maybe I wouldn't need them. After all, I knew perfectly well that it was all in my mind, that there was nothing *real* to be afraid of. So what was the worst that could happen?

Chapter 5

Client name: GlobalSeas Fisheries, Inc.
Corp. Headquarters: Hafnargarta 2, Grindavik, Iceland.
Primary Contact: Baldur Baldursson, President and CEO.
Odysseus Case Manager: Laura DiMarco, Associate Director.
Company Précis: GlobalSeas was established in 1974 as Fiskvélar, a small saltfish processor and wholesaler serving Iceland, and later the North Sea market. By 1990, when it changed its name to GlobalSeas, it was supplying seafood and fish to markets throughout Western Europe. Two trawlers are currently operated by the company, and additional purchases are made from dozens of other fishing vessels. Currently, GlobalSeas is also one of Iceland's main producers of saltfish for domestic consumption. In addition, the company operates extensive halibut-

and turbot-farming operations and is at the forefront of research on the genetic modification of Atlantic halibut and arctic char. The original fish-processing factory in Grindavik remains in full operation and serves as the company's headquarters.

Pertinent History: *As a result of GlobalSeas' international activities and its pacesetting experimentation in seafood farming and bioengineering, it has been a target of criticism and threats by environmental, anti-globalization, and anarchist organizations, but no overt action against them occurred until last year, when an abduction attempt on the company's president and CEO, Baldur Baldursson, was made by armed members of an organization calling itself the Verkefnið Björgum Jörðinni (in English, Project Save the Earth) or VBJ. The attempt . . .*

What?

I sat up with a jerk. I'd been browsing the Global-Seas case file in the Odysseus library, a pleasant room overlooking the neat rock walls and well-maintained grounds of the institute. We were located in the wine country near Woodinville, and the building itself had started out as a winery. One of the cellars had been just below what was now the library, so that a rich wine-barrel smell was generally in the air, particularly when the heat was on. Invariably, I found it sleep-inducing. Lulled by the aroma and the warmth, along with Laura's relentlessly passive constructions, I'd been on the verge of drifting off.

Now I stared at the file, aghast. What had I gotten myself into? *An abduction attempt by two armed members?* This wasn't just another ho-hum training program at all, it was . . . I read on.

The attempt resulted in the shooting deaths of two of the abductors by police. In addition, one police officer was wounded during the hour-long siege. Mr. Baldursson was unhurt, and the remaining abductors escaped. The VBJ is also believed to have been behind an earlier, highly amateurish kidnapping of a Danish baby-food company executive. It is unknown whether the group is still in existence. Our State Department contacts tell us that they have no record of . . .

Enough. I closed the file, put it back in the secure cabinet, slammed the drawer shut and locked it, and went grimly down the hall to Wally's office. The sweat was pooling in the small of my back.

In the reception area, the secretary tried to head me off. "Oh, wait a minute, Bryan. He asked not to be disturbed until—"

"The hell with that," I muttered, storming past her.

When I flung the door open I found Wally at his desk in the center of his plush, linen-paneled office—everybody else, me included, had glass-partitioned, utilitarian little cubicles—with his finger on his wrist and a ruler and penciled graph in front of him.

His hands disappeared under the desk. "What?" he demanded with a hand-caught-in-the-cookie-jar scowl. Wally was under the delusion that nobody knew that he regularly took his pulse and charted it, recording it sometimes twenty times a day, as part of some outlandish, self-designed health regimen. In fact, it was the frequent subject of jokes.

"I've just been reading the GlobalSeas file," I said menacingly.

"Good, it's about time. You leave pretty soon, don't you?"

"Wally, be straight with me. Did you know about this VBJ group and the kidnap attempt?"

"Well, sure. Sit down already, will you? I hate being loomed over."

I stood my ground, leaning forward onto the desk. "You knew there'd been shooting? *Killings?*"

"Of course. That's precisely why they're so eager to get you. So?"

"So why didn't you tell me?"

He shrugged. "I knew you'd look at the file for yourself. You're a big boy. I trust you to do your homework."

"I mean, why didn't you tell me in the first place?"

Wally blew out his cheeks in perplexity. "Why would I? What's to tell? What the hell business do you think we're in? Bryan, what exactly is your problem?"

"What's my problem?" I began, my voice rising. "What is my problem? My *problem*—"

I stopped myself. Wally's confusion was genuine enough. To Wally, I was a reliable, useful analyst and policy wonk among whose oddities happened to be a dislike of travel and of hands-on work. As for kidnappings and killings, they were the meat and potatoes of the institute, pored over in the cubicles and chatted about, even joked about (not by me!) over lunch and coffee. So what exactly was I supposed to tell him now? That the fact that GlobalSeas had been through an abduction attempt changed everything? That the shirt of his "heavy hitter" in these matters was soaked with perspiration at the idea of coming anywhere near them?

Besides, I'd already given my word, and I couldn't ask someone else to do it on a few days' notice. And anyway, they'd made it clear that it had to be me, or no one. There was Lori to think about too; Lori who had bought a new winter outfit, and hiking boots, and a drysuit for kayaking, and who had spent her evenings planning an elaborate, out-doorsy couple of weekends for us, and who was lighting up my own life with her sparkle and anticipation.

"Never mind," I said grumpily.

"Hey, if I thought it would bother you so much, I would have—"

But I was out the door before he could finish.

"THAT was a rough one last night, wasn't it?" Lori asked a few mornings later, over lox, cream cheese and toasted bagels, and the *Seattle Times*.

I'd been shocked awake by one of my more spectacular panic attacks in the middle of the night. Lori had sat up with me until the Xanax had taken hold and I could stop the humiliating cowering and shaking that goes along with them—I mean, talk about wimpy!—and lie down and sleep again. We had said little; there wasn't much to say. Of course, Lori had tried many times to understand what was happening inside my head when one of these things hit, but, aside from the fact that you're not in the mood for communicating at the time, it's not the sort of thing you can explain to anybody else anyway. You had to be there to appreciate it.

"Oh, not that rough," I said with a smile. "I'd give it a seven on a scale of one to ten. Sorry about waking you up. Did you get back to sleep at all?"

"Oh, sure, you know me."

She went back to her bagel and her reading, but I could see that she was barely skimming the paper, that she had something on her mind and was deciding whether it was better to bring it up or let it lie. I even saw the firm little nod of her chin when she came to her decision.

She put down the newspaper. "I'm worried about you, Bryan."

"Lori, I've been having these things for years, you know that. They come and go. In cycles. This time around, they've been a little hairier than usual, that's all. They'll pass, they always do. I'm fine, really."

"It's the third night in a row you've had one. When was the last time that happened?"

I thought for a moment. "A long time ago. Three years, maybe?"

"Try five. So the question is, what's bringing them on? I think it's got to be because this Iceland thing is worrying you."

I went on tranquilly spreading cream cheese on a bagel, but she'd struck home. When I'd first decided to accept the assignment I'd felt good about it, as if finally determining to take on my old bugaboos had made me stronger; as if, by standing up and facing them, perhaps I had them on the run at last. That was the way the psychologists said it worked, and I figured maybe it was true.

Then, three days ago, I'd read the case file. And three nights ago, the attacks had started again.

I responded with a shrug. "Maybe. Hard to say. Sometimes they just seem to come for no reason, you know that."

"Not three nights in a row. That's stress, Bryan, and you know it."

"I do *not* know it. Lori, honest to God, I am not stressed about this. There's nothing to be stressed about." I hadn't told Lori about the file, and I didn't intend to. Maybe after we got back home.

"I think maybe the whole thing was a bad idea, maybe we—"

"Absolutely not. We . . . are . . . going," I said. "I'll be fine. I'm looking forward to it. I am. Really." I picked up the paper, searching for something to change the topic.

She pushed it down with the flat of her hand, so she could look into my face. "Well, then, maybe it's time for you to see someone. I mean it, Bryan. You don't know what you looked like last night. You looked . . . you looked . . . Bryan I was *scared*."

"I tried seeing someone once, you know that. He was crazier than I was."

But Lori wouldn't be put off. "That was six years ago. There have been a lot of developments since then."

"Lori, I'm sorry. Psychiatry is not for me. You know I just don't buy all this endless regurgitation—"

"All right, then what about psychology? Remember that psychologist you were telling me about, the emeritus from the U—Zeta Something?"

"Zeta Parkington."

"Yes. What about talking to her? Her specialty is anxiety, isn't it? You said you liked her. Why don't you give her a call, make an appointment?"

"Aw, Lori, don't push me into it. I don't want—"

"Why not? Give me a reason."

"Oh, hell, I don't know. It's just . . . I don't know."

"Oh, that's a great reason."

"Lori, we're leaving next week. She's not going to cure me by then."

"So? It'll take a little longer. At least maybe you'll be on your way. Come on, let me hear a real reason."

I sighed. In the morning after a panic attack I was usually calm—maybe *drained* is a better word—almost to the point of somnolence, but along with it often went a shattered, empty feeling, as if I were disconnected from my body. Other people, even Lori, seemed out of focus and unreal. I felt fragile and vulnerable; minor work problems were unscalable obstacles; trivial decisions unmanned me; I was incapable of arguing a point.

"You're taking unfair advantage of me," I grumbled. "You know the way—"

"You're being evasive. Come on." She rapped the table. "Reason."

"I just—"

"You don't have one, do you?"

"I—okay, all right, I'll call her. All right? Are you satisfied?"

"Today?"

"Well, I'm not sure I can—"

She put on her fiercest mock scowl and leaned threateningly toward me. *"Today?"*

When Lori does that, I'm a goner. It's not fair, really. She's just so damn cute, it's impossible to resist. "Today, yes," I said.

"All right, then. I'm satisfied."

I shook out my section of the paper with a rattle and started reading again. "Jeez." I wasn't angry, of course, just a little grumpy about giving in, even though I knew she was right.

A minute later her hand reached across the table and covered mine. "Bryan?"

But I was still making my point. I shook out the paper again and kept reading.

"Bryan? Come on, honey, look at me."

I lowered the paper and met her eyes. Whatever the situation, I'm always glad to meet Lori's eyes. They are wonderful, a deep chestnut with flecks of amber and gold. It's like looking deep into the interior of a sun-dappled forest. It's impossible to get tired of looking into them.

She was smiling. "You know you're not mad at me."

"Well . . . not very."

"And you know that the only reason I get pushy like that is because I care so much about you. I love you, Bryan."

Well, that melted what reserve I had left, which wasn't much. The smile I'd been keeping in check could no longer be held back. "I know, sweetheart, and believe me, I appreciate it." I lifted her hand to my lips and kissed the back of it. "I love you too. And I think seeing Zeta is a good idea." I was feeling a lot better, a lot more grounded, than I had a few minutes ago. The woman had that effect on me.

"Still," she said, sipping her coffee and looking at me, her head tilted, her chin on her fist. "I think I'm coming around to thinking Wally's got a point. You *are* a hard case."

I couldn't help laughing. "A head case is more like it," I said.

Chapter 6

I'd first met Zeta Parkington at a University of Washington
function and then had run into her a few times at the
Starbucks on University Way when I showed up there for
some caffeinated fortitude on the two days a week that I
taught at the U. Zeta was in her seventies, a bluff, straight-
talking, chain-smoking emeritus professor of clinical psychology who favored boxy black granny dresses and kept
her stiff gray hair chopped off just below the ears. I'd taken
to her right away, even trusted her to the extent of telling
her a little about my problems over lattes one day, once I
learned that her specialty was anxiety disorders. Zeta had
said she'd be glad to try to help if I liked, and to come and
see her anytime; an unrepentant smoker, she had given up
her practice a few years earlier, the day a state law was
passed prohibiting smoking in "adult care facilities." However, she still kept her old office right around the corner, just
off campus, on Forty-fifth Street, and I was more than welcome to come in for a session or two, as long as I promised

not to report her to the authorities if she smoked. I'd give it some thought, I'd replied, and I'd meant it at the time. Still, that had been months ago, and there it had lain.

Until today.

Zeta's office was like the woman herself, forthright and unpretentious. What you saw was what you got. There were a couple of framed diplomas on the pale yellow walls, along with a Nature Conservancy calendar and a movie-lobby placard from *Casablanca*, signed by Sydney Greenstreet; nothing else. There was a plain, serviceable industrial carpet and a simple, standard-issue metal desk with an old-fashioned, leather-cornered blotter on it, and two side chairs, and over by the window a couple of marginally more comfortable armchairs and a coffee table. It was in the armchairs that we'd been sitting for the last forty minutes, during which I had talked steadily and Zeta had listened, mostly to my story of the hostage shootout and its aftermath. As for my childhood kidnapping, I'd spared myself a detailed description by giving her a copy of the narrative I'd written for Dr. Benson.

While she read it to the accompaniment of an occasional murmur or commiserative shake of her head, my mind drifted for the first time in years to my life immediately following the kidnapping. After the corrective surgery on my toe, I had returned home to the compound near Istanbul where the company's management staff was housed, and found that everything had changed. My mother and father were broken people, financially and emotionally. Dad, once a big, jovial man always joshing with me—a friendly jab in the ribs, a funny face made by sticking his glasses in his mouth to poke out his cheeks—seemed to fold in on himself and visibly shrink. He had always been a ready drinker from the moment he got home in the evening, but now I could smell it on his breath in the morning, and the bourbon that had made him pink-faced and twinkle-eyed in past years, a sort of beardless Santa Claus, now turned him sullen and reclusive.

Before, Mom had been the more energetic and adventurous of the two, the one who most encouraged my independence, but now she sniped and fretted at me when I was even momentarily out of her sight. Making things infinitely worse, there was a polio epidemic in Istanbul that year and my brother Richard caught it and died just a few months later. After that, she spent almost all of her time in the apartment murmuring and shaking her head over her private thoughts. Sometimes she forgot to make dinner or to turn on the lights in the late afternoon. I worried that she was going crazy.

The strain took its predictable toll on job and family. Before the project was completed, my debt-laden, grieving, increasingly incompetent father was demoted to crew chief, then fired altogether. My parents' marriage disintegrated, first into mutual repugnance and blame, then separation, then, not long after they returned home to Pasadena, to divorce. A few weeks before it became final, dad was killed when his Ford Fairlane sideswiped a garbage truck on San Gabriel Boulevard. His blood alcohol level was 0.28. You can imagine the load of guilt that lay on my six-year-old shoulders. No one ever said to me that all of this was on account of me, but no one had to say it.

I was eight when mom remarried and things really turned around. From then on I lived a blissfully unremarkable childhood; my stepfather was a generous, quiet, older man, grateful for the opportunity to nurture a second family. He was more step-grandfather than stepfather to me, but there had been genuine love there. Mom was happy too, I think. It lasted twelve good years, and then he died. Mom died a couple of years later.

"Well, that all explains a lot," Zeta said with a sigh as she put the narrative down. "Tell me, do you and your brother ever talk about it?"

"My brother?"

"Your brother Richard." She tapped the paper. "The one you were playing with. I was wondering how he felt about *not* getting kidnapped—how you felt about it, for that matter—if it created any issues between the two of you."

"Oh." It had been a long time since I'd thought about Richard. "Richard died just a few months later. There was a polio epidemic in Istanbul that year. That had a lot to do with my mother and father's breakdown too. It was all just too much for them."

She was shaking her head. "I should think so. Well, in any case, this is all in the long-ago past, it's done, and we can't change it. We need to work from the here and now and move forward."

"Good. I've had all the psychoanalytic depth interviews I'll ever want." Two, to be exact.

"But what you'd better understand right from the start," she went on, leaning forward with one hand propped on each black-draped knee and her cigarillo burning in the ashtray on the table, "is that the key to ridding yourself of anxiety that's rationally groundless—phobias, panic attacks—is to face it head-on. The minute you stop running from the fear and decide to start confronting it and to start gaining some control over the situation and over your own life, you're on your way. It's not very complicated, but it does take nerve."

I shook my head. "I don't know, Zeta. I *am* facing my fears. I'm actually leaving the country, going to Iceland. I'm working with an organization that's just been through a kidnapping attempt and is worried about another. These are huge steps for me, but things have gotten worse, not better.

I've had panic attacks three nights in a row. And last night I only headed off another full-blown one because I'd popped a pill the minute I thought I felt it coming on."

Zeta snorted and waved her cigarillo to brush away my protest. "No, you're not facing your fears. You're taking your trusty little bottle of happy-time pills to Iceland, aren't you?"

"My big bottle."

"Exactly, there you go. And when you get nervous because you think you feel an attack coming on, what do you do? You pop a pill—thereby avoiding the fear, not facing it. If you were going without your pills, *then* you'd be facing it."

"Are you asking me to do that?" I shook my head and laughed uneasily. "Because—"

"No, that's not what I'm asking you to do, although you shouldn't laugh at it, because it very well might do the trick if you could see it through. It's a relatively new approach, and for a lot of people it works. *Flooding*, we call it. Or exposure therapy. Or implosion therapy, although I find the term a little threatening. You just face down your fear all at once, with no crutches to lean on—you just *do* it. Panicked about riding in an elevator? You grit your teeth and get on one and ride it up and down and up and down until you're over it, and by the time you get out you might be sweating, but you've pretty much got it licked. It's extreme, all right, but it's the quickest way to be done with it once and for all. It's worked for other people, Bryan. It just might work for you. Same philosophy as beating your fear of horses by climbing right back up on the thing after it's thrown you."

"Yeah, or learning to swim by being dumped in a lake." I shook my head. "I don't know, Zeta. It sounds as if it might be reasonable, just sitting here talking to you, but if push came to shove . . ."

"Bryan, my boy, let me give you Dr. Parkington's theory

of panic-attack therapy in one sentence: In order to be rid of the damn things for good, you have to face whatever it is you're most afraid of—the very worst thing. That's the rule, no exceptions." She paused to let this sink in. "You don't fight it, you don't try to avoid it or moderate it with pills, or relaxation techniques, or slow breathing, or anything else. You face it down, once and for all. In fact, you purposely make it as bad as you can for as long as you can, so you can prove to yourself that you can do it. That's the price you have to pay."

"Pretty expensive price."

"Look, Bryan, what's the worst thing you can imagine? Just tell me. The most panic-inducing situation you could possibly find yourself in." She leaned interestedly forward.

"Well, it would be a repeat of what I gave you to read."

"Yes, but let me hear you say it."

I hesitated. It didn't strike me as the keenest idea I'd ever heard, but then, I was there for help and Zeta was offering it. I took in a breath. "The worst thing I can conceive of would be to . . . to . . ." *Would be to wake up suddenly, startlingly, in the middle of the night and find that my current life had been a dream, that in actuality I was still chained by the neck in a dank, pitch-black cave* . . . But I couldn't even think it through, let alone say it. I just sat there mutely shaking my head, conscious that I was breathing through my mouth in little gasps. Over and above the rest of it, I was both angry at myself and embarrassed. What a pusillanimous, lily-livered weakling this panic thing turns you into.

"Easy there, big fella," Zeta said. "Never mind, you don't need to tell me. But don't let it go entirely either. Let's say you did find yourself in the situation you're thinking about. What exactly do you think would happen? How would you react?"

"React? If it happened to me again? I'd lose my mind, I'd come apart. 'Implosion' is right. It'd kill me, Zeta."

She paused to relight the cigarillo—and, I suspect, to give me a chance to collect myself, which I did. I could feel my breathing return to normal.

"*Au contraire*," she said when she'd gotten it lit. "Nobody ever died from a panic attack, Bryan."

"Oh? And how could you know that?"

Zeta laughed, a robust, two-note *har-har*. She even slapped her thigh. "Well, you've got me there; I can't prove it. But we do know that extreme anxiety—panic—is a self-limiting phenomenon. It runs out of gas and ends on its own. You think it's going to spiral up and up and blow you apart—"

"Boy, do you."

"—but it doesn't, does it? Has it ever? No, it can't, because when the stress gets extreme enough it automatically activates the autonomic nervous system to kick in with a shot of beta-endorphin, and you calm down. Didn't you ever have a panic attack when you didn't have anything to take for it?"

"Sure, the early ones, when I didn't know what they were, before I had any medication. They were horrible. I was positive I was going crazy. I thought I *was* crazy." I shivered. "It's still what happens when I get one, in that brief period before the Xanax starts to act. Even now, when I know in my head that it's only a matter of minutes before the med goes to work, it doesn't do me any good until it actually kicks in. In my gut I *know* I can't last, I know there's no way that little orange pill can cope with this. I'm either going to lose my mind or die."

"Ah, but you don't die, do you? And you don't go crazy either. It all just quiets down after a while. Just the way it did in the old days, even without the medication. It just took a little longer."

"A lot longer. And yes, it quiets down. Until the next one comes along."

"Which takes . . .?"

"I don't know; days, weeks, months if I'm lucky. But sometimes it's the very next night."

She jabbed the cigarillo at me. "That's right, the *next* night. But never, ever the same night. Have you never wondered why? It's because it takes a while for the beta-endorphins to filter out of your system and let the panic syndrome start building up again."

"Okay, all right, I'll buy that. Tell me, then, how do we attack this thing? Short of this flooding idea. I'm not spending the night in a cave with a chain around my neck, I can tell you that."

"Well, if you're serious, we do need you to do something along those lines—work through a panic-inducing situation without the meds—but not all at once, if that's too much for you to think about right now. We build up to it, and in an analytical, modified way, with me right beside you. Now that's not so awful, is it?"

"Not so awful, is it," I echoed, smiling. "Zeta, no offense, but I'm guessing you've never had a panic attack yourself. Am I right?"

"Well, there have been moments when I—"

"No. I mean a genuine, honest-to-God, full-blown panic attack."

"Well, no, not personally, but I've sat through them with a good many patients, and, in any case, you don't have to have appendicitis in order to treat it, or . . ." She stopped. "No, you're right, I haven't," she said more softly. "Why don't you tell me what it's like, Bryan? For you, specifically, I mean. Or would that be too nervous-making?"

"No, not nervous-making, but not so easy to put into words," I said with a sigh. I got up and went to the window. I was looking down at the lively, grungy, student-infested corner of Brooklyn Avenue and Forty-fifth Street, and at the old-fashioned marquee of the old Neptune Theater. One of the last of the single-screen movie houses in Seattle, built in the 1920s, they had a rerun of *The Sting* playing. "How are you about heights, Zeta?" I asked after I'd gotten my thoughts in order. "Comfortable with them?"

"I'm not phobic about them, if that's what you mean, but I'm not crazy about them either. If I'm stupid enough to get myself anywhere near the edge of someplace high, I generally wish I was someplace else."

"Okay. Then imagine that you're standing right at the lip of a sheer two-thousand-foot cliff and not feeling too keen about it. No guardrail, nothing to hold on to. Your companion, standing next to you, suddenly, inexplicably, turns on you and shoves you—hard—and over the edge you go, out into space. The feeling you have at that moment, the exact moment when your feet leave the earth and you hang over the abyss, staring down—that heart-stopping, overwhelming, mind-shattering *terror*—that's what a panic attack is like."

"I see. Well, I can certainly—"

"*Except*," I continued, "that it goes on and on and on, full-force, unabated, for thirty or forty-five *minutes*, or even an hour, never letting up in the least, your heart banging against your ribs as if you've got this panicked horse inside, trying to get out."

"I see," she said more soberly, and I could tell that she was really trying to imagine it.

"And while forty-five minutes of that hardly sounds like fun, it does sound endurable, doesn't it? Especially because you know that there isn't really any danger since there isn't really any cliff and nobody's pushed you off it. Besides, you've lived through this before, so you know it'll be over soon, and all you have to do is wait it out, right?"

"Not right?" she said.

I turned from the window. "Ah, if only it worked that way, but it doesn't. The thing is, you are absolutely, incontrovertibly convinced that *this* time you've slipped for good over another edge, from sanity to wherever the hell you are now, and there's no way back. It's like one of those science fiction movies, where you go through an opening to some other horrible dimension, and when you turn around the opening is gone: You're in an alien world and there's no way home."

Back to looking out the window now, speaking quietly, musing, talking as much to myself as Zeta. "Now you see—with absolute certainty—that all along your other, 'sane' self was the mirage and this horrible, unendurable state of unending terror—*this* is reality. You're trapped in it with no possible way to get out, until your heart or your brain explodes with it, which can't be very long because who could possibly take this for very long? As for knowing there's no actual danger, that doesn't compute at all. Your thinking mind is shut off. There isn't room in your head for anything but the panic."

She'd sat through this without smoking, and her cigarillo had gone out. She relit it before saying anything. "Oh, my, my, my. That's very graphic, Bryan. I think my own pulse is up a few beats."

I let out a nervous laugh. "Mine too." I came back and sat down again. "Zeta, the one thing I've never understood about this: Why *can't* I think my way out of an attack? I mean, if I *know* that nothing is really there, why can't I tell myself that? That is, I *do* tell myself that, but I don't believe it. Why is that?"

Another wave of the cigarillo. "Ah, there's the rub, all right. Sure, we like to think that our upper brains are in charge of things, because that big, round prefrontal cortex is so smart and advanced, and the funny little limbic system way down in the neck—which controls emotions like fear—is so primitive and squiggly and funny-looking. And it *is* primitive. But it's also powerful. You see, by the time the cortex figures out what's going on, the limbic system—specifically, the amygdala and the hippocampus—are running the show and it's too late. Your head, as you so vividly put it, has no room for anything but the panic. Unfortunately, gut-level terror trumps reasoning and logic, whether you're a mouse, a monkey, or a human being; an unfortunate biological fact. *Thinking* winds up doing you more harm than good, because your perceptions are all screwed up at that point, and you see things all wrong."

I nodded. It made sense to me. I came back and sat down. "So tell me, how do we attack this thing? Short of this flooding idea. I'm not spending the night in a cave with a chain around my neck, I can tell you that."

"Well, if you're serious, we do need you to do something along those lines—work through a panic-inducing situation without the meds—but not all at once, if that's too much for you to think about right now. We're talking about cognitive behavioral therapy here. It's more self-treatment than treatment. What we'd have you do is work through a series of graduated exercises to create a panic response—a very limited panic response—and help you analyze it while it's going on. Your job would be to dissect exactly what you're feeling, to focus on it and learn—"

"*Focus* on it? Zeta, that's the last thing I want to do."

"Bryan, listen to me. As long as you keep running from it, you'll never get over it. You have to get used to it, that's the only reliable way. You look objectively at exactly what you're feeling and you prove to yourself, deep down, that you really *can* live through it, that your perceptions, your fears, are all wrong and you can beat them back. It's like finally standing up to this bully that's been terrorizing you and telling him: 'Do your worst, you sonofabitch. Take your best shot. I'm not running anymore.'"

She mashed out the cigarillo and paused—as if to prove to herself that she wasn't *literally* chain-smoking—and then immediately pulled the next one from a pocket pack and lit it. She smoked Hav-a-Tampa Jewels, vanilla-scented little mini-cigars with wooden mouthpieces. Unlike most cigar smokers, she inhaled. "You see, avoiding it—taking a pill, for example, or just staying away from airplanes or telephone booths or whatever—does avoid the panic for the time being, yes, but it makes things worse in the long run because avoiding it is temporarily satisfying, so it reinforces the avoidance behavior—making you less likely than ever to give up the pills, or get on a plane, or go into a telephone booth. Does this make sense to you?"

"I guess it does, yes," I said without much enthusiasm. Simply staying on the pills and suffering the occasional attack was sounding better and better.

"Frankly," Zeta said, "given your line of work, I'm surprised that you don't already know all this."

"This isn't my line of work. This is the part of my work I go to great lengths to stay away from."

"Har-har! Well, you see, there's my point right there."

I managed a pale smile. "Yes, I see. How long would this take, Zeta?"

"Well, look, it's never a sure thing, but for you—you're a brainy, analytical type—I would say the outlook's good. Assuming you don't want to go the all-at-once implosion route . . . ?" A questioning lift of one eyebrow.

"Not at the present time, thank you."

"Maybe later, we'll see. I'll leave it up to you. Sometimes we have the patient drink a couple of cups of coffee first to get the heart going and to accentuate the sensations. That really makes it fun."

"If it's all the same to you, I don't think I'll need the coffee. If I do it at all. So, about this cognitive behavioral theory—how long?"

"Oh, I'd say, oh, something like twelve or fifteen sessions, probably once a week, plus a little homework for you to do in between. Altogether, say three to four months. And I'll never try to make you do or think anything. I may ask you, but it will always be up to you, it'll always be at your pace, and that's a promise. We might not totally cure you, but I'm betting you'll be in a whole lot better shape."

"Okay, I'm game. But you know, I'm leaving the day after tomorrow and I'll be gone all of next week, so I don't suppose there's any point in starting now."

Zeta put her blunt-nailed fingers to her temples, as if calling up psychic powers. "I seem to be receiving these thought rays telling me to please, for God's sake, agree with the man that we don't have to start now. I wonder where they're coming from."

"Zeta, it's no joke. Frankly, the whole thing terrifies me. Let me have a couple of weeks to get used to the idea. Besides, I want the trip to be as much vacation as work. It'd be nice to just, well, relax. If I have to pop a pill or two, so be it."

"I understand. Far be it for me to push you into anything. It wouldn't do any good anyway. And there's something else you'll have to understand. Once we start—bye-bye, Xanax."

"For three months? That's a little scary."

"I know it is, Bryan," she said in a gentler tone than she'd used with me so far, "but if you're on a tranquilizer, you're not going to benefit. The drug turns off the entire autonomic fight-or-flight response, so you can never really experience the full force of the anxiety. And that's just what it is that you have to come to terms with before you can get yourself over the hump. And once you have, trust me, you won't need the pills anymore. Well, not as much."

I sat quietly, slowly shaking my head. "I don't know, Zeta," I said once more.

"It's worked for plenty of others, Bryan. Give it a try. If you find you can't tolerate it—which, to be perfectly frank, happens with some people—you can always quit, and you won't be any worse off than you are right now. But remember, I'll be right there to help you when you need it. In fact, I'll give you a magic mantra right this minute to help you through any attack you do have, just two words: *self-limiting*. Just keep saying it yourself. Let me hear you say it."

"Self-limiting." I smiled. "Okay. We'll start . . . but not until I get back."

"Good enough." She stubbed out her cigarillo and got to her feet. "Come on into the file room. I'll give you some reading material in the meantime."

Chapter 7

In the restaurant Brim in the harborside village of Grinda-vik, a sober, working community of fishermen, jetties, cranes, and fish-processing plants some thirty-five miles from the bustling capital of Reykjavik, the aproned, housewifely woman behind the counter had taken the man's money, 1,200 krona, and pointed him to the buffet table. She had then forgotten about him, which was what most people did after encountering him. He was easy to forget: in his mid-forties, five-eleven or so, stockily built, with limp, mouse-brown hair and a bland, squarish, unremarkable face. Spare in speech, unassuming in manner, keeping to himself, there was nothing about him that would attract the notice of others.

Had they taken a closer look, however, they might have seen something troubling in the blank expression and the milky, gray-blue eyes: a deadness, a cold detachment, indifferent and unfeeling. He was, in fact, a psychopath; officially certified by a court-appointed psychiatrist as having psychopathic personality disorder. Not the raving-lunatic kind, or the glib, charming, crazy, serial-killer psychopathic personality of the movies, no—it had never occurred to him to eat anybody's liver—but more than enough unsettling: an inability to feel empathy for others, a nonexistent conscience; a strong sense of entitlement; and, just below his unreadable surface, a vengeful, simmering, soul-eating sense of the "humiliations" visited on him by others.

He took his tray to an inconspicuous corner table near a window and sat down to eat: a thin fish soup, sautéed haddock (the only entrée available), boiled potatoes, and cold mixed vegetables. If salt, pepper, or any flavorings at all had been added to the food, he was unable to detect them. But this seemed to be standard in Iceland. Strange, he thought. One would think that it would be the cold countries that had the spicy, hot foods, and the warm countries that went for the bland ones, but in his experience of travel, which was considerable, it was the other way around.

Still, the saltshaker was available and the haddock was fresh, and so he ate, steadily and without complaint. Food was little more than fuel to him. While he chewed, his eyes wandered, apparently absently, to the activities taking place at the loading dock of the GlobalSeas fish-processing plant almost directly across Hafnagarta, the two-lane street that ran the length of the town, right on down to the docks. Occasionally he would glance at his watch or jot something down in the notepad at his elbow.

"Eleven-thirty . . ." he said to himself. "*Now*." And as if on cue, a white refrigerator truck turned onto Hafnargarta a hundred yards up the block, bringing a smile to the man's face. On its side, in an arc of Gothic lettering, was the word *Saegreifinn*—Sea Baron. This was a Reykjavik seafood wholesaler, and the truck had come to pick up its semi-weekly load of saltfish, which would go to local restaurants.

As he watched, the electrically operated gate in the ten-foot chain-link fence that surrounded the plant rolled open—the man pressed the start button on the watch's stopwatch function—and the truck pulled in, turned around, and deftly backed up to one of the three loading bays; the only one with its corrugated metal door rolled up and open. A forklift stood by waiting with a pallet of crated salted fish. Once the truck's rear door was open, the forklift operator levered the pallet into it. Then, while the truck driver pulled down the door and locked it, the forklift operator went to a wall telephone and spoke a few words.

In the restaurant, the man pressed the stop button and looked down. Four minutes, twenty seconds had passed since the gate had opened. Good. Excellent. He jotted it down in the notepad.

Now his attention shifted to the structure attached kitty-corner to the warehouse. This was a two-floored, metal-sided building without windows but with an outside staircase that led from the loading bay up to a door on the upper floor; the only opening in the wall. Behind this door, he knew, was the office of GlobalSeas' CEO, Baldur Baldursson. As expected, the door opened—the man pressed the start button again—and Baldursson, in shirtsleeves rolled halfway up his forearms, trotted down the steps. A few moments' kibitzing with the forklift operator and the truck driver while he signed the manifest, and then back up he trotted. The door closed behind him.

Another glance at the watch. Baldursson had been outside for fifty-four seconds. This was the fourth time he'd observed the CEO's appearance for the Saegreifinn pickup, and there had been hardly any variation in the amount of time he was exposed. Forty-eight seconds was the shortest; one minute, thirty seconds the longest. Now, as the truck left the grounds, the forklift operator pressed a keypad at the loading dock and the gate rolled slowly closed behind it. It had been open a total of eight minutes and ten seconds, also about the usual. Most important, this made four out of four times Baldursson had come out alone—no bodyguard—to sign the manifest, standing there in plain view with the gate wide open. Was it simple carelessness? Stupidity? A sense, even after what had happened last year, of invulnerability? A desperate need, if only for a few seconds twice a week, to be on his own for a while? To take a risk? After all, no one can be on guard every minute of every day. Besides, with Baldursson exposed for such a short time—and not really that out in the open, but well within the compound— right at the loading entrance to the building, a good fifty yards from the street—what could happen?

Plenty, the man thought, getting up to pour himself another cup of coffee. Icelandic food was a disaster, but when it came to coffee, there he had to give them credit. Their coffee was unfailingly excellent: dark, richly bitter, velvety. Of course, they practically lived on the stuff. Reykjavik must have had more coffeehouses per square block than Seattle did.

When he'd drained the cup, he got up again, pulled on his inexpensive gray quilted parka and knitted watch cap, also gray, and, having paid when he entered, left with a barely perceptible nod of thanks to the woman behind the counter. The woman nodded back without really seeing him.

He then strolled the two blocks to the gas station that served as Grindavik's bus terminal, arriving five minutes before the twice-daily bus to Reykjavik pulled in. A dozen others were waiting, and he boarded in the middle of the crowd and took a seat halfway back.

By the time he walked out of the Reykjavik bus terminal forty-five minutes later, his presence on the bus would already be forgotten. Or rather, it would never have been noticed in the first place.

IT was not because of financial considerations that the quiet man in the gray quilted parka and knitted cap had traveled from Grindavik to Reykjavik by bus. Had he wished, he could easily have afforded the most luxurious limousine service in Iceland. It was his custom to use public transportation when on business, regardless of the inconvenience or discomfort. In a pinch he would take a taxi, but only in a pinch. Rental cars, never. The fewer times he signed whatever name he was using, the less often he had to show one of his driver's licenses or passports, and the fewer people he came into one-to-one contact with, the better.

The man's name was George Henry Camano, but to the world at large he was known as "Paris," and in the more sensationally oriented media he was said to be "a vicious killer," a "master of disguise," and "an ardent revolutionary." He considered none of them to be close to the truth.

It was the "vicious killer" label that got his goat the most. The "killer" part, well, that he had no problem with, but *vicious*? As if he were some kind of slavering, mindless, wild beast? No, that was uncalled for, and it hurt him deeply. It was true that in the last half-dozen years circumstances had required eliminating four of his hostages, but never once had it been mindless. Always it had been done out of necessity. Or at least there had been a rational purpose. Or at least there had been some point to it. Once it had been simple expedience (the captive had gotten too much information out of his simpleminded guards to be allowed to live), but for the others there had been more to it than that: retribution, justice, belated punishment. Simply put, some people just plain didn't deserve to live, and in having removed them from this earth he took not only pleasure but pride.

A master of disguise? That was even more laughable. For one thing, he rarely found disguise necessary, having solved the problem of invisibility some years earlier. He had gone to Dr. Reuben Girard, a respected plastic surgeon in Virginia, a man who assisted the FBI in altering the appearance of turncoat gangsters who were entering the witness protection program and wished to keep their identities and whereabouts secret from their old colleagues. Dr. Girard, as it happened, pursued a vastly more profitable sideline as well: altering the appearance of gangsters who wished to keep their identities and whereabouts secret from the *FBI*.

Camano's request to the surgeon wasn't the usual plea to be made unrecognizable. Instead he asked to be "smoothed," to have any features that might conceivably be "distinctive" made as undistinctive as possible. His aim was to look as ordinary, as average, as a person could be made to look, and Girard had obliged. It was easy work, since Camano's face was quite ordinary to begin with. The underlying skeletal structure was left as it was, but the curling tops of his ears had been made less prominent, the pitted acne scars on his cheeks erased, a couple of irregular teeth replaced, and the slightly off-center nose, the result of a deviated septum, straightened. Camano had taken care of his black hair himself, dying it a dull, mousey brown. That had been it, and it didn't really change his appearance that much, in the sense that anyone who'd known him before would have had no trouble recognizing him afterward.

But that wasn't the point. Unlike the witness protection people, it wasn't old acquaintances he was hiding from, it was new ones. And to strangers Henry Camano was now Everyman, Mr. John Q. Public, the kind of guy you saw but didn't really see a hundred times a day on the bus, in the street, in the Safeway. Once in a while a passerby would stop him with a query: "Say, aren't you the guy that was in that old episode of *Seinfeld* (or *Boston Legal*, or *House*)?" But it was never the same show, the same bit part, the same actor. It wasn't only that he didn't really look like anybody in particular, it was that he reminded people, vaguely, of just about everybody.

And as for the "ardent revolutionary" label, it was too absurd even to discuss. He wasn't ardent—indeed, he prized coolness and forethought among his most useful virtues—and he certainly wasn't a revolutionary.

Basically, what he *was,* as he saw it, was a businessman much like any other businessman, an entrepreneur providing a service for a fee in a volatile and demanding market.

His business happened to be kidnapping for ransom. This, as he saw it, was in itself neither good nor bad (an interest in moral philosophy was not among those self-claimed virtues), but rather an expression of the application of certain basic economic principles. If you were searching for a textbook example of the free market at its purest and most uncluttered level, how could you come up with anything better than the exchange of a hostage for an amount of money agreed to solely by the parties concerned and no one else, without any outside strictures or interference?

George Camano had organized more successful abductions for profit than anyone else in the world. In so doing, he had built up a certain amount of fame, if you could call it fame when nobody knew what your name was; when no one had any idea of what you looked like, other than from two fuzzy photos that Interpol had been circulating to police departments without success for years (no wonder, since neither of them was of you); when half the people who have heard of you doubt your existence; and when your most successful operations were private matters unknown to the police or the press and thus ipso facto unknown to the general public—but every unsolved, high-profile kidnapping on the face of the globe was assumed to have been your handiwork.

Being a realist when it came to his actual abilities, he was aware that he didn't have the daring or the cunning that was attributed to him. What he did have was a system, and the system was organized on the need-to-know principle.

First, he never worked in the United States, his home country; he accepted only foreign jobs. He would hire out to plan and oversee the kidnapping of a specified individual (never more than one) and to have him (never a her; a female hostage was asking for trouble) held captive for the time necessary, but not to exceed one week, if at all possible. Four to five days was the time he shot for, after which tensions and differences between the captors built up to too high a level, along with developing relationships with the captive. The result was a precipitous increase in the risks and a decline in the prospects of full success.

As part of the system, Camano alone would be responsible for planning and execution and would use only his own handpicked people for the abduction, and then a *separate* set for the subsequent detention. The kidnappers would not know where the prisoner was to be held, and the captors would not know whom the kidnappers had been. The client—that is, the individual or group that was paying him—would be told next to nothing: not where or when the abduction would take place, not where the captive was being kept, not who Camano's henchmen were. Most important, once the project was initiated, they would not know where Camano himself was or have any face-to-face contact with him. Disposable cellular phones only.

Because what they didn't know they wouldn't be able to tell the police in the event that things went wrong and they were picked up. Or, in the far more likely event that things went right, they wouldn't be able to prattle anything important to their girlfriends; nothing that would get *him* in trouble, at any rate.

It was safer for the clients too. There would be no traceable connection between them and the kidnapping. And since they knew nothing, there was nothing for them to inadvertently reveal. As for Camano, none would know his real name either. If the police ever found out about the mysterious man who had engineered everything, which did happen now and then, he would be long gone, thousands of miles away, back home in the States.

This was the system, elegantly simple in concept, complex and tricky in execution, with which he had organized and managed thirteen kidnappings for ransom in the last six years. In that time, eleven ransoms had been paid, and only one person, one of his hired kidnappers, had even been brought to trial, and that case had been thrown out on the first day. Which was why Paris could command the fees that he did. Camano himself, it goes without saying, had never been arrested, detained, or even questioned.

At least that was the way the system was supposed to work, and the way it did work most of the time. But sometimes the conditions required changes, and the conditions in Iceland had required the most drastic changes yet. The problem was, the damn place had almost no serious crime and no competent criminals. Thieves and rapists, yes—Icelanders were human, after all, and some things just went with the territory—and even the occasional murderer; an average of three homicides a year in the whole country. There were plenty of pothead protester types who went around banging pans and metal spoons in front of the Parliament building, or throwing green yogurt on "corporate polluters" or the police, but they had nobody he would call professionals—grown-ups—to whom he could feel comfortable delegating the sensitive tasks that were required. Or if they did exist, he had no idea where to locate them. If any kind of criminal underworld network existed, he hadn't been able to find it.

So this job had to be approached differently. The clients themselves would have to handle everything: the kidnapping itself as well as the ensuing captivity. And since the client here was an organization consisting of exactly three people, not enough for twenty-four-hour guarding, and in any case not reliable enough to trust on their own, Camano himself would have to be there on site, a first for him. That made everything hugely more problematic, and he was charging accordingly. He had, in fact, turned them down when they offered his usual fee of $250,000, turned them down again at $300,000, and yet again at $400,000. But when they offered $500,000—*half a million dollars*—it was too much to resist. He'd even squeezed them for an additional hundred thousand before accepting. But he was deeply apprehensive. He was, for all intents and purposes, abandoning the system that had served him so well.

But there was one absolutely crucial element that wouldn't change: Beyond providing direction, Camano would have nothing personally to do with the ransom, not arranging for it with the payees, and certainly not picking it up, matters of which he washed his hands. He was able to operate on this inscribed-in-concrete principle because he dealt only with clients who could provide his fee up front. Oh, they would pay him out of the anticipated ransom? No deal. And he stuck with it. Camano got his money in the form of two payments: a standard initial $100,000 nonreturnable advance, which was already in his possession, and a negotiated final payment—in this case, $500,000. This had been placed in a numbered escrow account in a Cayman Islands bank last month, to be released to him on successful completion of the job.

And he knew just where that money was going too. The advance was already gone, spent to finish paying for his third home, a small but charming stone country house on the French Riviera, on the hillside above Saint-Jean-Cap-Ferrat. And the coming half million, every dollar of it, had been promised to a yacht broker just up the coast in Monaco, who was holding *Callisto*, a glorious, beautifully refurbished, sixty-five-foot Jongert cruising sailboat, for him. A buy like that didn't come along very often, and then only if you could pay for it outright. He had lusted after such a boat for years, and he wanted—needed—this one the way most people needed oxygen. A boat like that—in a place like that—signified that a man had made a success of himself, that he had arrived.

And after that, he just might cut back on his assignments—perhaps one a year, just to keep his hand in—while he was still young and hale enough to enjoy the many pleasures that came with a fancy, two-stateroom yacht in the marina at Saint-Jean-Cap-Ferrat.

Unlike Camano, the majority of his clients had a deep and foolish distrust of banking wire services, and when it came to the rewards for their own labor, they almost always wanted a ransom they could actually see and hold and count; a big bundle of cash; paper money. Camano thought of it as his duty to tell them they were being stupid, but then left it to them. It was no affair of his. By the time a cash ransom was delivered, he would be gone.

In this way, he kept well clear of the most dangerous phase of the process: ransom delivery. If anything were to go wrong—not that it ever had before, but not wildly improbable, given what he had to work with here in Iceland—it would go wrong for the client. For him, the worst that could happen would be the loss of the $500,000 in escrow—and the *Callisto*—a bitter pill, but a lot easier to swallow than a term in prison.

Chapter 8

GlobalSeas was putting us up at the Hilton Nordica Reykjavik, the same hotel in which the training sessions would be held. When we checked in, a little before seven a.m. on Friday morning, the night clerk was still on duty, a skinny kid of twenty, the very height of grunge fashion, circa 1990: spiked green and orange hair, tie-dyed T-shirt, ring in nose, safety pin in lip, etc. But he looked friendly, so I smiled at him and tried out two of the twenty or so words of Icelandic I'd managed to learn. *"Godann dagit,"* I said confidently. *Good morning.*

Whether he was pleased because I got it right, or amused because I screwed it up, I don't know, but he laughed with real delight. *"Godann dagit,* dude!" he yelled back and offered a high-five, which, of course, I accepted.

Other than the clerk, everything about the hotel was as advertised: sleek, up-to-date, and businesslike. Our ninth-floor "executive suite" room, ready for us despite the early hour, had blond hardwood floors, immaculate, minimalist, modern furniture, and floor-to-ceiling windows that looked out over the harbor area, the gray, uninviting waters of the bay, and snow-streaked, table-topped Esja Mountain beyond.

So far, things had gone more smoothly than expected. No problems at all, in fact, except a minor one at the very start, back at Sea-Tac, as we were boarding our flight to Boston. I'd pushed things a bit by deciding to try out Zeta's total immersion technique then and there, simply facing the terror head-on and analyzing the hell out of it. That had lasted about three minutes; by the time the plane started taxiing I had a Xanax inside me, but for once it didn't do its job; I'd begun to hyperventilate. By the time we lifted off, though, I'd had a second, and that had done the trick. To my great relief, no one seemed to have noticed my distress.

At our stopover in Boston, a long one, we'd had a decent dinner at the airport, where Lori ordered scrod, bringing forth the following from our waiter: "Okay, you ready for this? Woman arrives at Logan, asks the cabbie to take her someplace where she can get scrod. Driver turns around and stares at her, amazed. 'Gee, lady, that's the first time I ever heard anybody say it in the past pluperfect.'"

Lori smiled politely but I was goofy enough from the tranquilizers to be still snickering over coffee and dessert. Three hours later we caught our Icelandair plane to Reykjavik. Since it was an overnight flight (as were all flights from the US to Iceland) we'd each done what half the other passengers had apparently done as well: taken a sleeping pill and conked out for the duration. The coffee service with which we were awakened five hours later, twenty minutes before descending to Keflavik Airport, got our blood flowing again, and by the time we stepped off the plane, we were both reasonably refreshed and wonderfully relaxed.

. . .

RELAXED and refreshed we might have felt, but the seven-hour time difference between Seattle and Reykjavik had taken its toll, and after showering and doing a little unpacking, we fell heavy-eyed into bed. We slept from eight until ten-thirty and then we had to hurry to make the only appointment on our schedule that day: a get-acquainted morning coffee with GlobalSeas President and CEO Baldur Baldursson. Fortunately, he'd picked a place that was a five-minute stroll from the hotel: Café Paris on bustling Austurvöllur Square, across from the Icelandic Parliament building. A few brave locals sat at the outdoor tables, but it was too cold for us, and we were inside, surrounded by décor that was more Danish modern than French brasserie. Baldursson was a handsome, hawk-nosed man of fifty, lanky, laid-back, and self-confident, wearing an expensive but bagged-out corduroy jacket with leather elbow pads over a bulky gray turtleneck. Like just about everybody else we'd encountered, he spoke a slightly Europeanized English with complete fluency, and with a soft, agreeable Icelandic lilt, to our ears very similar to a Danish accent. In fact, everybody under forty or so seemed to use English at least as much as Icelandic, even when speaking with each other. In Baldursson's case, there was also a playful tongue-in-cheek quality to his speech, and in his manner as well, an impression of laughter just behind his words, as if he found the world around him, most definitely including you, a continuing source of entertainment.

"I'll say this for you, you've certainly come to Iceland at the right time," he told us as we waited for our coffees and the Icelandic crêpes that we were having on his recommendation. "Late March, early April, this is the perfect time. In the fall, you see, we are all quite deranged, having been driven gaga by months of never-ending daylight. In early spring, on the other hand, we are still catatonic from the long winter darkness. But now, now for this brief moment in time, we are as normal as we get."

We laughed at this and chatted a little more and asked about places to visit. Baldursson named a few scenic wonders but told us by all means to stay away from the much-touted Blue Lagoon. ("All you'll see are other tourists. By the busload.") "And make sure you save time for Reykjavik itself. Here we have many unique sights. A good many places have monuments to their Unknown Soldier, but only in Reykjavik is there a monument to the Unknown Bureaucrat."

We smiled politely, not sure if he was joking, but he insisted he was serious and drew us a little map on a napkin. "It's not far from here. A matter of great civic pride."

The waitress put out three absolutely wonderful-smelling cups of coffee—this was our introduction to Icelandic coffee—and our crêpes. Icelandic dessert crêpes, it turned out, were like their French namesake in that they were filled with whipped cream and jam and covered with strawberries, but the pancakes themselves had been crisped in a deep fryer and served folded in two, rather than rolled, so they looked more like whipped-cream tacos than crêpes. But just as good. Lori rolled her eyes with pleasure after the first bite.

"Baldur," I said, after we'd chewed for a while, "I think we should talk a little about the seminar."

He waved his fork in a little circle. "That's what we're here for."

"When we start on Monday morning, I'd appreciate it if you introduce me and talk a bit about the importance of the training. It helps me if they know it has your backing."

"Of course. I'll be happy to." He used the fork to indicate the crêpes. "Good, huh?"

"They're wonderful. Once the training gets started, though, I'd like it if you more or less took a backseat, or at least let the others get in their two cents before you put in yours. Otherwise, with the boss sitting right there . . . What?" He was waving the fork again and shaking his head while chewing.

"Oh, I won't be staying for the training itself," he said when the cream and strawberries had gone down. "I thought you understood that. There's no reason for me to take it."

"What?" I couldn't believe it. Here was the man who only a few months ago had been the object of a kidnapping attempt—in which two people had gotten killed in a wild shootout—and there was no reason for him to take a training program in kidnapping prevention?

Before I could get any words out, Baldursson laughed. "You should see the expression on your face, Bryan."

"Well, I hope it shows disbelief, disapproval, and total disagreement with that decision, because that's what I'm feeling. You of all people—"

"Bryan, calm down and listen to reason," he said easily. "Believe me, no one can get near me. I pay a lot of money so that I don't need any training. In the first place, I am now guarded around the clock by a firm of armed protection specialists. Interestingly, it's a Danish firm, because Iceland has no such—"

"You're here now," I pointed out, "in a public place, and I don't see any 'armed protection specialists,' Danish or otherwise."

He smiled and waved a hand in the general direction of an ordinary-looking guy in an unzipped parka a few tables away, coffee and pastries in front of him, but facing in a direction that took in both the entrance and our table. When I looked at him, he gave me a tiny nod.

"That's Petrus. There are three of them altogether. They serve as my chauffeurs as well. I don't drive anywhere myself anymore."

"Okay, that's all well and good, but there's more than that to protecting yourself. Do you understand that the fact that they came after you once makes it *more* likely that they'll try again?"

"Yes, I do, and I've taken precautions." He had bought a new home since the kidnapping, he explained, and equipped it with the finest security systems available (also from Denmark). In addition, the house was in the middle of two acres of walled lawns with motion detectors. The Grindavik plant, which housed his office and was where he spent his days, had a ten-foot, razor-wire-topped steel fence completely surrounding it, and his car was armored, was equipped with a rearview camera and bulletproof glass, and possessed Iceland's only internal car alarm button that linked directly to the police.

"Well, I admit, that's pretty thorough, but I don't see what the problem is with sitting through a few days of training. There's a lot of new information, new approaches in it. You could pick up a single tip that could save your life."

"The problem," he said with a first hint of asperity, "is that I refuse to let my entire life be consumed with keeping myself safe. I do enough. There are other things to live for."

That was hard to argue with. "I can understand that."

"Bryan," Lori said, "isn't there a trainee manual that goes with the course? Maybe you could make a copy for Baldur to read through."

"Good idea," said Baldur, smiling again. "I suppose I can make that much time available."

And there we left it, except for one other issue.

"Baldur, do you carry a gun?" The bulkiness and looseness of his jacket had seemed to me to suggest he might be wearing a shoulder holster, and I'd been trying to see if I could spot the strap when he moved one way or the other. I thought I did at one point, but I wasn't sure.

We had finished our crêpes. The waitress came and took them away, and Baldur ordered fresh coffee for the three of us. I got the impression he was using the time to decide how to answer.

He decided, as I thought he might, on not answering. "Should I? What do you recommend?"

"Have you had training? Do you know how to handle a gun? Do you practice?"

"No. Well, a little."

"A little's not enough. Having a professional armed bodyguard"—I tipped my head toward the other table—"yes, good idea. Carrying a sidearm yourself? Not a good idea. Unless, that is, you're comfortable with it and well trained, in which case, in my opinion, it *is* a good idea, although a lot of experts wouldn't agree with me. The thing is, your best chance of escaping is right there at the beginning, before they take you, and with a gun you stand a better chance of being able to do that. But you also stand a *much* greater chance of getting yourself killed."

"What would you do if you were me?"

"If I were you? I wouldn't carry a gun." This was a bit deceitful, because if I were *me*, and I was in any danger of being a target, I'd have a sidearm on me, training or no training. But then, I'm a special case, or so I like to think. From my point of view, avoiding capture is worth just about any risk. But Baldur wasn't me. So there you are, yet another example of *Do as the teacher says.*

We wrapped up after that, without Baldur's ever answering my question, and Lori and I went out looking for the Unknown Bureaucrat. We found him too, in a public courtyard only a block from the café: a life-sized bronze statue of a man in a business suit carrying an attaché case, with his head and shoulders encased in a giant rock. A one-of-a-kind, all right.

THE rest of the long weekend was as advertised by Wally: interesting and enjoyable. We rented a car and drove the Golden Circle out of Reykjavik, *ooh*ing at the plumes of steam and water at Strokkur and Geysir (*geysir*, we were informed, is the only Icelandic word to make it into international use) and *aah*ing at the truly magnificent two-tiered Gullfoss falls, still partly frozen. On the Reykjanes peninsula near Hafnir, we stood on the Bridge Between Two Continents and looked down at the surface rift that marks the separation between the European and North American tectonic plates. There, two different Icelanders, apparently lying in wait for foreigners, told us the same joke: Because the plates are drifting apart at the rate of one inch annually, Iceland gets an inch wider every year. So it is on its way to becoming the biggest country in the world. Just give it sixty million years.

And of course we ignored Baldursson's advice and spent a happy late afternoon, as has every other tourist who has ever visited Iceland, lolling in the warm, milky blue waters of the Blue Lagoon, wreathed in veils of geothermally heated steam and surrounded by ice-covered outcroppings of lava rock, watching snowflakes spiral down around us and melt into tiny water droplets a foot or so before they hit the surface. We laughed a lot, and we made love in the middle of the afternoon for the first time in a while. At the restaurants, we tried a few Icelandic delicacies—minke whale (other than being purple, not unlike beef), smoked puffin (a cross between burnt rubber and cod liver oil), and Icelandic lamb (sensational). All very interesting, but other than the lamb, once was enough; more than enough in the case of the puffin. Other local specialties, we lacked the courage to face (singed sheep's head, rotting shark). In general, though, the restaurant food was simple, fresh, and surprisingly bland.

The weather wasn't as bad as we'd feared. We both had brand-new high-tech Iditarod-approved parkas, but they were overkill. Reykjavik in late March wasn't that much different from the Pacific Northwest in early March. No, let me take that back; the weather here was an improvement over Seattle's. With the sun coming up at six and not going down till nine, there were almost twice as many daylight hours, which was a welcome change. It was cold but not unbearably cold—up in the mid- to high thirties in the daytime, lower at night, with snow flurries or sleety rain coming down out of a pewter sky once or twice a day, so that there was usually an inch or so of melting snow on the sidewalks (frozen over and slippery in the mornings), but no more. We wound up spending a good many hours walking on those sidewalks because, even equipped with a good city map, we were lost half the time. Mostly, it was the street names that flummoxed us.

Who but an Icelander could pronounce, let alone keep straight, street names like Bolstaoarhlio, Braedraborgarstigur, and Vatnsmýrarvegur? And they were all like that: Frikirkjuvegur, Kringlumyrarbraut, Sjafnargata. To make it even more fun, there wasn't one simple right-angle intersection in the whole city; every conceivable, multifaceted set of angles but. Still, it gave us plenty of excuses to stop in at a coffeehouse to warm up over a couple of steaming, aromatic cups and ask for directions. Sample of directions: "No, no, this is Laufásvegur. It's Laugavegur you're looking for. Just go up Njardargata, left on Skólavöroustigour, right on Klapparstígur, and you're there—Laugavegur. Although, come to think of it, it might be called Bankastraeti by that point. But don't worry, you can't miss it." Miss it we could and did, but in the end we wound up seeing a lot more of Reykjavik than we would have otherwise. And happily drinking a lot more excellent coffee.

At sunset on two of the three days we bundled up and sat out on the balcony of our room. The view over the bay, bleak and glowering most of the time, was stunning at day's end, when bands of riveting, fiery orange lit up the gloomy skies and turned the snow on distant Esja to molten lava. Twilights of the gods.

All in all, by Sunday night I was more confident than ever that accepting the assignment had been the right thing to do. I was starting to think that I'd turned a real corner. There had been no more panic attacks. Tomorrow after lunch the training would begin, and not only wasn't I dreading it, I was looking forward to it, or at least to the opportunity to prove to myself that it was no big deal, that I could not only handle it, but handle it with ease.

Of course, I understood that a big part of this upbeat frame of mind was the knowledge that I had the Xanax right there with me in case of need. In fact, my plan was to take one before going to bed the night before each session just to be on the safe side. It was something I didn't like to do, but I wanted to make sure I'd be upbeat and energetic for the training, not drained from a possible panic attack the night before. I knew very well, of course, that taking the pills that way could start me on a dangerous slide. Xanax was a benzodiazepine, a central nervous system depressant, and as with all of them, there were the risks of muddle-headedness and dependence if I overdid it. It may not sound like it, but I was anything but an eager consumer of happiness pills. I was careful; I'd always been careful. Never more than that one a day—well, hardly ever—and never increasing the dosage. Well, from .25 milligram tablets to .50 milligram ones, but that had been a few years ago, and I'd stayed with the fifty ever since. Besides, I'd only be doing it for five nights, and I wasn't going to become a dope addict in five nights; not at half a milligram a pop.

Chapter 9

Like most of her kind, Zeta Parkington had learned to leave her patients' troubles at the office (most of the time). It hadn't come easily to her, but it had been either that or find another line of work, and so she'd taught herself to do it. Only rarely nowadays was she unable to keep the psychological torments of some wretched soul in her care from intruding on her Monday morning rotating bridge gatherings or her Friday dinners in Issaquah with her thrice-divorced daughter's latest family. Psychologists should not be allowed to have children, she thought, not for the first time; they all turn out to have a few too many screws loose.

Bryan Bennett was hardly one of the wretched souls, but in the few days since their session she had found her thoughts straying to him at odd moments, so much so that today with the bridge party at her condo, she'd confounded her partner by absentmindedly fooling around with other suits when any novice would have known to pull trump. She had resolved then and there that she needed to take some time to determine what it was about him that was nagging at her. As was true with most of her resolutions, she was acting on it at the first opportunity.

The girls (some "girls"; the youngest was sixty-three) had left fifteen minutes earlier, and the living and dining rooms were littered with lipstick-smeared glasses of melting ice, half-filled coffee cups, and plates of leftover cherry cheesecake. All that could wait. For now, she had reheated a mug of coffee in the microwave and carried it out onto her terrace with her first cigarillo of the afternoon (five before noon, five in the afternoon, two in the evening; those were her limits, strictly adhered to). From the twelfth-story terrace she looked across Puget Sound toward Bainbridge Island, or would have had the sound not been shrouded in March's usual fog. On the other side of the water the Olympics were invisible in the gray pall, but it was nice to know they were there, and after the staleness of the indoors, it was wonderful to feel the clean, cold air flowing down from the glaciers and across six miles of open water, as if directly to her. *I am the first person in all of Seattle to breathe this fresh, good air,* she liked to tell herself, usually followed by a smaller voice, easily ignored: *a lot of good it's doing you, with you smoking these damn things.*

She lay back in the recliner, got her swollen feet out of their shoes, started on the coffee, and devoted her mind to thoughts of Bryan Bennett.

What was it about the man that was so intriguing?

By the time it came to her she had finished the cigarillo and was nursing the last of the coffee with both hands around the mug for warmth. She had been about to get up to bring out a sweater and maybe a little more coffee—with a jot of brandy this time—when the pieces fell suddenly into place.

He wasn't sick enough; that was the problem.

No, not exactly. The problem was that he should have been either in worse shape or in better shape—anything but the middling shape he was in. Assuming that the root of his difficulties was the kidnapping episode when he'd been a kid (exacerbated many years later by the hostage incident in which the two little girls died), what he was suffering from was surely a form of PTSD, posttraumatic stress disorder. And in her experience, people's reactions to traumatic stress—rape, combat, torture, near-death encounters—fell into two general classes. Either—and this was most of them—they put it behind them and moved on, suffering at worst an occasional bad dream, unpleasant association, or bout of melancholy; or else they fell over the precipice entirely, to become loners, haunted through the years by frightening, realistic flashbacks during the day and harrowing nightmares in which they relived the most terrible of their experiences. To greater or lesser degrees they were emotionally numbed, they had marital difficulties, and they had trouble holding on to their jobs. More often than not, heavy drug or alcohol dependence came into the picture.

There wasn't much doubt about which class Bryan fit into. He was happy in his marriage and successful in his work, with no drug or alcohol problems to speak of. His occasional reliance on the Xanax was minimal, no cause for concern. And he was untroubled by the two most reliable criteria of PTSD: the nightmares and those sudden, overwhelming flashbacks that could be triggered by a simple knock on the door or the sound of a car starting up. Panic attacks were surely awful things, but they were different from nightmares, and his relatively generalized phobias and aversions were a long way from the debilitating, highly specific hallucinations that went along with PTSD flashbacks.

In fact, from what she could tell, he thought only infrequently about either his months of captivity or the shootout in the celery field.

Bryan Bennett, in other words, was hardly any worse off than your run-of-the-mill neurotic, which left Zeta with an intriguing question: If he was fragile enough to still be bothered so many years after the original incident with his rather pedestrian range of neuroses, how had he withstood his fifty-eight days in a dungeon without *really* crumbling? Or ask its converse, and the question was no less provocative: If he was mentally and emotionally sound enough to withstand those two terrible months without turning into an emotional puddle, how was it that years later he'd fallen victim to his set of commonplace but troublesome neuroses? Either way it didn't add up, at least not on the surface.

But underneath the surface? Well, maybe it did, after all. This could turn into something interesting, she thought. She sat quietly for another minute, then shivered in the chill and went inside. She dialed the number of the departmental secretary they still allowed her as an emeritus at the U and requested a few hours of graduate research assistant time over the next few days. A little research in the U's library stacks was in order, and she thought she knew just where to look.

EVERY job, George Henry Camano had learned through the years, had a fly in the ointment somewhere, no matter how straightforward it was made to seem on the surface. In this case, it was one huge monster fly: the client organization. The VBJ, the *Verkefnid* Something Something. This was a pretty hard crew to take seriously, and not only because they had no more members than they did letters in their acronym. It went considerably beyond that.

The first thing that had caught his eye in their "citizens' command center" (a swishy apartment in an unabashedly upper-middle class section of Reykjavik, toward which he was now walking) had been two big quotations, clipped from cheap newsletters, highlighted with yellow marker, and taped to the wall.

Property is theft.

The substitution of the proletarian for the bourgeois state cannot be accomplished without a violent revolution.

Lenin and Proudhon. Mr. Communist and Mr. Anarchist. Camano had come close to laughing, not just at the flyblown slogans themselves, but at the murky thinking that went into taping *both* of them up. Which were they, anarchists or Marxists? Did they honestly think the two systems—if you could call anarchism a system—could peacefully coexist? Yes, they did, subscribing to a muzzy concept called anarcho-communism. It made no sense to Camano. How did they suppose real anarchists felt about submitting to a "state," whether proletarian or bourgeois, liberal or reactionary? What did they imagine dedicated Marxists thought about the "self-organized" social revolution that was the cornerstone of anarchism?

Not that he was interested enough to ask. Long ago, during his student years, Camano himself *had* been an ardent revolutionary, a fiery young Marxist-Leninist, an adoring disciple of Marcuse and Guillen. But by the time he was twenty the windy rhetoric had worn him down. All they had to do was keep it up, he'd finally told his "comrades," and in the end they wouldn't have to shoot the capitalists; they'd all have been bored to death. Soon afterward he had become an only slightly less fervent anarchist. That had lasted until he realized he was surrounded by addled juveniles who might just as well have been walking around with *loser* tattooed on their foreheads. If there had been anti-corporatists or eco-fanatics back then, he probably would have given them a shot too. But then his great epiphany had come: There was money to be made from these airheads, real money. Since then he'd been more concerned with efficiency and cost-effectiveness than with the depredations of the global capitalist monoculture. Oh, there'd been a setback or two early on, but he had learned what he could from them and put them behind him. And he had prospered.

The VBJ had come into existence two years earlier as an off-the-wall group of five University of Iceland graduate students, acolytes at the altar of a middle-aged professor of sociology, Magnus Halldórsson. Decidedly uncharismatic at the lectern—disorganized and stammering and given to swallowing his words—Halldórsson was a tiger when it came to writing incendiary tracts, and it was his prose that had given the movement its impetus.

At first, meeting periodically in one or another of the students' apartments, in the spirit of irreverent fun they had called themselves, in English, the Free Radicals. But things changed early on in what had started out as one more stunt that was supposed to end in nothing worse than a yogurt pie in the face of the CEO of a baby-food company that used biologically engineered meat in its products. Somehow, without meaning to, they'd wound up with the executive in their possession. Having no idea what to do with him or how to do it (their original goal had been nothing more than to get the pie-in-the-face picture into the papers), they had ended up more or less inadvertently extorting a million-and-a-half dollars from his parent company in Denmark. The whole affair had been handled privately; no one outside of the company had even known that there had been a kidnapping.

But other people soon did. Kidnapping for ransom was unheard of in Iceland, and the thrilling news had quickly run through the coffeehouse grapevine that served the substantial community of disaffected Reykjavik youth. Here was something *real*, not just more high-flown, airy locutions or silly pies in the face, but something that made a *difference*. The escapade brought the Free Radicals thirty new members, with cells in three of the island's districts, and they had earnestly set about the job of rescuing the planet, renaming themselves accordingly: *Verkefnið Björgum Jörðinni*—Project Save the Earth. Humor, especially self-deprecating humor, was now a thing of the past.

But their first serious undertaking had been a catastrophe: a slipshod attempt to kidnap Baldursson, the GlobalSeas CEO, in which two of their members had been killed and a police officer wounded. This was a bit *too* real for most of them. The chapters vanished, the new recruits melted away, and half the founding members as well.

Now, only these three were left, and Camano wasn't too crazy about any of them. The professor himself, Magnus, was still aboard, but he was the weak sister of the crew. Yes, he had propounded the anarcho-communist gobbledygook that was the underpinning—in Camano's view, the decidedly wobbly underpinning—of the VBJ. "Willing submission to authority is the root cause of the earth's ongoing destruction," blah, blah, blah. This and other gems were taped to the wall too, but these days Magnus wasn't propounding very much or doing anything else that was vaguely useful either. He was a disgraced ex-professor now, and keeping a low profile.

Within half an hour of meeting him, Camano had him pegged. He was well acquainted with the type: It was one thing to sputter on about class struggle and capitalism-induced ecosystem degradation at his computer with a jelly Danish and a cup of coffee at his side, but getting involved in the brawl at ground level, that was something else altogether. Magnus Halldórsson was a weak, unhappy man, dismayed at what he had wrought and desperately wondering how the hell he was going to get out of it without getting himself either killed or arrested.

Camano didn't know and hadn't asked to what purpose they planned to put the ransom money, but he was willing to bet that if Magnus got his hands on any or all of it, he—and it—would never be seen again.

Once upon a time, but not anymore, the mercurial, unreliable Stig Trygvasson had been one of those worshipful acolytes, and although he'd long ago stopped admiring the man—contempt was closer to the mark now—he still held deeply to his old professor's "teachings." Magnus had spent his life preaching the virtues of an anarcho-communist-libertarian world; Stig actually *lived* in it. A furtive, squinchy-eyed thirty-year-old, feverish and reptilian, Stig scared the hell out of Camano. He was trouble waiting to happen, a grenade ready to explode, a loose cannon if ever there was one. Put a black beard on him and he could be the wild-eyed anarchist in the old political cartoons, about to lob a black, fuse-sputtering bomb at one societal institution or another ("Patriotism," "Government," "Capitalism"). Camano had so far handled him with kid gloves, but it was a tricky situation. He had not the least doubt that Stig would come to a bad end; he just didn't want to be around when it happened.

The third member was the lone female, Gullveig Válisdóttir, which wasn't really her name. She'd been born Dagnyár Eyjólfsdóttir, Camano knew. Gullveig Válisdóttir was a nom de guerre she'd picked for herself: Gullveig, Norse goddess of war and rebirth, Váli, god of vengeance. Personally, Camano liked Dagnyár better, but he was in no position to object to fake names. At this moment, the three passports in the left inside pocket of his parka had three different names on them.

Gullveig was a question mark. He couldn't figure out what she was doing there, and he suspected that she wasn't sure either. Although she readily mouthed the platitudes of the feminist/anarchist/communist/eco-nut role she'd constructed for herself, he sensed her heart—and maybe her mind—wasn't in it. His impression was that what had kept her in the group had more to do with inertia than with enthusiasm. She reminded him of the plain-Jane coeds back home who had hung around the foreign students' clubs because no one looked at them twice at the regular frats and social clubs. The fact that she had had an affair with Magnus and was now sleeping with Stig (after a period of overlap) did nothing to increase his confidence in her judgment. Or in theirs: Gullveig was a slow, dumpy, moon-faced girl who eschewed makeup, wore great galumphing combat boots, and probably didn't shave her armpits (although that he didn't know and hoped never to know).

Fortunately, judgment was a nonissue. This operation would not depend on Gullveig's judgment, or Magnus, or even Stig, who was the de facto leader, or at least the de facto mover, of the bunch. It was Camano who was directing the show, and from the very first of their dealings he had made it crystal clear that he wanted no suggestions, no creative ideas, nothing but unflagging adherence to the plan he would lay down. That was the only way he operated; take it or leave it.

They'd taken it. It had been only a few weeks after the Baldursson catastrophe that they'd had the good sense to contact him for their next try, using the last of their baby-food money to recruit him. When he learned that it was GlobalSeas they wanted to go after again, he'd advised choosing another target—weren't there any other local companies that were raping the environment or exploiting the working class that they could hit? But no. As they saw it, GlobalSeas had been responsible for the two deaths of their members (they were wrong; they were the ones who had bungled the operation from the beginning), and now it was once again Baldursson they wanted. Camano had accepted the commission in the end, once he was certain that they didn't have a messy, dicey assassination in mind, but merely another ransom extortion.

And that was a state of affairs that he knew how to manage better than anyone else in the world.

Chapter 10

Everything was going just fine; couldn't have been better. GlobalSeas had booked the Hilton's ninth-floor Executive Lounge to hold the seminar, so my morning commute to work was a twenty-yard walk down the hall from our room. Coffee, pastries, and soft drinks were set up for us each morning, the tables and chairs were comfortable and informal, and the attendees were receptive and friendly.

It was Thursday morning now—I'd made it past the half-way point, and I was still flying high. There had been only one shaky moment, and that had been more laughable than disturbing. On Sunday night there had been a reception and cocktail party in the famous Ice Bar at the Restaurant Reykjavik, a big old yellow warehouse of a place down near the docks. The entire bar—that is, the room itself—is made out of ice, ostensibly from the glaciers: walls, counter, pedestal tables, chairs (they're covered with furs), even the glasses. Bottles of vodka are stored in recessions in the walls. (Vodka, unlike wine and other spirits, doesn't freeze or turn to a gel.) Illumination is by way of spooky blue lights that shine through the ice from the other side. The place is kept at a steady twenty-one degrees Fahrenheit, so at the door they hand you a quilted parka and a pair of gloves, plus a healthy jigger of Brennevín to get your furnace going, which it most certainly does. Brennevín is a Scandinavian schnapps made from fermented potato pulp and flavored with caraway. Unfortunately, it tastes about the way it sounds, but it does turn up your temperature. The Icelanders call it the "Black Death."

The whole thing is hokey but fun, or would have been fun, except that the room is only about twelve by twelve, and low-ceilinged to boot, and with a dozen people already crammed into its dim blue interior, it wasn't for me. I'd taken one look, handed back my parka and gloves (too late to give back the Brennevín), and headed the other way.

"I don't think this is my kind of place," I'd said to Lori, and we'd both laughed.

Other than that, there had been no problems. I'd fretted about the possibility of panicking right out in public, if something sensitive came up once the training itself got under way, but no such thing had happened. So far it had been a snap; I was enjoying myself. Of course, it was the easy, abstract part of the program we'd been through: contingency planning, security measures, that kind of thing. I'd covered the establishment of corporate policies and crisis committees; the following of simple precautionary rules of life at home and in the office—avoiding personal and family publicity, keeping an eye out for cars that passed more than once in the neighborhood, not accepting telephone requests to go someplace unless you were sure of the caller's identity; and the taking of defensive steps when on the road: not stopping at the same gas station more than a couple of times in a row, taking care not to be boxed in by two vehicles (especially vans or trucks), not getting into the first taxi in line or the one that comes up to the curb where you're standing, and so on. Special watchfulness on the way to or from work is paramount, since that's when something like ninety-eight percent of all kidnappings happen.

Unfrightening, relatively impersonal stuff, all of it. Nothing to get me unstrung. But this morning we were due to get into the other part of the material, the tough part: what happens *after* a successful abduction—negotiations, ransom, and, worst of all, the ordeal of being a hostage if you have the wretched luck to be taken despite all your precautions. That was the part that had me worried. Sure, I'd been able to make myself write about that aspect of it and to read about the experiences of others, but, except for Lori, Dr. Benson (that long-ago psychiatrist), and now Zeta, I had never, not once in all these years, talked to anyone about the devastating personal horror and emotional dislocation of captivity.

This morning I'd gotten to the lounge early and staked out an isolated nook in which to review my notes and fret about how well I was going to be able to cope with the upcoming subject matter, while the attendees gathered at the buffet table in the meeting area to sip coffee, munch pastries, and gossip.

There were sixteen people in attendance, all senior executives: ten corporate types from the Grindavik plant, four headquartered in Reykjavik, and the two regional directors. By now I knew them all by name: Ingimar, Alvar, Lilja, Lara, Tryggvi, Ragnar, and so on. What their last names were, I didn't have a clue. In Iceland, nobody bothers with surnames. If you bump into Prime Minister Jóhanna Sigurðardóttir on your way to work one morning (not all that unlikely in Reykjavik), you don't say "Good morning, Prime Minister Sigurðardóttir"; you say "Good morning, Jóhanna."

It's not a question of disrespect or informality; it's a matter of practicality. The thing is, for ninety percent of the population, your surname isn't really a family name. All it reveals about you is your father's name—his *first* name. It works like this: If your father's first name is Gunnar, then your last name is Gunnarsson. That's if you're a boy. If you're a girl, than your last name is Gunnarssdóttir. This is, of course, something like the way most European naming systems worked in ancient times. Your father was named John? Then your name's Johnson. Robert? Robertson. Jack? Jackson. But eventually these turned into family names and stuck, generation after generation.

Except in Iceland, where they last just the one generation. And when you add to this the fact that women keep their own names when they marry, the result is that in a conventional family of four—mom, dad, son, daughter—nobody has the same last name. Not only that, but all four surnames disappear in the next generation. You don't have the same name as your grandparents or grandchildren either. As a consequence, even the telephone book here is alphabetized by first name, not last; otherwise, nobody would be able to—

"Bryan, it's after nine, shouldn't we be getting under way? Everybody's waiting for you."

I started. My mind had wandered quite a ways away from my notes. "Right you are, Ingimar, be right there."

Ingimar was GlobalSeas' vice president and director of operations. Older by ten years than anyone else in the group, and older than Baldursson as well, he was second in command at GlobalSeas. I'd gotten the impression from him, and from the way the others responded to him, that he'd been promoted once or twice too often, having reached his level of incompetence years ago. Whatever he'd been before, he was serving out his time now and doing it strictly by the book.

I stood up to follow him, but lagged behind a little, fingering the vial in my pocket. I'd resolved not to swallow a precautionary pretraining Xanax (so far, I'd stuck to my resolve of one daily tablet, taken at bedtime, no more), but now that the moment was here I was wavering. Already, I could feel my breaths become shallower and more rapid.

To hell with it. I pulled the cap off the vial and tossed a little orange pill into my mouth, doing it quickly before I could change my mind. Almost immediately, my breathing slowed down. I was kidding myself, of course. That is, I knew perfectly well that the drug couldn't possibly get into my system that quickly, so at this point it was no more than a mental crutch, a placebo. The mere act of taking the thing was what was propping me up. But after all, an imaginary crutch for an imaginary problem, why not?

I repocketed the vial and stood there for a while longer, letting the strength and calmness, real or perceived, flow back into me. Maybe I'd take one tomorrow morning too, the last day of the program, in addition to the one I'd been popping at night to ensure that I slept through. The stuff wasn't making me dopey or slow, as far as I could tell. It just kept me levelheaded and calm, so that the terrors and heebie-jeebies couldn't get their claws into me. It made me better at the training, more able to deal honestly and helpfully with the subject matter. It wasn't as if I really *needed* them, you understand, or couldn't stop myself from taking them if I'd wanted to; but clearly it'd be better to head off the anxiety that had been building all morning before it got a foothold. Anyway, it would only be for one more day.

No big deal.

Chapter 11

The plan was simple and straightforward, but it depended on precise timing and quick action. The full massed army of the VBJ—all three of them—would be waiting in their vehicle, a dusty gray Ford Econoline passenger van with tinted windows. It would be parked and ready in the lot beside Grindavik's Saltfish Museum (the world's one and only), across a narrow alley from the sliding gate that provided the sole access to the GlobalSeas loading yard. Gullveig would be at the wheel. Behind her, in the body of the van, would be Magnus and Stig. Three minutes after the electric-powered gate rolled open for the Saegreifinn refrigerator truck, Gullveig would start the van's engine. As soon as the pallet of fish had been loaded and the truck's door pulled closed, Stig would slide the van's door open but remain inside with the others.

When the red metal door to Baldursson's office on the upper floor of the metal-sided building next to the loading dock opened and he started down the stairway, all three would pull on black ski masks and Gullveig would move the gearshift to Drive, but keep her foot on the brake pedal. Then, the instant Baldursson reached for the truck driver's manifest, she would stomp on the accelerator, and the truck would hurtle across the alley and through GlobalSeas' open gate. As it skidded to a stop at the loading dock, Stig and Magnus would leap out, screaming and rapid-firing their blank-loaded semiautomatics, thereby shocking and intimidating the hell out of the truck driver, the forklift operator, and Baldursson. Gullveig would quickly get the truck spun around so it faced the open gate, Baldursson would be muscled into the van by Stig and Magnus, and they would be on their way. They would be through the gate in three to four seconds (at Paris's insistence, they had rehearsed the operation a dozen times in an empty lot with markers laid out to scale), so even if someone pressed the button to roll the gate shut, it wouldn't come close to catching them.

They would speed north up Hafnagarta, then swing left at the corner onto Ránargata, as if they were heading toward the Reykjavik highway, but after two blocks they would turn right into the unmarked alley that led to a nameless, little-used dirt road that meandered inland through the lava fields toward Kleifarvatn, an unvisited, slowly disappearing lake in the middle of nowhere. Four miles down this track, out of sight behind one of the many rocky outcroppings alongside it, the transfer vehicle would be waiting, a 1988 Cadillac hearse with black-curtained windows and a blind rear quarter, into which they would pile. They would leave the Ford in its place and head back in the opposite direction toward their hideout, a rented three-room apartment on the ground floor of a newly constructed, half-occupied complex of four six-story apartment buildings in Kópavogur, a nondescript residential municipality along the N1, on the sprawling southern outskirts of Reykjavik. There Baldursson would be kept while ransom negotiations proceeded. Paris had assured them that it would take one week at the most.

That was the plan. But in kidnappings, even more than in life in general, plans have a way of not exactly proceeding according to plan.

THE problem was that Baldur Baldursson wasn't cooperating. In the first place, he wasn't where he was supposed to be, upstairs in his office next door; he was in the warehouse itself, where the back of the building had been outfitted with giant experimental marine tanks swirling with char and halibut at all stages of maturation from newly hatched fry to adult.

Second, he was not alone.

And third—unknown to the VBJ, to Camano, and to Baldursson's own security people—he was armed.

Chapter 12

"I'll tell you what really terrifies me about the possibility of being abducted," said Lilja, one of the regional directors, a dignified older woman who wore her graying hair in an old-fashioned bun and her glasses on a lanyard around her neck. "Not so much the possibility of physical abuse—of torture—but the psychological aspect. The idea of being cooped up, all alone, for day after day, maybe in the dark, maybe chained up, in some roach-infested dungeon . . . And what about the humiliation—I mean, how do you even handle—" The next part was difficult for her to say, but she shifted her gaze to the window, and got the words out through set lips. "—how do you handle, well, for example, going to the bathroom in a bucket or something if you know they're watching you? I just . . . I mean, I can't imagine—"

Oh, great, just what I needed. I inhaled deeply, grasping the lectern with both hands. This was getting too close. "It's a good question," I said, speaking slowly and evenly. Even with the tranquilizer in my system, I could feel the familiar stirrings of that skittish, sickish feeling in my chest. The key here was to treat the matter abstractly, not personally; to answer it with what I knew from my research, from the studies I'd read, from the experiences of others, and not with what I knew from my own childhood. *Don't think about menacing figures in faceless black hoods with holes for eyes; don't think about a befouled plastic bucket in the corner, or cowering under a plank bed while . . .*

"If it should happen to you," I said, "what you have to understand and accept is that you *are* going to undergo one of the most devastating experiences that a human being can have. There's no getting around it. You pass in an instant from being in command of your activities, with friends and family and a daily routine, to being utterly isolated, completely unprotected, and in threatening, unfamiliar surroundings. Your dignity, your ability to order your own life, what you like or don't like—they're all things of the past. But you *can* deal with it, believe me."

The trainees, not all that attentive in the earlier part of the program, were listening so intently now that they didn't seem to be breathing.

I realized that I wasn't either, and I made myself expel the air I'd been holding in, take in a fresh breath, and relax— try to relax—the tightening muscles at the base of my neck. "And the first few days are going to be the hardest of all, and the first few hours, once you get over the numbness and disbelief, are going to be the hardest of those. That's just the way it is, and it's better if you know it ahead of time, because even then, in those terrible hours, what you *don't* want to do is sit around pitying yourself, analyzing and reanalyzing what happened, asking yourself again and again, 'Why me, what could I have done differently?' You have to fight back, and there are plenty of ways to do it.

Memorize your surroundings, observe everything you can so you can help the police afterward. Plan your survival, plan escapes. Do math puzzles in your head, or write poetry. Exercise, keep yourself in good shape, so you're ready if an escape opportunity comes. Above all, there are two critical things you have to try to do . . ."

The silence in the room was as brittle as spun glass.

"First—and it's impossible to emphasize this too much— for your own sanity, you have to establish some control over the situation; you can't just let yourself be completely passive, completely in their control. Cooperate to the extent that you have to, yes, but at the same time look for ways that you can assert your independence—"

The hotel desk manager, fussy and self-important in the time-honored manner of hotel desk managers at ritzy hotels, had come into the lounge and leaned over to whisper something to Ingimar.

The vice-president listened for a moment, then pulled back to stare at the man. "You can't be serious," I heard him say, and a second later he was making for the elevator bank with the manager scurrying after him. The others paid no attention. It wasn't uncommon for Ingimar to be called away from the sessions by one "emergency" or another, not to return again that morning or afternoon. Still, a little shiver of apprehension crawled down my neck.

"Let's see," I said, "we were talking about . . ."

"The two critical things," someone prompted.

"Right. Extremely critical. Second—and this is vital for your physical safety—you have to try every way you can to get them to recognize you as a human being, a real person, just like they are, and not simply as an object to— Tryggvi, did you want to say something?"

Tryggvi, pale-haired, pale-eyed, slow-moving, and soft-bodied—a sluggish guy in the most literal sense of the word—was the head of quality control. Squirmy by nature, he'd really been fidgeting away for the past couple of minutes.

"Yes, I do," he said nervously. "I *am* worried about physical abuse. I'm pretty sure I can handle taking a crap in a bucket, but. . . . well, physical things . . . for example, what if they want us to confess our crimes against the earth or something, and they . . . you know . . ." His voice trailed away.

"Torture you? That's extremely unlikely, Tryggvi. If your abductors were political or religious terrorists out to shock or intimidate, that'd be one thing, but assuming that your captors—if you *were* to be taken—would be after a ransom of one kind or another, there'd be no percentage for them in torturing you. Or in mutilating or killing you, for that matter. It doesn't happen very often."

This wasn't good enough for Tryggvi. "But it does happen."

"Yes, it happens." *Here, let me show you where my little toe used to be.*

"So, how do you recommend we deal with it?"

"My advice is to resist it for as long as you can possibly stand it."

Tryggvi looked shocked. He didn't like the advice at all. Neither would I. Who would? "The thing is, I'm not sure how brave I am," he said, looking down at his plump, clasped hands.

"Tryggvi, it's not a question of being brave, it's a question of strategy. If you knuckle under and do what they want without putting up at least some resistance, then what you're telling them is that the way to get whatever they want from you is through torture. You're reinforcing their behavior. And that means that from then on there's going to be more of it, not less of it. Which is probably something you'd rather not have happen."

"Yes, but I've never been tested, you see. I just don't know how I'd stand up to physical pain." A few of the others nodded uneasily. Someone's nervous titter was quickly cut off.

I came out from behind the portable lectern and sat on the front edge of the table. From the other five tables, gathered into a semicircle, the trainees watched me silently. Most had put down their pens. "Look, people," I said, "I'm not telling you to stand firm while they cut you up into little pieces. Remember, if you do get abducted, the chances are good—way, way better than even—that you're going to get out of it alive, and your first responsibility is to yourselves and your families—to be in decent physical and mental shape when it's all over. If you do give in and deliver some kind of phony confession in front of a video camera, it's no big deal. People know the difference between a real statement and a confession under duress."

"Mr. Bennett, do you have a minute, please?" The desk manager was back, leaning in from the doorway and looking distinctly put out. "They'd like to see you downstairs. They're in the lobby bar."

"Take a break," I told the trainees, and followed him to the elevator down the hall, feeling much relieved. The training had gotten into pretty squirmy territory for me as well, and I too really needed a break.

Then I thought: *They?* and got a touch queasier. "Who's they?" I asked on the way down. "What's happened?"

He withdrew almost visibly into his desk-manager shell. "I think it's better if you hear it from them, Professor," he said gravely. A fist closed around my heart. *Lori*, I thought. *Something's happened to Lori.*

The Nordica's lobby bar was a modernist, minimalist gathering of petal-shaped violet chairs and small cocktail tables in a wood-floored, white-walled nook formed by the arc of a curving white staircase. Closed at this time of the morning, it was empty except for Ingimar and a large man in a tweed sport coat and loosened tie at one of the tables and, in a far corner, a uniformed cop—short-sleeved pale blue shirt with epaulets, dark tie, dark pants—whispering earnestly into a telephone. *Oh, Jesus.*

Ingimar was gray. He looked sick to his stomach. "Ah, Bryan, we have a situation, ah—"

The other man, sandy-haired and sandy-mustached, with a kindly, deeply lined face, stood up slowly, took an unlit calabash gourd pipe, a huge pipe, a Sherlock Holmes pipe, out of his mouth, and handed me a business card. "I'm Ellert Ragnarsson, Mr. Bennett. How do you do? Please sit down."

I looked at the card as I took my seat: *Reykjavik Metropolitan Police Department, Ellert Ragnarsson, Detective Chief Inspector, Criminal Investigation Division.* I nodded and mumbled something, but my heart was in my mouth. A detective chief inspector. *Please, God, let her be all right.* I had to wet my lips to speak. "What's happened?"

"It's Baldur," Ingimar said. He was staring miserably at a couple of sheets of paper in front of him. Beside it was an untouched cup of tea on a saucer. "He was—we don't have all the details yet, but it appears he was—that is, we know he was, ah . . ."

Mercifully, the chief inspector cut in. "He's been abducted, I'm afraid. It happened a little less than two hours ago, in Grindavik." He had the usual pleasant Scandinavian accent and a slow, deep, wise, comforting voice, like an old-time family doctor's. The old-fashioned pipe suited him perfectly. "There was gunfire. We have reason to think he may have been hit."

"I'm very sorry to hear that," I said (a bald-faced lie; what I was feeling was nothing less than a joyful billow of relief—Lori was all right). But something more seemed to be required of me, so I said, "Is there anything I can do?"

"Indeed, yes," Ragnarsson said. "We understand you're an expert in these matters, and we consider it a stroke of luck that you're here. We'd be very glad of your assistance."

"Of course," I said. "Anything I can do." But the joyful billow was gone. *Yes, Lori was okay*, but *God help me, I'm right back in it*, I thought. *How could this be happening to me?* Immediately, I was ashamed. Baldursson kidnapped, maybe wounded, maybe dead, and all I could think about was my own mental devils? I was staring down at my clasped hands, unwilling to look Ragnarsson in the eye, afraid I wouldn't be able to keep my own eyes from jumping around.

The chief inspector took one of the sheets of paper from in front of Ingimar—he moved the way he spoke; slowly and with conviction—and slid it across to me. The smell of pipe tobacco rose from the tweed of his jacket. "Approximately thirty minutes after the kidnapping this was faxed to *Morgunblaðið*—"

"Pardon?"

"*Morgunblaðið*. It's a newspaper," Ingimar said, surfacing from his trance.

"—and also sent to my chief superintendent's office," Ragnarsson finished.

"Do you know where—?"

"It was sent from a post office in Hafnarfjörður."

"Which is?"

"A few kilometers south of here. Maybe thirty north of Grindavik."

"And there's no clue as to who sent it? Man? Woman? No witnesses?"

"None as of yet. Bryan, may I say with no offense intended"—his gentle, tolerant smile made his point for him—"that I am not requesting your help in our investigation, but in the way the situation, as it stands, is best handled?"

"Of course. Sorry."

A couple of beats passed. "So," he said patiently, "it might be a good idea if you read that fax."

Yes, but what the detective chief inspector didn't understand was that I'd been doing everything I could *not* to read it. Until I did, I wasn't really involved, but once I did there'd be no going back. I'd be in it up to my ears. I looked at it a second longer, fought with myself, lost (won?), and, with a sigh, focused my eyes on it. It was neatly typewritten in English and headed "Communiqué No. 1. Operation Baldur."

At 1:30 p.m. on Thursday, April 1, the earth-raper Baldur Baldursson, president of GlobalSeas Fisheries, was arrested and taken prisoner by citizen-soldiers of Project Save the Earth, the Verkefnið Björgum Jörðinni. This action was carried out as a strike against the bio-colonialism of the New World Order's continuing assault on biodiversity.

For too many years, the GlobalSeas corporate monoculture has been at the forefront of the environmental nightmare known as "bioengineering," particularly in its reckless aquaculture operations, which have caused havoc among wild species due to infection and interbreeding with escapees. THIS CANNOT BE PERMITTED TO CONTINUE.

Unless reparation in the amount of $5,000,000 is made to repatriate the prisoner, the prisoner will be tried and sentenced for his crimes against the biosphere by a war-crimes committee of the VBJ.

We are aware that the police, in their capacity as servile minions of the global elite will try to involve themselves in this. They are to be left to their own devices. ANY ATTEMPT ON GLOBALSEAS' PART TO WORK IN CONCERT WITH THE POLICE WILL RESULT IN THE TERMINATION OF COMMUNICATION AND THE IMMEDIATE EXECUTION OF THE PRISONER.

We would like to make our purposes clear to all. Unlike GlobalSeas, we are not gangsters motivated by greed and profit. The profit motive, created and reinforced by the Amerika-dominated international-capitalist complex, is systematically destroying life on this planet. Therefore, only by taking the profit motive OUT of this wanton destruction can it be stopped. The reparations demanded by the VBJ are a first step in that process; a war tax. Furthermore, these reparations will be used solely to repair, to the extent possible, the damage to our native ecosystem caused by GlobalSeas and its human meatpuppets.

"The liberty in man's laws consists solely in this, that he obeys the laws of nature because he himself has recognized them as such, and not because they have been imposed upon him by any foreign will whatsoever, human or divine, collective or individual."

Note: This communiqué is to be published in full in tomorrow's (Friday's) *Morgunblaðið*. Failure to comply with this initial step will be seen as noncooperation and will end negotiations. Further instructions will follow upon publication.

This communiqué has been issued under the direction of the Executive Coordinating Committee of the Verkefnið Björgum Jörðinni.

"Bakunin," I murmured.

"I'm sorry?" Ragnarsson said. He was in the act of lighting up, so he was looking at me the way pipe smokers do, head down, squinting over the jetting lighter, through a cloud of fragrant blue smoke.

"The quotation. Mikhail Bakunin."

"Ah. Well, I'm glad that's cleared up." Another couple of puffs to get the pipe going for good. "Bryan, the truth is, we're not very familiar with affairs of this sort. They don't really happen in Iceland, you see. The only similar instance during my tenure—and I've been with the department since 1999—was the previous attempt on GlobalSeas by the VBJ, and that one was over before it started. Any help, any advice you can give, we'll appreciate. I know Ingimar feels the same way."

Ingimar came out of his funk with a start. "What? Oh, absolutely."

"Certainly," I said. "I'll do anything I can." Strangely, reading the fax had settled me. The turgid diction, the bizarre, clumsy locutions—*earth-raper, servile minions, Amerika, meatpuppets*—were familiar, almost reassuring, the kind of thing I'd seen a thousand times. You had to convince yourself it was the real thing, not some kind of parody. Of course I could help, and I would help. I could deal with something like this practically by rote. There were rules, principles, established ways of doing things and, more important, of not doing things. If I stayed in the background and worked through Ingimar or Ragnarsson—and stayed the hell away from the upcoming negotiations themselves— there was no reason I couldn't get along just fine. And be of some use too.

"That's good," Ragnarsson said. "All right, then, advise us. What's to be done first?"

"First, *Morgun* . . . that newspaper . . . has to decide whether or not to publish the communiqué. My advice would be for you to recommend that they do so. Second . . ." I

looked at Ingimar. "You'll want to get your board of directors involved immediately. They'll have to make some quick
decisions—" I stopped. Ingimar was shaking his head.
"What is it, Ingimar?"

"There is no board. Just Baldur. He's the sole director. I
serve as the assistant director."

"So—you'll be making the decisions?" *Hoo boy.*

He looked even sicker. "That's right."

"Okay, then, first decision: Is GlobalSeas going to ignore
their warning and work with the police? With the detective
chief inspector here? Or are you going to try to deal with
them on your own?"

Ingimar looked from me to Ragnarsson and back. "Well,
I . . . How would they know if we cooperated with the
police?"

"I don't know, and I doubt that they could, but I think it's
safest to assume they might be able to find out."

"So then . . . what's your advice, Bryan?"

"I think you should involve the police in everything you
do—and vice versa, for that matter. The likelihood of a
successful resolution is a lot better if the two of you are in
it together, as a team. Otherwise the left hand doesn't know
what the right hand's doing, and you can create a
disaster."

Ragnarsson looked pleased. Ingimar gave a hesitant nod.

"And if they do find out, the chances of their actually
killing Baldur on account of it it are just about nil," I went
on. "Look, if this was a terrorist group that took him, if this
was some kind of military or political leader they had,
there'd be more risk. They could make a statement with
murder. But if they kill Baldur, what does it get them? They
don't score any points, they no longer hold any cards, and
they wind up with nothing except a murder charge and a
manhunt."

"Exactly what I've been telling him," Ragnarsson said.

"All right, then, yes, I agree," Ingimar said. "Yes." The more he could spread the responsibility around, the happier he was.

"Okay, assuming that's taken care of," I said, looking at Ingimar, "we'll need a spokesman for GlobalSeas, a single, high-ranking person to serve as liaison with this group. I guess that's you."

"Me! But can't you do that? You're the expert."

"Well, yes, but . . . sure, if you want me to, but I think it'd be better if you actually spoke for the company. I'll be right there with you, but behind the scenes."

Ingimar looked as if he was about to cry. "But I don't . . . I wouldn't know how to . . . what to . . ."

"Look, Ingimar," I said gently. "Is GlobalSeas insured against this kind of thing?"

Ragnarsson raised a quizzical eyebrow. "There's insurance against kidnapping?"

"Yes, we are," said Ingimar. "With Argos Risk Management in London."

"Ah." This was not good news. Not only was Argos a notoriously tight-fisted company, but they weren't like the newer outfits that specialized in this kind of thing. For them, kidnapping insurance was just a profitable sideline. They didn't provide training to their clients, and while they did send out ransom negotiators, I'd met two of them and was greatly underimpressed. But this was GlobalSeas' affair, not mine. "Well," I said, "they'll want to send one or two of their people over, and I'm sure they'll be able to do the negotiating for you."

"But that might take *days*. Don't we need somebody now? What if— I mean, who knows what they're going to do? Couldn't you at least . . . at least . . . We'd be happy to pay whatever . . ."

I closed my eyes for a second, filled my lungs with air to steady myself, and said, "Until then, sure, if you prefer, I'll be the contact. Don't worry about payment." The prospect terrified me, but what else could I say? GlobalSeas couldn't just refuse to communicate for the time it would take to get someone there from London. Especially not with a bona fide, super-duper internationally recognized expert sitting right there.

"You'll do the negotiating?" Ingimar said, brightening.

"Until whoever's coming from Argos gets here, yes." *Sheesh, I'm really in it now,* I thought. *Damn it. I knew this would happen.*

"Thank you," Ingimar practically sighed, but a moment later his face fell again. "But the policy is only for two million dollars. These people are demanding five million."

"Well—"

"And there's a two-hundred-thousand-dollar deductible. Oh, my God, five million! That's . . . that's over half a *billion krona*! I'm not at all sure that we'd be able to—"

"Let's not worry about that right now, Ingimar. You wouldn't want to pay it even if you could. If you cave in too fast—at the first demand or the first threat—they'll most likely realize they didn't ask for enough and they'll up the ante. It happens all the time—double-tapping, we call it. They'll also have learned that GlobalSeas is an easy mark . . . for the next time."

"The next time," Ingimar echoed woefully. "Please."

"Besides," I said, "if past history is any guide, they're not really expecting to get anywhere near that much. This is a first offer."

"How much are they expecting to get, then?" Ragnarsson asked. "If the past is any guide." I detected a bit of an edge to his voice.

"Maybe I'd better rephrase that, Chief Inspector."

"Ellert."

"Ellert. Naturally, we have no way of knowing what these people are really expecting. Sometimes a group demanding ten million dollars will settle for five hundred thousand. Other times, they'll refuse an offer of five million. But statistically, when ransoms are finally paid, they generally come to about twenty-five percent of the initial demand."

"And does the payment of the ransom generally result in the safe release of the hostage? Statistically speaking."

I knew only too well what was bothering him. No cop could like the idea of even considering, let alone caving in to, ransom demands. Neither did I, but I knew there was another side. And the truth was the truth.

"Yes," I said, "it does."

"And therefore," said Ellert, "your advice to GlobalSeas is to pay the ransom?"

"If the objective is to get Baldursson back, yes."

He leaned forward, eyebrows bristling. "And if the objective is to apprehend a vicious gang of kidnappers and killers?"

"Well, then, maybe not. But you see, that wouldn't be my objective. I couldn't afford to be perceived by them as being on anybody's side. I'm a middleman, a facilitator, a neutral. I'm not emotionally involved. The same will go for the guy from Argos. If we get out of this without anybody else getting hurt, we've succeeded as negotiators, ransom or no ransom."

"Have you, now?" Ellert's tone was distinctly less warm than it had been a few minutes ago. "And what happens the next time they abduct someone, since you've made it so easy and pleasant for them this time? And what about all the nice new automatic weapons they might well be going to buy with their precious ransom, and all the terrorist organizations they might fund, how do you feel about that?"

Now I was the one who was getting irritated. "Look, Chief Inspector—"

"Ellert, damn it."

"Look, Ellert, I said 'perceived by them,' didn't I? You think I like them any more than you do? I want to see them put away too. But I'm not a cop. Catching them isn't my primary job."

"What is, then?"

"What I said: saving lives."

"Oh, I see. Like a doctor, is that it?"

"No, not like a doctor, because once it's over, then—"

"You'll pardon me," Ellert said gruffly, and turned his head. The officer who'd been on the telephone had come up to him and bent to whisper in his ear. Ellert whispered back.

I took advantage of the break to go to the soft-drink machine in the lobby, got a Coke (Iceland, I'd read somewhere, consumed more Coke per capita than anywhere else), and returned to my purple tulip chair. Aside from letting myself show more annoyance with Ellert than I should have, I was doing fine. True, most of what I'd been saying had been straight out of the books and monographs, so I could speak the words without internalizing them, but still, I was doing all right. I had no sense whatever that I was in danger of going over the edge, of losing control. How much of this was the meds talking I couldn't say, but what did it matter? A crisis had erupted and here I was, pitching right in and doing what I could to help.

One of the things that Zeta Parkington had told me stirred at the back of my mind: "The minute you stop running from the fear and decide to start confronting it and to start gaining some control over the situation and over your own life, you're on your way." Well, I was confronting it, wasn't I? Xanax or no Xanax, I could have chosen to run and hide, but instead I'd taken it on. "You can feel the difference from the first minute," Zeta had told me, and it was true. Already I sensed an inner strength building, a steady, dispassionate capability that hadn't been there before.

Which lasted for all of one second. Then, with a mere dozen words, Ellert emptied me of air the way the smack of an open hand collapses a paper bag. The floor opened up underneath me.

"Bryan, I have some disturbing news. It seems they have your wife."

Chapter 13

As to Lori's condition—Ellert's voice softened—they didn't believe she'd been hurt. The forklift operator and the truck driver, who had been there, told identical stories. Baldursson had begun firing first but had quickly been shot—twice, they both thought. While still slumping to the ground, he'd been caught by one ski-masked man on either side, half-carried the few steps to the van with his toes dragging, and roughly thrown in. One of the men had then turned, caught hold of the stunned Lori, and jerked her into the van as well. As far as they could tell, she hadn't been shot or otherwise harmed.

I closed my eyes. "Unh," I said, an inadvertent release of the air I'd been holding in without knowing it. I'd listened numbly to Ellert's account with a sick, disembodied sensation of being there and not being there. The chief inspector was looking at me now, waiting for a response, but I felt as if I were locked in some vast sea of ice, deep in the earth, unable to manufacture thought or action. When Zeta had asked me what was the worst thing I could imagine, I'd told her it would be to wake up with the metal collar around my neck again. Now I knew there was something worse. When Lori's pretty, smiling face suddenly swam up in front of me, my world started shaking. I could feel all the little cogs and wheels of my mind begin to wobble and come loose.

"I wonder why they didn't mention her in their message," Ellert mused to bring me back.

"Because . . . because she wasn't part of the plan," I said, thinking out loud as I clawed my way up out of my funk. "That message went out only half an hour after the kidnapping, so it had to have been prepared before, and they weren't expecting to take her, so she wasn't mentioned. It was an afterthought." *An afterthought!*

"So why would they have done so?"

I shrugged. How the hell did I know? "Maybe they thought she heard something, or saw something. Maybe it was just an impulse: She was standing right there, so they grabbed her. People do crazy things under pressure."

"But then wouldn't you think they would have revised the message to—"

"Ellert, damn it, I don't *know*," I snapped.

He stiffened. "Sorry."

"No, I'm sorry. I apologize. I guess I'm just a little crazy myself, worried that . . . you know, that . . ."

He nodded. It wasn't necessary for either of us to say. If they had taken her on no more than the impulse of one overexcited kidnapper, what would they do with her? What *had* they done with her? My mind flinched away from the possibilities.

"What happens now?" Ingimar asked me. "They said instructions would follow. How will they get in touch with us—with you?"

I shut my eyes again for a moment and pulled myself

together—relatively together. "It could go one of several ways. Written message, newspaper ad, e-mail, but most likely a phone call. So everyone who might be on the receiving end—the phone secretaries at GlobalSeas, you, your family—all have to be ready for it." The question had done me good, calmed me down, put me on familiar ground. I was operating on automatic, practically reading aloud from one of my own manuals. "The minute they get off the phone they should write down everything they can about the caller: voice, accent, sex, age, how excited or calm he or she seemed. And any background noises they might have heard, even if they think they might have imagined them. Also, they'll have to have a telephone number for me, so they can tell the caller I'm the contact person."

"We have cellular phones," Ellert said. "We'll give you one. You have no objection to it being monitored?"

"Absolutely not." A cellular phone was a good way to go. For one thing, it could stay with me twenty-four hours a day. For another, as Ellert obviously knew, cellular phones are the easiest of telephones to tap. Operating on radio waves as they do, it isn't necessary to attach any gizmos to the phones themselves. You just tune in to the right frequencies—as long as you know what frequencies to tune to.

"Also," I said, "the minute a call comes in, whoever gets it immediately informs the police. Ellert, we'll need a contact in your office."

"That'll be me. I'll give you my home number too."

"That's helpful. Now, back to these people who might receive the first call: We want them to be polite and efficient. Just give the caller my name and number and tell him I'm the one to talk to. No anger, no pleading, no trying to resolve the case. And no trying to keep him on the phone longer so that the call can be traced. Nothing clever, nothing that might make him nervous. Clear?

Ingimar swallowed and nodded. "I think so."

"I'll write everything down for you. We'll make a form everyone can use." I already had one in an appendix to the training manual.

The idea of a form reassured him. "Oh, that would be wonderful, Bryan."

My mind had been pretty much free to work on its own while I recited all that boilerplate material, and I had come to understand, with some surprise, just what it was I was feeling. Anger. Outrage. At God, at fate, at the monstrous flukiness of life, at the violent men who now held Lori. How was it that this could have happened to her? *I* was the one who was supposed to get kidnapped, wasn't I? It had hovered over me, circled around me, almost my whole life. In any kind of logical, orderly universe it should have been me, not Lori, who'd been destined to stand on that particular loading dock, in that particular town, with Baldursson, at that particular moment.

And there was something else that was gnawing at me too. I'd chosen not to tell her about the earlier attempt on him; I hadn't wanted to make her uneasy—one basket case was enough. But what if I had? Would she have taken greater care? Would she perhaps have decided not to go to Grindavik at all? I remembered now that she'd told me this morning that she'd be spending some time at GlobalSeas, but I'd been deep in my prep and it had barely registered. I suppose I'd assumed she'd be at the Reykjavik office. How had she even gotten to Grindavik? Why hadn't I—

"What?" I murmured, conscious that Ellert had said something.

"I was wondering, given what's happened—about your wife, I mean—whether you still feel all right about handling the negotiation."

"Absolutely, why wouldn't I?"

"Well, if I were in your place, I might find it a little difficult to maintain the neutrality you referred to earlier." He paused. The sad, pouchy eyes looked at me keenly. "Let alone remaining emotionally uninvolved."

I finished my Coke, set the can on the table, and gave him my steeliest gaze. "I can handle it just fine," I said.

His response was an acquiescent, you're-the-expert shrug, but before his shoulders had settled back down, my saner self had taken charge. I let out a long, apologetic sigh. "No, I can't handle it just fine. You're right, Ellert. I'm the last person we want negotiating. Tell you what. Let me call Odysseus back in the States. I'm sure they'll send over one of our negotiators. He should be the one who handles negotiations for Lori. I'll stay in the background." It was going to kill me just to stand by, but it was the right—the sensible— thing to do, and surely the best thing for Lori. "And then whomever Argos sends from London will want to handle the negotiations for Baldursson. Me, I'll just help however I can."

"I think that's wise. But until they arrive—if the VBJ should get in touch—you're still the man?"

I nodded. "Until then, I'm the man."

THE first contact came at 3:30 in the afternoon, about four hours after I'd finished talking with Ellert and Ingimar. I was on the balcony of our room at the hotel, where Lori and I had watched the sun go down only twenty hours earlier. The coffee cups we'd used, missed by the cleaning crew (who in their right minds would be having coffee on an outdoor balcony in Iceland in March?) were still on the round glass table. I'd been sitting there, zipped up in my parka, thinking hard for the last three of those four hours—or maybe *thinking* wasn't the right word, because

I'd made no notes, come to no conclusions, devised no plans. I'd just worried and agonized and dithered the time away, with barely any memory of what had passed through my mind besides what I knew to be the typical recriminatory what-could-I-have-done-differently-to-prevent-this-from-happening questions. Unfortunately, I came up with plenty of answers.

Other than that, I'd been concentrating my mental energies, such as they were, on the cellular phone that the police had supplied me with, and willing it to ring. I know, I was supposed to be out of it now, waiting for the arrival from Odysseus of someone not emotionally involved. But with Lori in their hands, how could I not want to hear something *now*—*do* something now?

How many movies have we all seen in which someone stares hard at a telephone and mentally commands, "Ring!" How stupid was that? And yet here I sat doing the same thing.

When it did ring at last, I leaped to hit the receive button and waited, holding my breath. There was nothing.

"Hello? Hello? Is somebody—?"

It rang again, but, confusingly, from inside the room. Well, of course; how could they call me on the police phone if they didn't have the number yet? Stupid! Even while running to answer the other phone I realized this was a warning to me of just how messed up my thinking was. I had to stop beating myself up and start thinking like the expert I was supposed to be.

This time when I picked up the phone I could hear start-and-stop traffic noises in the background. That figured. The call was probably being made from a pay phone on the street somewhere.

"Bryan Bennett," a woman's voice said. Robotic, harsh, even when softened by the gentle local accent.

"This is Bryan Bennett. Who am I talking to?"

"You can call me Gullveig." Possible meanings: *It's my real name. It's not my real name. It's my real name, but I'm putting it that way so you think it's not my real name.* "I am speaking for Project Save the Earth. In order to ensure the repatriation of the criminal Baldur Baldursson, we demand reparation in the amount of five million US dollars." She was reading the words. "The money—"

"No money, no talking, until we have proof of life."

"—is to be . . . What? Proof of what?"

Was it possible she didn't know what proof of life was? I didn't like that. I preferred to be dealing with people who knew the way the game was played. "I need to know he's alive. I need to know they're *both* alive."

"What do you mean, *both*?"

"I mean the woman as well. We're not paying for dead people." A shiver ran up my spine and squirreled in between my shoulder blades.

There was a rustly sound. Gullveig was covering the phone while she conferred with someone else. "They're alive," she said. "Definitely."

"I can't take your word for that, Gullveig. At this point, how am I supposed to know for sure that it's your group who has them, let alone whether they're alive or not?" It amazed me that I could make my voice sound so calm, so unconcerned. Or was I kidding myself?

"What kind of proof of life do you need?"

"The easiest thing would be to put them on the phone."

"That's—no, I don't—" The rustle again, and muffled whispers. "No, we prefer not to at this time."

It was what I'd expected to hear. Wherever Lori and Baldursson were, they weren't in the phone booth or wherever with Gullveig. "All right, later then. What about calling me back, say in an hour or so, and putting them on then?"

"No, not possible. What else would you accept as proof?"

I was ready with my reply. "Ask her what the dog gets as a lunch treat. Ask Baldursson where his Aunt Amalia lives." The question and its answer, South Africa, had come from Ingimar.

"I'll see," Gullveig said.

"What does that mean, you'll see?"

"It means I'll see. We'll call you back. Stay by your phone."

"I have a cellular phone," I said and gave her the number. "Better to use that one." Whenever the next call came, I wanted the police on the line too.

"Whatever," she said.

Chapter 14

Camano's head was killing him. He was boiling, trembling with anger and frustration. His trio of cretins had turned a meticulously planned operation—a beautiful operation—into a farce. They couldn't have done a better job of bringing it down in ruins if they'd tried. Every caution he'd laid down had been ignored—no, *subverted* was more like it. If everything wasn't *exactly* as anticipated, they were simply to forget the whole thing, quietly pack it in, and try again another day. How hard was that to remember? How many times had he banged it into their heads? And yet, when Baldursson had surprised them by appearing, not at his second-story door but down at the loading bay in the warehouse, they had proceeded merrily on. And when they realized he wasn't alone but had this damn woman with him? No problem, full steam ahead. What the heck, might as well grab her too while they were at it. What could go wrong, right? Duh!

And then, when Baldursson had produced a gun—all

right, there the fault was partially Camano's; he hadn't known Baldursson was armed, hadn't anticipated it—Stig had actually *shot* him—twice! This after Camano had laid it down as an absolute law that no live ammunition was to be used. Hadn't they had enough experience with live ammo the last time they'd tried for Baldursson, when two of their members had been killed in the shootout? He had made them show him the 9-mm parabellum blank cartridges they planned to use in their Serbian-made semiautomatics. He had actually watched them insert them into the magazines. And then Stig, crazy, dangerous Stig, had decided on his own that he'd better bring along a second handgun "in case things went wrong," as he explained afterward, when he was furiously confronted by Camano.

"It's a damn good thing I did," he'd said mulishly. "He could just as easily have hit me with his next shot."

If only, Camano thought, seething but silent. There was nothing to be done about it now; the deed was done. Baldursson was dead. Useless. Instead they had the woman, and what good was she to them? Well, there was the slim possibility that she knew enough about Baldursson for them to have half a chance of coming up with sufficient proof-of-life information to make it appear that he might still be alive. If so, Camano might yet be able to salvage the operation. But what an unnecessary frigging muddle it all was.

Now, if only Baldursson *had* managed to kill Stig, at least there would have been an upside, but no such luck. Instead, he'd hit Magnus, and now Magnus too was dead and useless (as opposed to being live and useless). But even dead, Magnus complicated matters. With him out of the picture, the logistical situation was turned on its head. For this kind of operation, a minimum of two people awake and available at all times was required. Which meant that Gullveig and Stig alone couldn't handle it, assuming they required sleep from time to time. Which meant one more of the essential ingredients of The System would be kaput: Camano himself would have to be right there, on site, cooped up with the two of them, twenty-four hours a day, God help him.

There had been a couple of times in the past when things had gone as haywire as this (*almost* as haywire; this one set a new record for fiascos), and he had aborted the operation and taken the next plane out. But this was different. That yacht waiting for him in Monaco beckoned him like a Siren. It was almost his now; he could practically see the two lounging, bikini-clad girls smiling back at him from the foredeck, and feel the smooth teak deck shifting and tilting under his feet as it knifed through gentle three-foot seas. How could he give that up without a fight?

Gullveig and Stig had quickly gotten rid of the two bodies, hauling them down into one of the numberless, narrow lava caves that perforated the barren brown moonscape of the Reykjanes peninsula, and there he had no complaint. It was the one thing they'd done right. The corpses would never be found. He doubted that even Stig or Gullveig could locate them again.

But what in God's name made them stop in Hafnarmumblemumble and send the fax that they'd prepared earlier, just as if everything hadn't gone so horribly awry? What was the hurry? Baldursson was dead; he wasn't going to get any less dead or more dead. There was no reason they couldn't have waited. Killing him had changed everything. Camano needed time to think it all through again, to replan, to consider whether it was even possible to continue. What would have been the harm in holding off on the fax for a couple of hours, or even a day?

The needless death had made things immensely trickier. They were faced now with the problem of *hiding* the fact that he was no longer alive. How were they going to do that?

How were they going to get around the inevitable proof-of-life questions, the kind where the guy on the other end of the line says, "Go and ask him what his ex-wife's mother's name is?"

The more he thought about it, the more he thought the sensible thing for him to do was to walk out (his retainer he would *not* return; it was little enough payment for what they'd put him through) and leave the Two Stooges to deal with their own mess.

Ah, but always his thoughts went to the *Callisto,* moored to its dock and gently bobbing in the sunny marina in Monaco. The damn thing called to him the way popcorn called to ducks.

And so, back to the woman. When the proof-of-life questions came up, with any luck they could get the answers from her, or at least enough information to finesse the negotiator. They could say that they couldn't ask Baldursson any follow-up questions right now because he'd been injured and was in a semicoma, but they'd learned some things from him as he'd drifted in and out of consciousness. Lame, but workable if played right. If that were the case, he would stay with it, at least for now. If not, he would be on a plane tonight.

As for the woman, now that he thought about it, the simplest thing would be to get whatever she knew about Baldursson out of her, then get rid of her—her body could go into one of those thousands of lava caves with the others. That way no guard duty, no tedious, dangerous period of captivity, and, best of all, no holing up with these imbeciles.

Yes, there was hope yet.

It was time to have a look at the woman.

Chapter 15

S omeone had come in. Or opened a door, or turned on a light, or rolled up a blind. She knew because the gray-black mesh that was her entire field of vision had lightened by a few shades.

"Is someone there?" she asked.

Even with her hearing deadened by the painfully tight rubberized bandage that encircled her head, she was sure she'd be able to make out the sounds, if not the words, if someone were to say anything. She ached to tear the thing off, but she'd been told—by a woman; Icelandic accent—not to touch it, and she wasn't about to. She understood that seeing their faces did not improve her chances of survival.

"If there's anybody there, I can't hear you." Her voice sounded muffled and small, but the strain in her throat told her she was shouting.

No reply. *Assume someone is watching.* That's what Bryan said you were supposed to do. Don't show fear or desperation or despondency. What she felt like doing was screaming, and that she wasn't going to do. She'd done enough of it earlier, when there had been all the shooting and confusion, and Baldur had spurted a horrifying gout of blood from the side of his neck and collapsed half on top of her. She'd screamed then, all right, and passed out—or perhaps taken a blow to the head?—because there was a gap in what she remembered. She had no memory of how the shooting had ended or how she'd gotten into the van, but only a gluey, dreamlike trudge toward the vehicle, with poor, blood-soaked Baldur, his legs barely working, being hauled along by the elbows. Now, looking back, it seemed like something that had happened to someone else, or like something she'd seen on television.

Her memory of the events immediately leading up to it was almost as blurry. (Traumatic retrograde amnesia, was that what it was called?) Baldur had been taking her on a tour of the Grindavik facility; she remembered that clearly enough. He'd been showing her around the marine research lab located at the rear of the warehouse: rows of big, floor-mounted tanks populated by halibut, char, and salmon at every stage of development. He was in the middle of a lively explanation of their plans to use microsatellites—repeating strings of DNA sequence—as means of isolating the genetic factors involved in herbicide-runoff tolerance in fish, when his cell phone had rung.

"Our major saltfish distributor just made its pickup," he told Lori when he'd hung up. "I like to go out and say hello and sign the manifest myself; just takes a few seconds, and it gives me a chance to get to know the men. Want to come?"

What had happened next was the hazy part—a gray van, tires squealing, gunfire, blood, screaming—but after they'd wrenched her into the van beside the semiconscious, incoherent Baldur, things had snapped back into focus. They'd quickly manacled her hands to the armrest and tugged this thing—an elastic support bandage, she thought, the kind you'd use to brace an injured knee—down over her face. Then doors had slammed, and the van had jerked to a start. Baldur had gone quiet and slumped against her, drenching her slacks with blood. She could actually feel the individual warm spurts as they pulsed from an artery. She'd shifted away as much as she could—it was impossible for her to aid him—but to her horror she could still *hear* the blood pumping—*hssh . . . hssh . . .*

As shocked and sickened as she'd been, she had tried to memorize what useful information she could during the drive, but with no sight and little hearing it was next to impossible, and after they stopped and bundled her into a second vehicle—Baldur too? She didn't know—trying to count seconds (one Mississippi, two Mississippi) or keeping track of left and right turns was hopeless. Even smells, which Bryan had told her could be valuable because kidnappers often didn't think to disguise them, were beyond her ability with the bandage over her face.

Even now, the canvasy, medicinal odor was all she could smell. She had no idea if she was in the city or the country, or how far they'd driven, or whether they'd gone in circles to confuse her. It seemed to her that she'd been sitting there on the bed frame for about twenty minutes, but it could easily have been much more. Because the floor under her feet seemed to be covered with a thick, coarse fabric that could be made to shift a little, she believed she might be in a tent. But indoors, not out in the country, because beneath the fabric the floor was hard and smooth. As she knew, kidnappers sometimes used indoor tents as a way to keep their captives from being able to identify their surroundings afterward.

Is that really what she was, a "captive"? Or merely an

incidental bystander caught in the crossfire and impulsively hauled off because they didn't know what else to do with her? There couldn't be any doubt that Baldur had been their target. Didn't that mean they'd release her when they'd gotten themselves straightened out? Or did it mean . . . *No, don't go there.* If she was going to make up scenarios, they'd damn well be on the positive side. Better yet, forget the scenarios, and start planning for—

"Do you need anything?" someone asked.

"DO you need anything?" Camano asked. He had been sitting on a camp stool just inside the entrance to the tent, watching her for some time. He liked to observe them in the first few minutes. You learned a lot about human behavior that way. Not this time, though. She had sat there disappointingly still and composed, revealing as much emotion as a potted rubber plant.

The woman straightened and raised her chin to face him, although he knew she couldn't see him. "No," she said. "Thank you. I'd appreciate it if I could take this thing off my head, though. It's starting to hurt."

"Not possible."

For three reasons: first, it wouldn't take long to occur to her that being allowed to see the faces of her captors was a pretty reliable indication that they planned to murder her, and then would come the hysterics and other such nuisances; second, keeping her face covered depersonalized her, made it harder for her to establish a connection with them, which might create some reluctance when it came to doing the deed. Not for Camano himself, and probably not for Stig, but about Gullveig he was less sure. Third, and most important, killing somebody was easier when they couldn't see you.

"Anything else?"

"How is Mr. Baldursson? Is he—?"

"Baldursson's all right. We're attending to him. What's your name?"

"Lori Bennett."

"Lori. What is that, a nickname?"

"No, it's my whole name."

"Okay, Lori. How well do you know Baldursson?"

"I hardly know him at all."

Bad news, if true. "Then what were you doing at the plant?"

"Mr. Baldursson was giving me a tour of the research laboratory."

"And what's your connection to GlobalSeas, Lori?"

"I don't have any connection. I was just visiting."

"You were just visiting, and the president and CEO of GlobalSeas . . . who you hardly know . . . personally gives you a tour?"

"Oh. My husband is conducting a training program for them."

"You mean in Reykjavik, the course in how not to get kidnapped?" He smiled. Camano had virtually no sense of humor, but he appreciated irony.

She hesitated. "Yes."

"Too bad Baldursson didn't take it, isn't it? He might have—" The smile died. "Wait a minute, *Bennett*? Is your husband *Bryan* Bennett?"

She jerked. The question had startled her. "Why . . . yes, he is."

"The hostage negotiator?"

"He used to be, yes, but . . ." Her sudden stillness told him that she sensed she'd made a mistake, but she didn't know what it was.

Camano rose slowly to his feet, his mind whirling with fantastic new plans and possibilities. A whole new world had just opened up to him.

And Lori Bennett was wrong about having made a mistake; she had just saved her own life.

Chapter 16

I'd botched the call from Gullveig. I realized now that I'd come across every bit as pushy and desperate as I actually was. I'd made her nervous, the last thing I should have done. This was *exactly* the reason your anxious, frantic spouse is the last person you want negotiating for you the next time you get kidnapped.

Earlier in the afternoon I'd put in a call to Odysseus to tell Wally what had happened and to ask him to send out a negotiator to take over. Wally, who was in truth at his best when the chips were down, had come through without hesitation. He would talk to the board immediately about freeing institute funds for Lori's possible ransom (Baldursson's ransom was GlobalSeas' affair), and he was dispatching former FBI special agent Julian Minor, a first-rate negotiator, to Reykjavik. Minor was already on his way and would arrive in Iceland in the morning, but I couldn't help hoping, despite knowing that Julian was the better point man in this situation, that the next call came before then, so that the process could get under way. I was desperate to do *something*.

But other than calling Ellert to tell him about Gullveig's call, there wasn't much I could do but wait. And worry. Gullveig's response, or rather nonresponse, to the proof-of-life questions had been troubling. And now almost four more hours had passed, with no follow-up telephone call. What did that mean?

I'd had a pastry for breakfast and nothing since, and I needed something to eat. I knew that at least some of the GlobalSeas people would be having their dinners at the Hilton's restaurant, and I didn't want to have to talk to them, so I slipped into my parka and walked a few blocks to Laugavegur, the main street, lined with restaurants and shops. I went into the first eating place I passed, an unpretentious Italian place with only a few occupants inside. I didn't want people and noise around me. I found a table at a streetside window and ordered a pizza margherita from the wood-fired oven. I was ready to kill for a Scotch, but that was out of the question, so when the waitress suggested something called Egils Malt Extrakt, which she assured me was Iceland's finest nonalcoholic beer, indistinguishable from the high-octane kind, I nodded, barely having heard her. If she'd recommended a glass of hot lava fresh from the volcanoes, I probably would have nodded too.

It did turn out to be vaguely reminiscent of a glass of beer, but a glass of beer in which you'd dumped two tablespoons of sugar. But since I could hardly taste it anyway, I sat there sipping it and staring out the window, waiting for the pizza and trying not to think bad thoughts—about Lori, and where she was right now, and what was happening to her . . . what they might be doing to her. I wasn't going to be of much use if I completely tied myself into knots, so I made myself focus on the scene outside instead. There were a lot of people out, as always on Laugavegur in the evening. Watching them, I found myself filled with resentment—these laughing, chattering arm-in-arm pairs or threesomes, on their way to yet another pleasant meal, their lives as normal and predictable today as they were yesterday, with no dreadful threats hanging over them. I wanted to strangle them. There was one couple in particular, obviously deep in love, lost in each other's eyes . . .

No, what kind of way was that to think? What was wrong with me? I shifted my attention away from them, tried to think about something else. Across the street there was a tattoo and piercing parlor, and I saw that its sign was in English only, not Icelandic as well, which was unusual. Was that because it was used basically by Brits and Americans, or because English seemed more hip? Or—

"Are you Mr. Bennett?" It was the hostess. "There's a telephone call for you."

"Thank you." Startled and a bit confused, I reached without thinking for the cellular phone that I'd laid on the table.

"No," the hostess said, also understandably confused, "you can take it up front."

I jumped up and followed her to her station at the entrance. How could anyone be calling me on the restaurant phone? No one knew I was here; I'd only decided myself a few minutes earlier. So someone had been watching me—and still was; they'd known at which table I'd been sitting.

The hostess pointed to a telephone on a small stand beside her podium. I snatched it up. "This is Bryan B—"

"Bryan, it's me! They—"

"Lori!" I yelled loud enough to make some of the diners turn around. "Are you all right? What—"

"Bryan, they won't let me talk long—"

"Have they hurt you? Are you—?"

"I'm all right. I just—" There were scuffling sounds—

they were taking the phone away from her—and I heard her shout, "I love you!" Then more scuffling, ending with a sharp "Ow, damn you!" from Lori that stabbed into my chest like a spike.

"Lori!"

More stares from the diners and a frown from the hostess, who approached gingerly, thinking she might have trouble on her hands.

I waved her away. "Lori . . . !"

"Hello, Bryan Bennett." A man's voice, steely and arid, no trace of an accent. He was American, maybe Canadian.

I lowered my voice. "I have to talk to my wife again. I need to know—"

"No, you don't need to know anything. Now, stay where you are. I'm going to call you right back."

I hung up, shaking, but wrung out with relief. She was alive. They'd maybe wrenched her arm to get her to give up the phone, but they hadn't really hurt her. When someone really hurts you, you don't say, "Ow."

The hostess took the telephone out of my numbed hand and put it on a shelf inside the podium, then gestured as if to lead the way back to my table.

I shook my head. "No, I'm sorry, I'm going to be getting another call. It's an emergency."

"Sir, our busy time is just starting. I can't let you monopolize—"

"Damn it," I snarled, "just—" It rang. I snatched it up. "I'm here," I said keeping my voice low. "Who am I talking to?"

"Now, Bryan, let me explain the situation—"

"Do I know you?" I blurted.

"As charming as your wife is," he went on, "she's not

much good to us, you know? I can't imagine you coming up with five million dollars, can you?"

"What do you mean? Is Baldursson dead, then?"

"You, on the other hand," the voice went dryly on, "with the foundational resources of the Odysseus Institute behind you, would be a damn valuable commodity. You understand what I'm driving at?"

I blinked. Could he be suggesting— "You want to exchange my wife for me?"

"Would you be interested?"

"Of course I'm interested. As soon as possible."

"All right. Tell me, then: Would the Odysseus Institute be willing to raise the money for your ransom? Be honest. Your life's going to depend on it."

"I'm sure they would." What else did he think I was going to say?

"That's good. All right, let's do it. I want you to go—"

"Hold on, I need some guarantees. I'm not just walking into this on your say-so. I need to *know* you've let her go—"

"No, you do not need to know."

"I—"

"Shut up. Don't waste any more of my time telling me what you need. Listen to me, Bryan. The raw truth is, your wife is a liability to us. If you agree to the exchange, we'll set her free, unharmed. Tonight, the moment we have you. You have my word on that. We have no reason to keep her. But if you don't agree, we'll kill her. You also have my word on that. Do you believe me?"

I took a breath. "I believe you."

"That's good. Trust me, I always keep my word. So, should we proceed?"

"No, not until—"

"And here's something else you have my word on: This

is not one of your famous negotiations, this is a one-time-only offer, nothing to negotiate. Either you accept now—*now*, not five minutes from now—or you don't accept. If you don't, it's over and done. I won't ever bother you again. Neither will Lori."

"Sir," the hostess said, "I really have to—"

I turned away from her, pulling the phone out of her reach. "All right, okay. What do you want me to do?"

"Don't go back to your table. Walk out the front door and turn left. At the first corner you come to you'll see a trash can. Drop your cellular phone into it."

"I don't have a—"

"Please, don't insult my intelligence. Drop it in the trash can. Keep walking four more blocks. Which will get you to Laekjargata. When you cross it you'll be on the corner of a large public square. You'll see a pink bus shelter there. At 7:50 the next bus should arrive. Take it—"

"Is there a number on the bus? What will it say on the front?" I scrabbled through my pockets for a pen, a scrap of paper. "How will I know which—?"

"Just take it, don't worry about the number. Get off at the BSI stop."

"BSI, what's that?"

"It's the out-of-town bus terminal." A quickening of impatience. "Stop talking and listen. Now, you speak to nobody, do you understand? Don't ask the driver to tell you when you get there. You'll know. When you arrive, get off and stand with your back to the terminal entrance. You'll see a parking area in front of you, then an open field, and then a smaller, isolated lot, graveled, not paved, two hundred yards from the terminal under a highway overpass. Walk straight out from the entrance to that parking lot and wait."

"Straight out from the entrance," I echoed. "Open field. Parking area. Got it." I don't think I'd ever before had so many feelings boiling through me at once. Yet at the same time, I felt weirdly weightless and removed from myself; floating and directionless, like a kid's balloon that's snapped its string.

"And one more thing, Bryan. We can see everything you do. I can see you right now. If you fail to leave the cell phone behind, if you try to leave a note, or if you say anything—*anything*—to anybody, it's off. If you try to make some sort of signal, even an eye signal, it's off. There will be nobody to meet you. Your wife will be killed. Now, tonight, instantly. Is there any part of this that you don't understand?"

It took a moment before I could get my own voice going again. "I understand," I said. "I'm on my way."

Chapter 17

At 7:50 on the nose, the number 1 bus, with *Klukkuvelli* on the front panel, pulled up to the shelter. I boarded it and deposited my three hundred krona, making sure not to respond even to the driver's nod. Was I really under observation every step of the way? I doubted it, but who knew? Possibly, there was someone in a nearby car who was following the bus. Maybe someone was on the bus itself, although none of the few passengers were paying me any attention. But then, of course, they wouldn't, so that meant nothing.

Once seated, I tried to force my mind to think through what I was doing. As a consultant I would have said—I already *had* said: Don't knuckle under to their first demands, no matter how threatening. Yet that was precisely what I'd done. But how could I have acted any differently? How could anyone? This, I thought grimly, was another reason you never used a negotiator who was personally involved. Hell, I was so emotionally fixated I hadn't remembered to ask for proof of life on Baldursson.

Well, naturally enough, it was Lori who took up all my thoughts, all the energy I had for worrying. And right now I was primarily worried about whether or not they would really let her go. ("If you agree to the exchange, we'll set her free, unharmed. Tonight, the moment we have you. You have my word on that." Yeah, right, what could be more reassuring than that?) How could I trust them to follow through? How would I know for sure if they did? I couldn't and I wouldn't, but I didn't see what there was to do about it. They held all the cards (this particular deck held only one card that mattered—Lori) and all I could do was hope they knew what they were doing. But the VBJ, from most of what I'd seen, was an amateurish group of bunglers, and that was cause for worry. Amateurs did stupid things. They went back on their word; they changed their minds; they killed their captives when they got scared. Experienced, more professional abductors, on the other hand, were usually more trustworthy, more true to their word—and more ruthless as well. When their demands were met, they generally released their victims. When their demands weren't met, they followed through on their threats. To them, a captive was a means to an end. Merchandise, nothing more. If it had value, you took care of it. If it didn't, you cut your losses and got rid of it.

The VBJ had been anything but professional to date. Could I count on them to live up to their word and release Lori? What could I do but trust them and hope for the best?

As we pulled away from the bustle of downtown and into the outlying neighborhoods, my own more personal situation began to niggle its way into my mind. For the second time in my life I was about to undergo the worst thing I could imagine: I was going into captivity once again. It had almost wrecked me the first time, when I'd been an innocent and untroubled child. Then, it had left me with a lasting legacy of panic attacks and night terrors. What would it do to me now? How long would it last? Assuming that Julian would do the negotiating, it might take two weeks; he was a famously slow, deliberate negotiator. Could I last two weeks?

My trusty vial of Xanax—actually, a travel-size plastic Advil bottle—was in its usual place in my right-hand hip pocket, and on the way to the bus stop I'd practically had to hold on to my right wrist to keep the hand from plunging on its own into that pocket and going after it. But I knew it would be crazy to fuzz over my senses or to muddle my judgment any more than it already was. So I hadn't, and as a result my head was in reasonable order, but my insides were twisted up in knots.

I was scared right down to my toes of what lay ahead. Not of the possible torture or degradation that had worried the trainees. Not of the confinement itself, either, or of the awful helplessness and dependency that came with it, or even of the possibility of death. Those things I could and would handle if I had to. No, it was the panic itself, the panic attacks that would surely go along with them that filled me with dread.

This was a distinction that nobody but a full-fledged, card-carrying panic sufferer could possibly grasp. *Say what? There's a difference between fear of something and fear of fear of something?* Oh, yes, you better believe there is, and anybody who's been through one knows all too well that the nightmare terror of an unmitigated panic attack is immeasurably worse than the mere fear of driving over a bridge or getting on a plane or being locked in a little room or whatever your particular bugaboo happens to be. In the horrific clutch of an attack, the source doesn't matter anymore. You aren't really even aware of the cause. You know only two things: You are paralyzed with fright, alarm, terror . . . There's no word in the language, in any language, that truly conveys its intensity. You are close to physically bursting with it. And you are either going to die from it or go crazy—right then, that second—because you know—you *know*—that nobody can stand this much stress and remain sane. That you've lived through them before, that they've always passed, that there is nothing actually threatening you; none of that signifies. Your mind is too disordered, too petrified, for anything like systematic thought. This time, you are utterly convinced, is different. This is the end, if not of life itself, then of reason.

I know, I know; I'm wasting my breath here, trying to explain it. It's impossible. If you have panic attacks, you know all this without my telling you. If you don't, there's no way you can really understand what I'm talking about. It's bad; I'll let it rest there. All I could do was hope they'd let me keep the pills. If they didn't . . .

As my caller had said, the BSI terminal was hard to miss, a big white barn of a building with bus bays all around it and "BSI" on it in six-foot-high letters. I was the only one who got off. At this time of day, eight-thirty, there wasn't much going on; no long-distance busses loading or unloading and only a few cars in the parking slots. Through the glass doors of the building I could see a few worn-out-looking travelers on benches, but the ticket counters were closed down. Sunset was still half an hour off, so although the day had been gray and gloomy (a perfect match for my spirits), visibility was fairly good. I could see that the terminal and its parking areas were on an isolated island of asphalt in a big, empty field that was in turn ringed by roads and highways heading into and out of the city. At the far end of the field I spotted the smaller lot that I was looking for.

Partially under a highway overpass, it held a few pieces of heavy equipment; no other vehicles. I guessed it was a parking area for road-maintenance crews.

It took two or three minutes to walk across the stubbly, snow-dusted field and when I got there I saw that I'd been right: nothing but a couple of snowplows, a sweeper, and something I took to be an asphalt hot-patcher. No likely looking kidnappers lurking among them. I leaned against a green snowplow, crossed my arms in front of my chest to stay warm, and waited. And fretted. I had nothing close to a guarantee that this guy would do what he said about Lori. I was confident that the Odysseus board would come through for me, but who knew how long it would take? I had no idea of what my confinement would be like. Everything I'd done since I picked up the telephone on that first call had been stupid, rash, and most definitely not by the book—and I truly believed in the book, or so I'd thought. Hell, I practically wrote it. Still, even given all that, what should I have done differently? Nothing I could think of, not with Lori's life in the balance.

The car's engine was so quiet that by the time I heard it, it was practically on me, having come from a direction I hadn't expected, on a narrow dirt road I hadn't noticed. No, not a car, but a long, low-slung, black limo with a window-less rear quarter and a hatch in the back, like a hearse. It circled me slowly, tires crunching on the gravel. The wind-shield was black, impossible to see through. I stood my ground, turning as the van turned, staring at where the driver had to be.

Having made one full circle, it stopped, facing me. The motor continued to purr. Other than that, the only sound I could hear was the intermittent swooshing of tires twenty feet above our heads. I could feel myself being studied. After a few seconds the two front doors swung silently open. This was it, then. My self-determination, my freedom, was at an end. I was in for it. Again. I couldn't help doing a quick mental check for the usual warning signs of oncoming panic: Pulse pounding in the ears? No. Heart-in-the-throat sensation? A little, maybe. Shallow breathing? A little. Burgeoning, formless dread? Burgeoning, yes; formless, no.

Now, it's not as if I didn't know that this kind of self-probing, hunting for cracks in my facade, was an extremely dumb thing to do: Seek, and ye shall find, right? But it's not something you can help once you've been through panic hell a few times, and you're anticipating a rerun. But in this case, thankfully, there wasn't much to find. Now that the moment of truth was here, my insides had actually settled down. What I was feeling more than anything else was a welcome sense of resolution, of determination to see this through, to face whatever lay ahead. I suppose what made the difference was that I was doing this of my own free will and that I was doing it for Lori. I was grateful for the opportunity.

Two men climbed out of the van, leaving the doors open, and approached me from either side. They wore ski masks (I would have been surprised if they hadn't) under parkas with the hoods pulled up. No gloves. And no guns, at least not in sight, but then, why would they need them for this? Both about average height, but even with those quilted parkas and hoods I could see that one of them was small-headed and wiry and the other one, a little shorter, was on the pudgy side. On second glance, I decided the second one was a woman. Gullveig?

"Where is she?" I asked. "Is she all right? Did you let her go?"

I didn't expect an answer and I didn't get one. "Let's go," the wiry guy said and nodded to the woman, who produced a pair of handcuffs. The accent was Icelandic or Scandinavian, the voice breathy and intense. This was definitely not the polished, confident character I'd been talking to on the telephone.

"Hey, come on, why do you want to do that?" I said. "I'm here voluntarily, aren't I? Why do I need cuffs?"

He made a get-on-with-it gesture directed as much at his companion as at me. "Let's go, let's go, let's *go*."

The woman approached with the cuffs, and I held out my hands, wrists together. I didn't know what was going to happen, but I knew that, whatever it was, I'd be better off with my hands cuffed in front of me than behind, and I figured that this gesture of compliance on my part might make that happen.

Not.

"Turn around," she said, and I did. Yes, it was Gullveig.

The cuffs clicked on. "Too tight," I said. "They're cutting into me."

"No, they're not. Be quiet." There was a brief discussion in Icelandic between them, and Gullveig started searching me, first nonchalantly patting down the obvious places for weapons, then going through my pockets. She removed their contents—wallet, coins, comb, tissue shreds—and put them into a paper bag. When she came to the vial of pills, she started to put it in the bag with the rest.

"Wait a minute," I said. "I need those."

The eyeholes looked at me. "Why, what do you have?"

"I have a heart condition. Um, cardiomyopathy." Cardiomyopathy? Where had that come from? *Was* it a heart condition? I thought so; it sounded like one. Damn, how could I have failed to figure out *exactly* what I was going to say beforehand? I'd had the whole bus ride to work it out, and all I'd done was dawdle and worry it away. *Okay, Bryan, focus! Get on the ball here.*

She read the label. "You take Advil for a heart condition?"

"That's just what I keep them in. It's a travel size and it's flat, so it fits in a pocket. Look, I have to take those every day. I depend on them."

She shrugged and looked at the man for guidance. He shook his head and motioned for her to drop it in the bag.,

"I think you'd better let me have them back," I said. "I'm telling you, I have a bad heart." I forced a smile. "You wouldn't want me croaking on you, would you?"

I heard a nasty, snorty chuckle from the guy. "No, but I bet we could live with it if we had to."

"Not if you're expecting a ransom."

"Forget it. You're not getting them. You don't have a heart condition."

"I'm telling you—"

"I said forget it."

"Suit yourself," I said with a don't-blame-me-when-you-screw-up shrug, although it now felt as if I *did* have a heart condition. At the prospect of going without Xanax, it seemed to have shrunk to the size of a walnut.

"Hey, didn't I already tell you once to shut up?"

In the meantime Gullveig had pulled open the rear door of the van. It opened not like a hatchback, bottom to top, but like a safe, from left to right, the entire rear end of the vehicle swinging smoothly on its hinges. She leaned in and arranged something inside.

"In," the man said.

When Gullveig moved out of the way, I got my first look at the interior, and it stunned me. It *was* a hearse. Not only that, there was an open coffin inside, complete with fluffed-up pillow, its head toward the front.

"You mean in the *coffin*?" I said. I couldn't believe it. The world started wobbling.

"That's the general idea," he told me. "Let's go, we don't have all night."

I stared at it. I could feel the sweat jump out on my fore-head. I'd thought I was ready to do anything to get them to release Lori, but climbing voluntarily into a coffin, and not a very big coffin at that, well . . .

"Hey, now look," I said, as the panic coiled and tightened inside me, "what's the point of—"

"Relax," the man said, "you're not going to be in it that long."

"Yes, but—"

"Oh, for Christ's sake." He put a hand between my shoul-der blades and shoved hard. Instinctively, I dug in my heels, literally dug them into the gravel, to resist. He shoved harder, pushing me up against the corner of the hearse, and I came apart. I just lost it. The panic took over completely. I remem-ber trying desperately to pull away and run—I don't know where to, but I know I would have run like hell, probably screaming all the way. I remember trying to butt them with my head, elbowing and kicking at them, snarling and beg-ging, crying, cringing—who knows, probably drooling—the whole ugly show. Loss of face? Gone and forgotten. Self-esteem? Nowhere in sight. Lori? Who?

"Jesus, this guy is really a wreck," the guy said with icy contempt, but I just fought harder. That's one of the worst aspects of this thing: You're oblivious to shame. There is no room in your head for anything but blind terror, and you don't care who's there to witness it. Not at the time, anyway. Later is a different story.

The man clubbed me on the ear with the heel of his hand, and while my head was ringing with it, the two of them bent me over and held me there, pushing my face down against the floor of the hearse. Something stung me in the right hip, and whatever tiny part of my mind was still functioning understood that they were drugging me. *Thank God*, I thought. Within seconds, the relief began to flood through me. I stopped squirming and was able to un-tense my muscles enough to let the burning fluid get into my system that much faster.

When they started shoving me into the hearse again, I went along with the flow, already getting giddy and uncoordinated. I remember giggling when I went sprawling on the floor of the wagon because I had the illusion that my arms and legs were ropes, not limbs, and that was funny. And I remember the man saying in English, "Goddamn it, give me a hand with him, will you?" and then both of them grabbing hold of me while I continued to flop around and snicker.

The guy grabbed a fistful of flesh at the back of my neck and shook, the way you'd shake the scruff of a recalcitrant puppy. The sudden pain took me by surprise, and I let out an indignant yell.

He squeezed harder. "Shut your goddamn mouth, you bloodsucking bourgeois flunky!"

"Stig, you'd better stop that. You'll really hurt him," Gullveig said.

After that, as the murderer explained to the TV detective, my mind went blank.

I awoke to the smell of disinfectant. My first impression, a calming one, was that I was looking down from a great height, onto the still surface of an immense, cloud-shadowed green sea, but when the world slowly tipped and righted itself, I understood through the torpor that I was lying on my back on a cot, looking up, not down, and that the distant infinity of green was five feet above my head; a bellied, sloping ceiling of green nylon fabric.

So. I'm not in the coffin anymore, knock on wood. Now I'm in a tent. Next question: What am I doing in a tent? With no answer forthcoming, I did another self-check. Naturally enough, I was feeling generally lousy—achy, cottonmouthed, and leaden-limbed—but I was rational, I was composed, and most of all, I was glad I'd done what I'd done. There was no intimation of imminent panic. The lingering sedative effect of the drug? Could be, but I preferred to think that I was starting to cope on my own. Maybe Zeta's implosion therapy theory was working after all: By facing up to my fears, I was overcoming them.

By turning my head I found the source of the disinfectant odor; a new-looking chemical toilet about a yard from my nose, a big, hassock-sized, top-of-the-line job. Well, if this was to be my prison, it was already quite an improvement over the squalid open bucket in the corner.

The whole place was a big step up from Turkey. The tent was a roomy, straight-walled, cabin-style tent with enough headroom along the center line to let me stand up—not that I was up to getting on my feet quite yet. There were cartons of supplies—food, water, toilet tissue, that kind of thing—on the floor nearby. The tent had been set up indoors, I knew because, besides the disinfectant, there were indoor smells as well: floor wax, kitchen odors, house dust. And no sounds except for a fat, drowsy fly that hovered near my head, buzzing and stopping, buzzing and stopping. No, wait, I could just barely pick up the hum of traffic too—a highway, because it was steady; no stopping and starting. But it was far away and muffled by windows or walls. So I was definitely indoors. A house? A garage? No, a house; who waxed the floors of a garage?

The ache in my head intensified. Too much thinking right now. I dozed again for a second—it seemed like a second—and was awakened when the fly settled on my cheek. I moved to brush it away, and was surprised to find my hands still manacled behind me. Damn, I'd forgotten about that. I knew the drug they'd shot into me was still working, because if it hadn't been, the panic would surely have started to build right then. Oh, well. I shook the fly off, shifted from one side to the other to give my shoulders a break, wondered what time it was, and dropped off peacefully again.

Chapter 18

"You don't mean to say they have *Bryan* now?" Julian Minor, his carry-on bag dangling limply from his hand, stared haggardly at Lori.

"Yes, Julian."

"But . . . you don't mean to say they exchanged you for him?"

"Yes, Julian."

"You don't mean—?"

"Julian, you look bushed. You've been traveling all night. Let's go get you a cup of coffee."

He nodded submissively. "I suppose I could use a little something."

Iceland's international airport, Keflavik, had only one place to eat, a snack bar consisting of a counter and three small, bar-height tables with stools. The English version of the sign above the counter said SANDWICHES, COFFEE, DRIED FISH, ETC. "My word," Julian murmured when he read it. "I do believe we're not in Kansas anymore."

They took an uncleared table, and Julian fastidiously wiped it down with a paper napkin and deposited the used cups in a wastebasket before measuring sugar and nondairy creamer into his coffee. He drank half of it down in five fast, tiny sips, shaking his head all the while. "I just can't believe it. Lord, Lord."

Little wonder he was rattled. He had been briefed by telephone not much more than twelve hours ago, then driven within the hour from Providence, where he'd been winding up a negotiation, to Boston, from which he'd gotten the red-eye to Iceland. He'd prepared himself to be met by Bryan and brought up to date on the status of a kidnapped Lori. Instead, it was the other way around, and the astonishment could have been read on his face from fifty feet away. "Oh my word, that's awful," he said mournfully, and then, in clumsy apology: "That's not to say . . . I mean, naturally, I'm glad *you're* all right, Lori. I meant only . . ."

She patted the back of his hand. "It's all right, Julian. I understand." It felt good to laugh. It was the first time in many hours, but immediately she felt guilty. How could she possibly be laughing when Bryan—

"By no means is it all right. You shouldn't be comforting *me*. I'm the one who should be comforting you. Are you really all right?"

"Yes, really—well, as good as can be expected. I'm . . . desperately worried about Bryan, Julian, but having you here is a tremendous relief. Drink your coffee. I'll fill you in as much as I can."

"You don't want any yourself? Something to eat?"

She shook her head. She'd been unable to eat, or even to drink, since she'd learned that she'd been released only because Bryan had exchanged himself for her.

Julian gulped down some of his coffee. "All right, what is the situation at this point in time?"

She almost smiled again at the choice of words: *the situation at this point in time*. As a negotiator, Julian Minor couldn't have been more of a misfit. A former FBI special agent (specialty: bank and tax fraud), he was a tidy, slightly overweight, middle-aged black man with neat, grizzled hair, dressed as always in a dark, pinstripe three-piece suit, crisp white shirt (being Julian, no doubt he'd changed to a fresh one before landing), and dark, solid-color tie. Even now he carried with him the finicky manner of an industrious tax accountant. Adding to this impression was a fondness for fussy, archaic phrases straight out of a 1920s secretarial handbook: "Be that as it may . . ."; "Thus and so . . ."; "In the normal course of events . . ."

As such, it was impossible for him to project the unflappable, super-laid-back manner of the textbook negotiator. On the contrary, there clung to him an aura of vague but constant fretting, and yet somehow for him it worked. Kidnappers trusted him. In critical situations, hostage-takers who might be wary or fearful of decisive, take-charge negotiators were disarmed by Julian's honest, earnest prissiness. When Julian said, "I doubt sincerely that such an arrangement would prove constructive under the present circumstances," or "I'll have to query the company on that before I can respond with confidence," he was believed, where others might not have been. According to Bryan, he was the most effective negotiator they had, and Lori was immensely glad to have him there.

Having been effectively interviewed by Detective Chief Inspector Ellert Ragnarsson the night before, it took Lori only twenty minutes to tell him her story. Not that there was much she could tell. She was fairly sure that Baldursson had died there in the van, right beside her. It was something that had become clear to her only later, under Ragnarsson's questioning. Those horrible sounds of the blood pumping from his neck, so clearly audible at first, had become weaker and less regular, and within a few minutes they had died away altogether. She'd never heard another sound from him and never sensed a movement. After a while, they'd stopped the van and moved him away from her. She'd heard the door slide open and closed, and had heard them moving around outside while it was open. Ragnarsson had said it probably meant Baldursson was dead and they had disposed of his body somewhere.

"An assessment with which I'd agree," Julian said. "It would appear to have been one of the carotids, which would have emptied within a regrettably short time. And inasmuch as it's the carotids that supply the brain, the loss of blood would have—"

Lori grimaced and held up her hand. "Julian, could we not be quite so graphic, please?"

"Of course. Forgive me, Lori. What can you tell me about the man who spoke to you when you were in the tent?"

"Not much. I think he was American. I couldn't hear any accent at all. Seemed well educated. He didn't threaten me or anything. Um . . . he knew Bryan."

Julian's head came up. "He knew Bryan?"

"Well, he knew who he was."

"That seems odd, doesn't it?"

"I don't know, does it? He knew about the training going on at the Hilton. Wouldn't he be likely to know the name of the person conducting it?"

"Yes, I suppose that's possible. Still, it makes one won-der— Well, never mind. He finished his coffee. "Go on, please."

At about eight p.m. (she and Ragnarsson had recon-structed the time afterward), she'd been informed she was to be released. When she'd started to ask questions, she was forcefully told to be quiet and then ignored, which didn't much bother her, not with the tremendous flood of relief she was feeling. When time, and then more time, passed with nothing happening other than her being given water to drink and being led, still blindfolded, to a bathroom, she grew concerned that they wouldn't follow through, but eventually they came for her—two of them, a woman and a man—and drove off with her. When the vehicle stopped—she couldn't tell what kind this one was: van, truck, ordinary automobile— she was told to close her eyes and keep them closed for a count of one hundred after they let her out. The blindfold was removed, she was helped out of the vehicle and left standing with her hands placed on a low stone wall for balance. She followed instructions and counted to a hundred.

"I don't suppose you were able to keep track of how long the drive took, or the traffic sounds, or that sort of thing?" Julian asked.

"I know it took a good half hour. Ellert—Chief Inspector Ragnarsson—said that meant they had to have been in the general Reykjavik area, but nothing more."

"That's so," Julian said. "They could really have been half an hour from where they let you off, or just as easily right down the block. Where *did* they let you off?"

"At the Tjörnin, which is a sort of a mini–Central Park for the city, with paths and a little lake—Bryan and I had a breakfast picnic there. It's only a few minutes' walk from police headquarters, which is where I went at once. I called the hotel from there to talk to Bryan, but of course he wasn't there, and then, later, while I was with Ellert, we found out that . . . that . . . that Bryan was . . ."

She shook her head as her throat closed and her eyes welled up. She had sat in the hotel's ninth-floor lounge until four a.m., looking out over the sleeping city with her arms around her knees, endlessly rocking back and forth, but her eyes had stayed dry. And now, here came the tears, pouring down her cheeks. The two tissues she had with her were sopping wads within seconds. "Oh, Julian, I'm sorry. This is silly. I'm not a crier, haven't cried for years. It's just—"

Now it was Julian who covered her hand with his. "Lori, I know how awful this is for you, believe me. But we'll get him back. I have absolutely no doubt. None whatever. Bryan knows what he's doing and I know what I'm doing. All right?"

She sniffled. "Okay."

"You trust me, do you not?"

"I do. Bryan says you're the best."

"As usual, he's entirely correct, and I intend to make sure he continues to think so when this is done. Now, then. I am going to get some more coffee for myself. I am going to get some for you as well."

"I don't need—"

"Yes, you do. I am going to get us something to eat too. What would you like?"

"Julian, really, I couldn't—"

"If you don't tell me, I shall bring you dried fish. But you *will* eat something."

She gave him a wan smile. "Some kind of pastry, then. Thank you."

He stood up, fished in his inside pocket, and came up with a packet of Kleenex, which he placed on the table for her, then went to the counter.

Her throat still closed up at the idea of swallowing anything, but she was as worn out and depleted as Julian seemed to be, and perhaps she could get something down. Julian brought back two more coffees and a couple of almond sweet rolls on a paper plate. "And you're completely sure they really do have him?"

She spread her hands. "If not, where is he?" And here came the tears again.

Julian waited until they stopped. "Now tell me," he said mildly, "have they made any new demands since this all happened? I have a copy of the first one, but has there been anything since?"

Lori made a final dab at her nose with a tissue and slid across the note that she'd discovered in her handbag at the police station. Julian, scowling, mumbled his way through it.

To whom it may concern:

We now hold the corporate lapdog Bryan Bennett as well as Baldur Baldursson. Arrangements for their release will be handled one at a time, with Bennett first. We will give you exact details on how to get Bryan Bennett back as soon as you have complied with the demands of this letter. The price is the same as it will be for Baldursson, five million US dollars. The money is to be in twenty, fifty, and one hundred dollar bills of approximately equal number. No series, no unused bills, no marked bills. Any deviation from these requirements will be considered nonfulfillment, and you will be responsible for the consequences.

We do not wish to hear from you at this point. However, as soon as the money is ready and physically available, you are to place a classified ad in Morgunblaðið. The ad is to be under Real Estate for Sale, and is to say in English: "Prestigious home, 400 acres, stables, woods. Near Akureyri. USD $5,000,000," followed by the name and telephone number of the person we are to contact. Do not waste our time with

*counteroffers, delays, or explanations. Also note
that we are not interested in discussing the status
of Baldursson at this time. That will be taken up
again at a later date.*

*If the ad does not appear by Monday, 5 April,
exactly as indicated, this transaction will be
terminated. There will be no further communication
from us and the prisoners will not be heard from
again.*

*It is of no concern to us whether the money is
provided by the Odysseus Institute or GlobalSeas
Fisheries or both. That is for you to decide. We
have carefully studied the financial situations of
both organizations, and we know that the amount
we require is within their capacity to pay.*

Then he read it through again, silently this time. "The
language . . ." he mused, still scanning it. "It's different, not
like the first one. Less doctrinaire, more straightforward,
fewer catchphrases. No 'meatpuppets,' no 'repatriate,' no
'soldiers,' no 'Amerika' with a *k*."

"Is that important? Does it mean something?"

"I don't know." He looked up, his lips pursed. "Lori . . ."
He hesitated, searching for the right words. "You do know,
as much as we want him back, we can't simply give in to
their demands right off the bat. That wouldn't be a good
beginning. It could make things worse, drive up the price,
lengthen the entire affair."

"I understand."

"If I thought the quickest, safest way to get him back was
to pay what they ask, that's what I would tell Wally to do.
But—"

She held up a hand to stop him. "I know how it works,

Julian. I'm married to him, remember?" She smiled. "It's just . . . just . . ."

"Just that it feels a little different when it's someone you love. But look, even if it takes a few days, I truly believe there's no reason to worry. They didn't mistreat you, did they?"

"They shot Baldur—"

"That was during the excitement of the abduction. I mean later, once they had you."

"No, they didn't mistreat me."

"Well, then, you see, there's no reason to think they'll mistreat Bryan. Besides, he knows how to handle himself, he knows how the game is played. We'll get him back for you, safe and sound, don't worry. I'll call Wally right away, and whatever money we have to come up with, we'll come up with, I have no doubt at all. We just want to play according to *our* rules if we possibly can. But Bryan's safety comes first." Then, as an afterthought: "And Baldursson's; that is to say, if he's alive."

She had been picking without appetite at half a sweet roll, forcing it down, but now she stopped. "You think he might be?"

"No, I don't. I believe he's dead, all right."

"So why would they say he's still alive?"

"In my judgment, because they consider that it benefits them for us not to know of his death, and by simply refusing to discuss him they preclude the embarrassing possibility of being required to get proof-of-life information from a dead man. But I strongly suspect Mr. Baldursson is no longer negotiable property. Bryan is all they have."

"Is that what he is now?" she asked softly. "Negotiable property?"

"Yes," Julian said bluntly. "And I am ready and eager to

begin negotiating for him." He put down the last of his roll and wiped his lips with a paper napkin. "Enough, I'm recharged. Shazam. And now I'd like to meet the detective chief inspector."

"Of course. I've got a car in the lot, and I promised to bring you over to talk to him. Would you like to stop by the hotel to freshen up first, though? We have a room for you."

"Freshening up can wait. Time is of the essence. Lead on."

On the way to the parking lot, Lori reached a decision that she'd been struggling with since the middle of the night. "Julian," she said falteringly, "time really *is* of the essence, more than you know. I . . . I don't think it'd be good for Bryan to be in captivity for very long. He . . . well, he's not really . . . not really able . . ."

"Lori," Julian said gently, "I take your point. I know what you're trying to tell me."

She shook her head, smiling. "I doubt it."

"Oh, but I do. You're worried he might not be able to cope. He has a few, ah, hang-ups, doesn't he?"

She stared at him openmouthed. Bryan—and Lori, for that matter—had been convinced that no one at the institute knew. They had worked hard to keep it that way.

"How did you know that?" she blurted.

"What is it, claustrophobia?" Julian went on, not pressing, but not backing off either. "Fear of heights, fear of confinement—?"

"Julian, does *everyone* know?" They had stopped walking now and stood in the parking lot, in the slanting early-morning sun.

"I don't know if they do or not, Lori. Whatever else we may be, we're not a gossipy group of people. I wouldn't be surprised if they do, though. The people at the institute aren't exactly stupid, and it's not really too hard to figure out. Even in the five years since I've been there, Bryan has never once flown anywhere. In automobiles he becomes, shall we say, not to put too fine a point on it, squirrely. He refuses to participate directly in negoti—"

"It's not that he's a coward!" she interrupted fiercely. "There are just some things that get to him."

Julian held up his hands as if to hold her off. "I know, I know. You don't have to tell me that. Some of the risks he took in his days as a negotiator are famous; they're in the textbooks. All I meant—"

"He was once kidnapped himself. As a child, did you know that?"

He goggled at her. "You don't mean it."

"He was held for two months. In Turkey. In appalling conditions. He almost died. He was only five years old."

"How terrible. My word, I had no idea."

"And it's left him with a few scars," she said, calming down under Julian's gentle concern. "He has panic attacks sometimes; that's the worst thing. If they've taken away his pills . . ." She shook her head mutely.

Julian took her elbow. "Come then, let's get going. Lori, I'll have him free by the close of Monday. Four days. Whatever it takes. That's a promise."

"It's not the days I'm worried about, Julian," she said soberly. "It's the nights."

Chapter 19

"Are you calm now? Can you speak rationally?"

My eyes were closed, but I recognized Gullveig's voice, and with its recognition came a playback of the way I'd behaved in the parking lot. It hit me like a brick in the face. My God, it had been one of the wildest, worst attacks ever, and they had seen it all, they had watched as I groveled and raved and whimpered. They'd had to *subdue* me. They'd *laughed* at me. I very nearly groaned with remorse and embarrassment. How strangely the mind worked. Here I was, helpless, hands manacled painfully behind me, not knowing what awaited me, my life at the doubtful mercy of kidnappers and murderers, Lori's fate uncertain, and what was my overriding feeling? Mortification, acrid and profound.

Whatever happens, I said silently, *whatever is in store for me, you won't see me like that again.*

"What did you say?" The man's voice, the one from the parking lot.

So, apparently I hadn't said it silently. "Yes, I can speak rationally," I replied with all the self-possession I could dredge up, but my voice caught in my throat, thick and phlegmy.

I opened my eyes. I was alone in the tent.

"Are you there?" I asked, meaning "Are you *really* there, or is the drug playing games with my mind?"

"Oh, we're here, all right." The man again.

No, wait, not just "the man." I knew what his name was . . . Stig, that was it. In the parking lot, Gullveig had used his name in front of me. That in itself was something to think about. For obvious reasons, kidnappers who knew what they were doing didn't do that. So either these two didn't know what they were doing or she had inadvertently let the name slip. Either way, pretty amateurish.

Then again, "Stig" might be a fake name invented for my benefit, but I didn't think so; it had slipped in too spontaneously. Or—and this one I didn't want to dwell on—they might not care if I knew their names because they had no intention of ever releasing me. But if that were the case, why the hoods? Well, there was an answer for that too. It might be that they wanted me to think that they would eventually let me go, because that would make me less desperate and thus easier to deal with.

Or it could be . . . no, overthinking things wasn't getting me anywhere. Wheels within wheels.

I could see where they were speaking from now. There was a mesh window in one wall of the tent, and they had lifted the outside flap that allowed them to look through it. The light streaming through a window behind them turned their heads into featureless silhouettes, but it provided information as well. It was daylight, not artificial light. And it wasn't gray or rosy; it was bright yellow sunlight, so I knew that we were now well into the next day.

The flap was then drawn down over the window, and a larger flap over the entryway was zipped open. They came through quickly, with Gullveig carrying a tripod and a video camera. I was able to get another glimpse of the outside world through the open entry, but all I saw was a blank cornflower-blue wall and a section of hardwood flooring. Still, at least it confirmed that we were inside, not outside.

Gullveig set up the tripod near the entrance, about six feet from where I was, and fiddled with the camera, then started it running on its own and came a bit closer, careful not to block the lens.

Stig stood a few feet away, arms folded, eyes narrowed, keeping watch. They both wore black woolen sweaters, stiff, heavyweight black pants, and simple black ski masks, the cheapest you could find, with two teardrop-shaped openings for the eyes and a slightly larger oval one for the nose and mouth. Well, maybe not the very cheapest. In Turkey they'd used potato sacks with a couple of rough holes torn out.

They wore thick woolen socks, no shoes. That was to keep me from knowing when they were or weren't nearby.

"Can you stand up?" Gullveig asked.

"I'm not sure," I said truthfully. "I'm a little woozy."

"Give it a try," said Stig coldly.

Having my wrists clamped behind my back was more of a problem than the dizziness. As I swung my feet awkwardly to the floor I realized that I was without shoes too. And no belt. Along with my parka, they'd been taken away. Standing up brought a stab of pain to my head, but all in all I felt physically sound for the first time since they'd jabbed the needle into me. More important, my mind seemed to be working right again.

Gullveig waited until I was reasonably steady on my feet before starting. "We are informing you that you are being detained by soldiers of Project Save the Earth, *Verkef-*

nið Björgum Jörðinni. Please state your name for the record."

"What record would that be? What is this being filmed for?"

"Please state your name for the record," she repeated in precisely the same dull monotone. And I mean precisely, as if she'd hit rewind and play again. It occurred to me that she might not have been reading from notes when we'd spoken on the telephone, after all. It was simply the way she spoke.

"Okay, my name is Bryan Bennett."

"And you are an agent of the Odysseus Institute for Corporate Protection in New York?"

"I'm a research fellow at the Odysseus Institute for Crisis Management and Executive Security. In Seattle, not New York."

"State your duties."

No. Name, rank, and serial number were all they were going to get, and they already had their equivalents. "I'd appreciate knowing about my wife."

"State your duties."

"No, not until I know something about—"

Stig made an impatient noise. "Come on, this is ridiculous," he told Gullveig. "You can do this later. Look at him. He barely knows where he is. People will think we drugged him."

"You *did* drug me," I said, regretting it before the words were out of my mouth. Reminding them of last night wasn't something I wanted to do.

Stig had caught a glimpse of my manacled hands behind me and pointed at them. "You forgot his watch," he said to Gullveig. "He doesn't need a watch."

I began to object but caught myself and kept quiet. The more they knew that I wanted something, the more power they had over me. The thing with the pills had already given them the upper hand, and I wasn't going to add to it. Besides, I already knew enough about Stig to understand that asking for it would have been pointless.

So Gullveig unstrapped my reliable old $24.95 Casio and took it from my wrist. I stood submissively while she did it, but I wasn't as woozy as Stig thought. My mind was hard at work, sorting data, hatching plans. I knew things they didn't know I knew. They'd made sure to situate the tent's entry so that when it was opened it revealed nothing but that blank wall. However, they hadn't taken similar care with the mesh window, probably not thinking of it as a way to look *out*. Its flap had been up only five or six seconds before they'd come in, and their heads had blocked much of the view, but you can take in a lot in five or six seconds if you pay attention, and I'd been paying attention.

What I'd glimpsed was part of another wall, this one with a single shade-covered window, in front of which was a green plastic student chair, the kind with a tablet arm, with a folded newspaper on the arm. That would be the guard station.

Just to the left of the window was a small telephone table. A couple of feet to the right was a doorless corridor, perhaps ten feet long, leading to a kitchen, of which I could see a part. The place was not a dump by any means. Bright, cleanly painted walls, blond wood flooring, big, expensive, stainless steel refrigerator in the kitchen. It was all new, or at least newly renovated; the opened tent admitted smells I hadn't picked up before: wood dust, paint, plaster.

But it was the window that had gotten my attention. An ordinary enough window with two sliding panes, one above the other, with the top pane opened a few inches. It was covered by one of those shades that close not from the top down, but from the bottom up. The shade hadn't been pulled all the way up, but only to just above eye level, so I could see through the top foot of the upper pane. What I saw were the winter-bare top branches of a spindly tree a few feet from the window, and behind that, fifty yards or so away, what appeared to be two identical five- or six-story brick apartment buildings, so new that many of the units were unfinished; I could see stepladders and paint cans, and some of the windows still had crisscrossed tape on them. I assumed that I was in a similar building, part of a complex, and that this particular apartment had been chosen because the units around it were not yet occupied.

That window was going to be my escape route. Sooner or later there would be a letdown in vigilance. The guard in the chair would be deep in his or her newspaper, or possibly—even better—asleep. If I could figure out a way of silently getting the entrance flap up, I'd simply head straight for that window and hurl myself through it, praying that the canvas shade would keep me from being shredded by the glass. Somebody would surely be in the guard chair, but I had only a few feet to cover—it would take me less than a second to reach him—and I'd count on momentum and surprise to barrel right through him. The spindliness of the tree outside told me it was young and small, which meant we were on the bottom floor, so the ground would be only a few feet down. I'd launch myself through the window headfirst, or rather shoulder first, and hit the ground rolling. The headlong-through-a-glass-window thing was worrisome, but I wanted to make sure that I didn't break a leg by landing awkwardly on it. Better to be cut up than unable to run.

Even if I were still in handcuffs, I thought I could do it.

Okay, I agree, not what you would call an elegant plan, but for starters it wasn't bad. Was I serious? Would I really try it if the opportunity arose? Truthfully, I didn't know, but at some point I would have to come up with something. I was as sure as sure could be that the nights would bring on the panic attacks, and they were likely to be humdingers. While I was prepared to make it through one or two nights of them, or even three or four if I had to (or so I told myself), I knew I couldn't possibly stand much more than that without truly going bonkers.

In any case, what I did know was that concocting even a plan as rash and dubious as this one was a healthy way to occupy my mind, and that was good enough for me at that point. If I ever did put it into action, the part I'd have to worry about was getting the tent flap open without alerting them, especially with my hands manacled behind my back. If they caught me at it, there would be no second chance.

I realized Stig had been talking to me. "What?"

"I said, why aren't you dead yet?"

"I don't understand."

"Your pills. You need to take them every day. But you didn't take them today. Why aren't you dead yet?"

"Give me time. The day's not over yet."

Stig was not amused. He made an impatient motion at Gullveig. "Let's get on with it."

With what? I wondered nervously.

Gullveig produced a padlock and a length of chain from somewhere and locked one end of the chain to a corner of the bed frame. Then she asked Stig something in Icelandic, but her gesture toward my handcuffed wrists made clear what it was. She wanted the key. Stig gestured with his chin to the rooms outside the tent. "He keeps it," he said. "I'll get it from him."

A minute later he was back with it and handed it to Gullveig. "Turn around," she told me, and I did. Standing behind me, holding the free end of the chain in one hand, she used the other one to waggle the key into the key slot in the left cuff.

I guess my mind really was more sluggish than I thought, because it took until then for me to understand what was going on. Once she got that left cuff off my wrist, she was going to slip a link at the free end of the chain over one of its arms and snap it shut. I would be chained to the bed by my right wrist. *Chained!* Good God, I hadn't expected . . . The second I was hooked up to that thing, any plans for escape would become pointless fantasies. This "cot" of theirs was no lightweight aluminum job. The frame was heavy-duty steel; it had to weigh thirty pounds, minimum; more likely, forty. There was no way I would be going anywhere dragging that thing behind me.

Which meant—

The key clicked.

—that it was now or never.

I knew I had only a fraction of a second to act: the tiny window of time between the time she got the cuff open and the time the link was slipped over the cuff's free arm. Make my move too soon, and I'd still have my hands manacled behind me. Too late, and all was lost; I'd be shackled to the bed. I closed my eyes to focus on my hearing, waiting for the soft *snick* of the ratcheted arm opening out. Every muscle in my body was tensed and ready. Gullveig, holding both the chain and the key and having to keep the cuff steady as well, was having trouble, fumbling a little.

"Do you need some help?" Stig said irritably.

Say no, I commanded.

"No, I don't need any help. Ah, here it comes . . ."

And there it was, the sound I was waiting for, the almost inaudible slipping of steel on steel.

I bolted. I'd been standing facing the cot, my arms behind me, and I spun quickly around, at the same time pushing off from the bed frame with my foot to gain all the thrust I could. The plan, if you could call it that, was to head straight for the loosened entrance flap, bowling over anybody in my way. Gullveig, standing almost directly behind me, would be caught totally off guard and easily bulled out of the way. Stig was off to one side, two or three steps from my prospective path, and I didn't think he could react quickly enough to block me.

Once I made it through the flap I'd be home free; just a couple of yards, maybe two running steps, to the window. There, if nobody was right on my heels I'd use the little table to smash the glass. Otherwise, I'd just have to launch myself through it—a considerably less appealing prospect. Still, that canvas shade would surely provide some protection. And—for me, at any rate—a faceful of lacerations and a broken bone or two were risks I was more than ready to take to escape being chained up like that. Once through the window and on the ground, I'd be yelling like hell and running as fast as I could.

That was the plan.

But you know about plans.

Gullveig, standing right behind me, was first on the list of bowl-overees, and, exactly as planned, I lowered my head and rammed into her with one shoulder, assisted by the impetus I got from pushing off against the bed. But the blocky Gullveig turned out to be one of those people who are made of heavier, denser materials than the rest of us. My push got a grunt out of her and a single step back, but that was all. It took a second, more protracted thrust to force her back one more step, where she slipped on a roll of paper towels and went over backward, safely out of the way.

But.

The extra second that was consumed was enough to give Stig his chance. Moving with the darting quickness of a cat, he reached out as I shot by him and snagged the cloth of my sleeve. I spun completely around, tearing the sleeve and leaving him with a handful of cloth, and *he* went over backward too, helped more by his own momentum than by anything I did. That left both of them sprawled on the floor, and nothing in my way between me and the tent entrance.

But.

In flailing as he toppled backward, Stig knocked against the camera tripod, upending it, and wouldn't you know it, my legs got tangled up in the struts, so instead of eventually launching myself headfirst through the window as per said plan, I wound up launching myself headfirst through the open tent flap, getting tripped up yet again by a three-inch-high band of fabric at the bottom of the entry, and then managing to stagger two wobbly-legged steps before executing what I believe is called a right shoulder roll. I ended up on the wooden floor of the room, half sitting, half lying against the blank, windowless wall directly in front of the tent, with the breath partially knocked out of me. I was a good eight feet from the window. It was all over.

Chapter 20

My head hadn't finished bouncing off the wall before Stig came scrambling sidewise from the tent like a fiddler crab. When he reached me, he stood there, muscles taut, fists tightly clenched, watching me haul myself up against the wall.

What now? As near as I could tell, his intention was other than to lecture me on my misdeeds; the guy meant business. Stig was unsettlingly quick and obviously fit, but he wasn't a big man. At six feet and a hundred-and-seventy-five pounds, I probably had fifteen pounds on him and four or five inches in reach. My eyes wandered briefly back to the window. If I could get my hands on him the right way, I could probably throw him out of the way and still make it out before anybody else got to me. Maybe I could even throw him *through* the window.

But.

Did I forget to mention that my hands were still cuffed behind my back? Well, they were. Apparently the arms of the cuff hadn't quite opened completely when I broke free, and the sudden movement had jammed them shut again. So there I stood, not in the best shape of my life, with no usable weapons other than my stockinged feet and my head. I decided the latter was the better bet, and I lowered it preparatory to butting him in the midsection.

But before I'd gotten my head halfway down, it exploded with fireworks-like pinwheels of light. I don't think I've ever felt anything more painful. I didn't know what hit me—that is, I was reasonably certain it was Stig, but I couldn't imagine what he'd hit me *with*. I found out when he did again—to the same spot, just under my nose—every bit as excruciatingly as the first time. And then, yet again. I fell back against the wall and slid down it, blinded and near-paralyzed with pain.

As I sank, he came down with me, so that he was on his knees astride me, and what he was doing was hitting me with his fist, but not with your ordinary, everyday, ho-hum punch. He had formed the fist with the fingertips not folded into the palm, but up against the undersides of the fingers, so that the striking surface wasn't the big knuckles of the hand, but the far sharper middle row of finger knuckles. Something out of the martial arts, I assumed. And he wasn't swinging powerful, roundhouse rights and lefts but short, stiff, precise, stylized jabs, all to my upper lip, which I now knew to be one of the most devastatingly sensitive areas of the human body. The intent of punches like that wasn't to knock one unconscious, but to cause as much hurt as possible. And let me tell you, they do the job.

I was utterly helpless, my mouth full of blood, tears of pain streaming down my face, trying to twist away from him. But he was still at it, sometimes missing his target now, so that the rest of my face took some of the blows—not quite as painful, but bad enough—when he suddenly stopped with his right hand still cocked for yet another shot.

Only then did I realize that another voice had come into play. "For Christ's sake, do you think that's really necessary?" it had said tightly, a schoolmaster reprimanding a willful ten-year-old.

"I don't think I need you to tell me what's necessary," Stig grumbled, breathing hard. Poor guy was winded from beating me up.

"Get up," the other one said with a sort of weary distaste, as if Stig's behavior had been a source of disappointment to him for a long time. I recognized the voice now. This was the man who had called me at the pizza place.

Stig, showing reluctance, sullenly pushed himself off me, but halfway up he couldn't resist delivering one more of those stabbing jabs. I had closed my eyes for a moment, so it caught me by surprise, and an inadvertent whinny of pain escaped—the first cry I had made, I think. I tried to redeem myself with a snarled "God *damn* you!" but my mouth and throat were so clogged with blood that all that came out was a disgusting gargly noise—that and a spillage of blood down my chin and onto my shirt. I ran my tongue around my mouth, searching for missing or broken teeth. Amazingly, I couldn't find any damage.

"Now you want to tell me what the hell that accomplished?" the other guy asked.

"It made me feel better," Stig said.

"Moron," was the muttered reply. Then to me: "That was stupid, what you did. Where'd you think you were going? The doors are all steel and all combination-locked."

I shrugged. "I thought it was worth a try."

"All you got out of it was making this . . . my friend here mad, which is not a good idea."

"Tell me about it," I mumbled.

He was an average-sized guy, maybe a little taller than average, and aside from the usual black ski mask, he was the only one who wasn't dressed for a ninja movie. He wore a reddish plaid flannel shirt and brown corduroys. Unlike the others, he had shoes on his feet. "He belongs back in the tent," he told Stig. "And get him cleaned up, for Christ's sake."

"I'll take care of it," Stig said dully.

"No, I don't want you touching him"—a real edge of asperity here. "I want the other one to do it."

"Fine. Whatever."

I was still on the floor, sagging against the wall, hurt and bleeding from mouth and nose, but my mind was working fine, picking up information with almost every sentence. I now knew for sure that of the three people I'd interacted with so far, this new guy was the boss, which confirmed the impression I'd gotten over the telephone. And since he'd referred to Gullveig as "the other one," didn't that mean that the three of them were all there were?

Most important, I knew that they thought, or at least the man in charge did, that I'd been trying to get to the door. It hadn't occurred to them that I'd be crazy enough to jump through a closed window, especially when I had no idea, or so they thought, of how high up we were. That would make it easier to try again the next time. When and if.

"And when he's cleaned up, get him secured again."

"I will."

"*Properly* secured this time."

"I said I'll see to it."

"I'll come by and see for myself later."

"I *said* I'll see to it!"

Yes, definitely a little tension there. Maybe something else I could exploit.

NEVERTHELESS, Stig did dutifully see to it. In a few minutes I was well and truly secured, my right hand attached to the cot's frame via handcuffs and chain . . . and my right leg shackled to it with another chain that had one end padlocked to the foot of the frame and the other one firmly looped around my ankle and padlocked as well.

Only then did we get around to the clean-up phase. And indeed, Gullveig was "the other one," but Stig chose to leave it to me, tossing me a wad of wet paper towels to dab at the mess on my face while the others stood around and watched.

My face was swollen, but I could find only one injury worth mentioning: a split lip (no surprise there) that was still oozing blood. I kept the towel pressed to it.

Gullveig checked the padlocks one more time and gestured at various objects in the tent. "There's food in the cartons and water in the jugs. That's a chemical toilet over there. You know how to use it?"

"Yes, but it's going to be a little hard with these," I said, jangling the chains.

"Oh, that breaks my heart," said Stig.

"Is there anything else you need?" Gullveig asked.

If it sounds as if she was concerned about my welfare, then I've given the wrong impression. She came across as a technician assessing the maintenance and preservation requirements of a piece of perishable merchandise.

Which is what I was.

I shook my head. "I'm all right." I was too. One would have thought—*I* would have thought—that being bound hand and foot like this would have been enough to drive me around the bend, but I guess I didn't have enough adrenaline left in me to do the job. What would happen when the adrenaline well was filled again I didn't know and didn't like to think about. "Um, I suppose there wouldn't be any point in asking for those pills back?" I tried to make it a casual question but I don't think I succeeded.

"You got that right," Stig said with a laugh.

"Where are we anyway?" I asked. "How about at least telling me that?" Pointless, but it was what you did when you'd been kidnapped.

"Miles from anyone," Stig answered, "so don't waste your time yelling for help. There's no one to hear but us, and it would only annoy us."

"Well, I certainly wouldn't want to do that."

"No, you wouldn't. Also, don't move anything in here, you hear what I'm saying? That would bug me too. The bed stays where it is, everything stays where it is. You have everything you need within reach. And keep away from the walls of the tent. I don't want to see you touching them." He spoke to Gullveig. "Check him again."

"But I just—"

"Check him again."

Okay, the full chain of command was now firmly established in my mind. The other man, the one who had interrupted Stig's little exercise on my face was at the top, Stig in the middle, and, at the bottom, Gullveig.

She tugged on the chain around my ankle, jiggled the locks, and tested the handcuffs. I smelled body lotion and perspiration as she bent over me. "He's secure," she said, straightening.

"What happens now?" I asked.

Nobody answered. Stig motioned Gullveig to precede him through the tent opening, then bent, followed her through, and began to pull the flap across.

"Hey!" I yelled. "How about telling me what time it is?"

He laughed again. "What difference does it make to you?"

"Screw you," I muttered, loudly enough to prove I was still my own man (but not combatively enough to bring Stig back), and then, battered in mind and body, and nauseated from having swallowed so much blood, I turned over and dropped off into a fitful, edgy sleep.

Chapter 21 _____

Detective Chief Inspector Ellert Ragnarsson stood at the window of his third-floor office in the dingy, off-white monolith that served as headquarters for the Reykjavik Metropolitan Police Department, a building—cold in the winter, hot in the summer—as unloved by the personnel who had to work in it as it was by the general public. Twiddling his fingers behind him and puffing away at his beloved fifty-year-old calabash (the one he was forbidden to smoke at home), he gazed out at the mixed sleet and rain that had been slopping down all morning out of mud-gray skies. Ugh, nasty. He hated March. Like all Icelanders, he preferred the white stuff. At least you didn't get freezing water down your neck when it snowed.

When the pipe went out he tried once or twice to keep it going, then gave up and tenderly placed it in the antique pipe rest on the gray metal bookcase behind his gray metal desk and went back to looking out the window. Across the street, the hunched, soaked, unhappy-looking people scuttling roachlike in and out of the oddly Orientalized intra-city bus terminal did their part to contribute to the day's cheerlessness. A gloomy day in the far north, indeed, with little prospect of improvement in sight.

The arrival of the new man from Odysseus had done nothing for Ragnarsson's mood. Ordinarily, he was not given to snap judgments about people, and Julian Minor had walked into his office not even twenty minutes earlier. Still, the impression he'd made was anything but favorable, perhaps because the chief inspector had been expecting another Bryan Bennett, with all his confidence and ready certainties. But Minor, with his ear-lapped, fur-lined hat, his banker's three-piece suit, and his fuddy-duddy manner, had seemed more like a punctilious assistant office manager than a skilled and experienced hostage negotiator.

Seated on the visitor's chair beside the chief inspector's desk, Minor methodically clicked his sleek, silvery ballpoint pen one, two, three, four—Ragnarsson gritted his teeth—five, six, *seven* times, checked to see that the point was withdrawn, placed it in his inside jacket pocket, read what he'd written one more time, nodded his approval, and said: "I think that should do it, Chief Inspector. In my opinion, this should go into tomorrow's paper."

"Mmp," Ragnarsson rumbled, coming back to the desk and sitting down. Minor slid the paper across to him, and Ragnarsson took it without much confidence. The fastidious care with which he'd printed out the brief message in small, perfect, perfectly aligned block letters, hadn't helped any.

"Well now, let's see what we have here," Ragnarsson said with gruff, largely false good cheer.

The proposed advertisement was almost exactly what the kidnappers had demanded: *"Prestigious home, 400 acres, stables, woods. Near Akureyri. USD 850,000. Contact Mr. Julian Minor, Tel: 295-5266."*

Almost, but not quite. "They've demanded five million. I see you're offering eight-hundred-and-fifty thousand."

"In point of fact, yes." Minor had his hands resting on the desk, his fingertips touching. Unless Ragnarsson was mistaken, he thought sourly, the man went to a manicurist. He wore cologne too.

"Are you sure that's a good idea?" Ragnarsson said. "They were quite explicit—no counteroffers would be accepted. It's up to you people, of course; it's not my place to influence any decision as to ransom, but aren't you concerned . . . ?"

"I take your point," Minor said. "I do, indeed, but I believe we can assume with reasonable safety that their threats are empty. I assure you that they don't expect to get five million dollars. We'll offer the eight-fifty, they'll be 'outraged' and counter with four million, we'll offer one, they'll come down to three, we'll say two, and we'll settle for two-and-a-half. Three, if need be."

Ragnarsson's bristly, V-shaped eyebrows went up. Whatever the merits of the plan, he had to admit that when it came to ready certainties, Minor was no slouch either. "Ah? I understood from Bryan that twenty-five percent was the more usual figure. That would be one and a half, if I'm not mistaken."

"In the normal course of events, you might be right, but only when we have weeks of bargaining at our disposal. In the present circumstances, however, we are anxious to settle as quickly as possible. That being so, two and a half is a more likely outcome."

Ragnarsson couldn't help laughing. "If it's as cut-and-dried as that, why not settle it for two and a half million right now and eliminate all this busywork?"

"There's a right way to do this, Chief Inspector," Minor said in gentle reproof.

"Of course. I understand." The hell he did. If it were up to him, he wouldn't be handing them one damn cent, but Minor was supposed to be the expert here, not him, and the chief had said to give him plenty of leeway, at least for a while. Well, he would. For a while. It was their money, after all, but still it was hard not to say *something*. He went and got the pipe and took some time to get it going again with the fearsome lighter—a jet like a flame-thrower—his son had given him for his last birthday. "Now as to this money, this $850,000. Suppose . . . *huff* . . . they take you up on your offer—"

"They won't."

"But suppose for a moment that they do. Do you already have it . . . *huff* . . . available?"

"As it happens, no, not yet, but the difficulties are basically logistical. It's not easy to pull together that much currency, especially used currency, to say nothing of negotiating its way through the banking and finance regulations of both our countries. Fortunately, I have a good many contacts in that area and things should move quickly. The process is already in motion. I hope to have the first four hundred thousand dollars in a vault at Kaupthing Bank here in Iceland by tomorrow morning, and all the rest that we might need no later than the following day."

"You can do this on a weekend? Tomorrow is Saturday. The 'following day' is a Sunday."

"I have reason to believe it can be done, yes."

Ragnarsson was beginning to wonder if he'd been a little quick in his evaluation of Minor. "I gather from all this . . . *huff* . . . that your people—the Odysseus Institute—are . . . *huff* . . . determined to pay for Bryan's release, then."

Now it was Minor's neat gray eyebrows that lifted. "Determined? Hardly. Willing? Certainly, if that's what it takes. Understand, Chief Inspector, my first obligation here is—"

"The preservation of life," Ragnarsson said brusquely, looking to see that the pipe had been fully lit, which it had. "Yes, so I've been informed."

He got out of the leather-backed chair and went to the window again. Minor waited politely for him to continue.

"*My* first obligations, on the other hand," he said forcefully, "are the prevention of crime and the apprehension of criminals." His arms were crossed, his back was to Minor. The well-chewed stem of the big pipe was clenched between his jaws. This was the fourth bit he'd had to have made for the calabash, and it was about ready for a fifth.

"I take your point," Minor said respectfully.

"And so, my question to you, Mr. Negotiator, is: Will you work with me in those aims? May I count on your sharing information and keeping me abreast of events so that we can do our job too? It would work both ways, naturally."

"Of course I will," Minor said, surprised at the question. "That's why I'm here now. I'll do everything I can to help you arrest these people, and to recover the ransom too. It's only that Bryan's safety comes first."

Mollified, Ragnarsson turned from the window. "That's good, Julian." He saw Minor stiffen slightly at the intimacy. "We go by first names, here," he explained, "but if you prefer—"

"No, no, not at all . . . er, ahum . . . Ellert. Ahum." He fiddled with the knot on his tie.

Ragnarsson very nearly laughed. He was starting to like Minor. The man did have a certain antiquated charm to him, and so far, at least, he seemed to know his stuff. "Let me ask you about something else that worries me, though, Julian. You seem to be letting a lot ride on their knowing these 'rules' you talk about as well as you do. But this is the VBJ we're dealing with, you know; hardly experienced professionals."

"Perhaps, but they seem to be quick learners, Chief Inspector—ah, Ellert. Consider the differences between the first note—the one for Baldursson—and the second one, for Bryan, a mere eight or ten hours later."

Ragnarsson squinted through tobacco smoke. "Differences."

"The first one," said Minor, "was ninety percent harangue, with nothing whatever about method of payment, and so on and so forth. The second is all business, very professional. Not a word about earth-rapers or war crimes."

"A reference to Bryan as a corporate lapdog, as I recall."

"True, but that was all. And the intent is entirely different. The first time it was 'Publish this or else.' This time it's 'Give us the money or else,' accompanied by highly specific instructions on how to proceed. I'm sure you made note of the contrast."

Ragnarsson, who had in fact failed to make note of the contrast, cleared his throat. It seemed he'd sold Minor short, all right. "And from that you infer?"

"Well, I've been giving that some thought, and it seems to me to indicate a sharpening of focus, a shift in their priorities from propaganda to profit. It's as if they've pulled themselves together and decided what they can realistically salvage out of all this, given the hash they've made of it thus far. There may well have been internal dissension, perhaps a change in leadership. Or it may be that they've sought the guidance of someone more seasoned—a professional."

Ragnarsson's eyebrows went up. "A professional kidnapper? Is there such a thing?"

"Oh, yes," Minor said. He had his fingertips together on

the edge of the desk and studied them for a few moments. "At this point in time, however," he said, "it would be premature to pursue these inferential hypotheses."

This time Ragnarsson did laugh. "I'll buy that," he said. "Now. About the money—the two and a half or three million dollars that you believe will eventually be required. I have a suggestion."

"I am eager to hear it," Minor said pleasantly.

Ragnarsson peered at him, not sure whether or not he was being sarcastic, but giving him the benefit of the doubt; the man certainly did have his own way of putting things. "It's this, Julian: Iceland is not as thoroughly behind the times as you might think. We have ultraviolet currency-marking equipment and scanners here, and some experience in using them. When those bills arrive, I'd like to get my people started on them so that we have some hope of—"

To his astonishment Minor let out a laugh before quickly resettling his face. "Indeed? And how many people did you have in mind?"

"Two, if necessary," he said, biting down on the pipe as he grew more irritated, "or even three. In all honesty, I fail to see what—"

"Forgive me, I meant no offense. It's only that the very idea of . . . Ellert, you say your people have marked bills before. On the average, how long would you say one needs to allow per bill?"

"On average? Two or three seconds, no more."

"Including marking, recording, bundling, and all?"

"All right, four seconds, if you like."

"Even considering that these would not be smooth, new bills?"

"*Five* seconds, then. If you would get to the point—"

"Five seconds," Minor said. "And how many bills would

you guess it would take to comprise three million dollars in equal numbers of ten, twenty, and fifty dollar notes?" He drew a tiny calculator from his jacket and began punching in numbers with his pinky.

"I have no idea," Ragnarsson said, "but I suspect you're going to tell me."

"It would take"—*dink-dink*—"a little under thirty-eight thousand notes in each denomination," Minor said, rolling along in his element, "a total of about"—*dink-dink*—"one hundred and fourteen thousand bills. At five seconds per note, that would come to five hundred and seventy thousand seconds, or nine thousand five hundred minutes, which is"—*dink-dink-donk*—"one hundred and fifty-eight hours. Now. Were you to assign three people eight hours a day to the task—which you couldn't do on account of unavoidable errors resulting from fatigue and boredom—it would take"—*dink*—

Ragnarsson held up his hand. "I take *your* point, Mr. Minor," he said dryly, sinking back into his chair.

"—almost seven days," Minor finished. "One entire week."

"Yes. All right then, I think we can dispense with the marking idea."

"And concurrently, you have no objection to my placing the advertisement as written?"

"None whatever. Julian?" He reached across the desk, offering his hand. "I'm glad to have you with us."

LYING on his bed with a moistened towel pressed to his eyes and his head pounding, Camano emitted a pent-up groan, partly of suffering, but mostly of exasperation. Both were the result of the increasingly absurd, frustrating, and dodgy situation in which he found himself.

Stig was even more dangerous than he'd thought. Stig

was crazy. Camano had entirely misjudged him. Wild-eyed Stig might be, but he was no anarchist, no communist motivated by airy-fairy dreams of bringing down a corrupt, greed-bloated world so that a free, fine, equable one might be rebuilt in its place. No, Stig was not an ideologue at all; he was a hater, pure and simple. He'd *hated* Baldursson. He *hated* Bennett. He *hated* all he thought they stood for. That summed up his worldview. Magnus Haldorsson's overheated, undercooked professorial rhetoric had provided a framework to hang it on by giving form, vocabulary, and even rationale to his instinctive, corrosive loathing for the agents of authority, for the corporate world, and for pretty much anything in or representative of the established order.

Worse, he was extravagantly, mindlessly violent. The shooting of Baldursson could be explained (but probably wasn't) by the excitement and tension of the moment, but pulping the face of the handcuffed Bryan Bennett like that? What was the excuse there?

It wasn't that violence in itself offended Camano's sensibilities; he had never shied from violence when the situation called for it. Several of his one-time captives were getting along nowadays with fewer appendages (fingers, ears) than they'd once had, and as four murdered hostages would attest—if murdered hostages could attest—he hadn't shied from execution either. But in every one of those instances he had acted with prudence and foresight, not animal passion, so that full ransoms had been collected even when the ransomees no longer existed. And then, come to think of it, there had also been a few other removals along the way—hirelings who turned out to be too greedy or stupid or inquisitive—but no great loss there.

As to the current situation: Bryan Bennett was going to be killed too, that was a given, and Camano looked forward to personally attending to it. But not yet. It would have to wait a little while. Killing him now would jeopardize the ransom negotiations. He would do it in his own time, in his own way. And, oh, the miserable sonofabitch would know who was killing him and what for; otherwise, where was the satisfaction in it?

Bryan Bennett had stolen seven years—*seven years!*—of Camano's life. No, worse than that, he'd turned them into seven blighted years of degradation, squalor, and wrenching despair; seven years of living hell. He'd done it through guile and lies, *and he'd gotten away with it!* Ever since, Camano's dreams and plans of vengeance—no, let's be more precise, of retribution, righteous and just—had nourished him, even kept him alive, in the darkest days. He had fed off them and hugged them to himself. The day would come when he would act on those plans; he'd known it would.

And then, against all odds, fate—it couldn't have been mere chance—had dumped the man into his lap without any work on his part. In a supreme twist of irony—how the gods must be laughing—he had come of his own free will, thinking that his expertise had prepared him for what he was in for, but having no idea of what awaited him. But when it was time, Camano would carry the act out coldly, surgically, and not, as with Stig, in a blood rage. To give in to your emotions that way, as Stig had done, was to admit you'd been beaten at your own game even though you held every possible advantage. And that, to George Camano—to Paris—was anathema. Had Stig been a mere paid helper rather than one of the clients, and had there been anybody else to replace him, he would have gotten rid of him as soon as Baldursson had been shot. But this was Iceland. There wasn't anybody else. He was stuck with Stig, and with Gullveig.

Gullveig. He had misjudged her even more fully than Stig. It was *Gullveig* who was the ideologue. Not only that, it was Gullveig and not Stig who turned out to be the VBJ's moving force. She was slow and plodding and heavy, yes, but she was dogged and insistent, and she never . . . ever . . . gave up. Stig grated on his nerves like sandpaper on raw skin. Gullveig was Chinese water torture: *drip . . . drip . . . drip . . .* insistent and unrelenting.

This he had discovered when he drafted the second letter, the one about Bryan Bennett. He had given the draft to them to look over in case he'd said something inapt from a local point of view. Stig, uninterested, had shrugged and passed it to Gullveig, who had used a ballpoint pen to insert the usual mind-numbing locutions: "Amerika-dominated," "anthropocentric ecodestroyers," "corporate leeches," and the like. Camano had crossed them out one after the other, patiently explaining that with the death of Baldursson things had changed; efficiency and stripped-down simplicity were now crucial. When it was all over, they would have plenty of money to get their message out. Gullveig had sulked, but she'd apparently accepted it.

Then, five minutes later she'd trudged up to him again with her face like a block of wood. "Why shouldn't we take advantage of getting our message out now?"

He'd explained again, and again she plodded sullenly off.

Then, five minutes after that: "Why *shouldn't* we at least . . ."

And then: "*Why* shouldn't we . . ."

In the end he'd won out, giving her a single sop, "corporate lapdog," to shut her up. But, Christ, she was wearing him raw. And then last night, after the pickup in the parking lot, she'd come to him with the insane idea of making a video with Bryan. Absolutely not, he had said. Too many possible clues for the police. Didn't she know that a trained police technician could bring up background sounds they themselves weren't even aware of?

"What trained police technician?" she had responded. "This is Reykjavik, not New York." And she'd stomped off in another sulk. Twenty minutes later she'd started in on him again. "Why couldn't we just . . ."

For the sake of his sanity, he had compromised: "All right, go ahead and make your damned video—but it is not to be released until after the ransom is paid and Bennett has been let go. *Is that understood?*"

He could see from her dully smug reaction that she'd considered it a victory, and so it was, he was forced to admit. But then there had come this morning's fiasco—while they were supposed to be recording—and Bennett had tripped over the damn camera and broken it. This was of no concern to Camano as far as making a propaganda video went, but that was the camera with which he'd planned to keep a constant, all-seeing eye on the prisoner and thus provide a little welcome relief from the pressure of guarding him, short-staffed as they were.

Afterward, Gullveig had come clomping up to him. "We'll need to buy another video camera now."

"Fine, fine," he'd said, his head already beginning to throb. But on reflection he'd changed his mind. This video recording thing was a bad idea, and sending one of these two to purchase another camera at a local shop was begging to turn disaster into catastrophe. No, things were complicated enough; the video was out. Period. And this time, he would not be cajoled or wheedled or pressured into amending his decision. Gullveig could sulk all she wanted; she would just have to live with it.

The only problem was that he hadn't told her about it yet. So now, here he was, hiding from her in his room until his headache relented enough for him to face her drudging, slogging persistence.

This wasn't the way it was supposed to be. Maybe it

really was time for him to retire. He refolded the towel so that a cooler surface lay against his eyelids, and tried to bring up visions of the *Callisto*, its sails ballooning, scudding along on a foam-flecked Mediterranean, under a deep blue, cloud-dotted sky.

Chapter 22

I woke up more angry at Stig for taking away my watch than for beating the bejesus out of me. This is not to say that I was willing to let bygones be bygones about being punched silly, but that was, after all, more or less a personal matter. But the watch . . . that was serious. The kind of situation I was in—isolated, inside a tent inside a building—was a kind of sensory deprivation, with much of the uncertainty, dissociation, and disconnect that went along with it. Every link to the real world, the world outside the tent, was precious, and knowing the hour was something solid to hang on to, proof that you still were a part of that world. Without it, without some way of measuring how long it had been from one event (or, more likely, nonevent) to another, you were adrift in time as well as in everything else. I was just going to have to figure out some way of approximating it.

I lay there with my eyes closed for a while, doing another self-assessment. How was my pulse? How was my breathing? Was I starting to panic? No? Good. But was I starting to panic about starting to panic? It was like poking at a toothache with your tongue to see if it still hurt or if maybe it had gone and healed itself, and it was just about as useful. I was depressed and anxious, yes, and I had a hell of a headache, and my upper lip was swollen and sore, but it didn't take a self-assessment for me to figure that out.

"*. . . what you need to understand, and accept,*" I'd told the trainees yesterday (only yesterday?), "*is that you're going to undergo one of the most devastating experiences that a human being can have.*"

And now here I was, living it (again!), while they were probably in the Hilton coffee shop, buzzing about this latest turn of events—assuming they knew I'd been taken. (And there was another source of disconnect—not knowing if anybody knew what had happened to me.) I shook my head; life was full of ironies. But looked at the right way, I was luckier than any of them would have been in my place. I knew what to expect, and I had some idea of how to cope with it. I was an expert; I got paid for thinking about this kind of thing and providing advice for others. I knew all about the mind games and the psychological stumbling blocks better than my kidnappers did. This time around, I wasn't a helpless five-year-old in a Turkish dungeon.

Looked at another way, though, things weren't so hot. It had been many years since I'd had to get along without Xanax; that vial in my pocket had been a happy crutch for a long time. Most of the time I took no more than two or three a month, but several times a day I'd check my pocket to make sure they were there, just in case. And now, "just in case" had arrived in spades, and no Xanax. The prospect of seeing a string of attacks through on my own was, to put it mildly, daunting. To put it not so mildly, I was petrified. Now that I was up against it, truly Xanaxless, Zeta's advice—focus on the feelings, face them down, stand up to the bully—seemed childish and even cruel, the kind of advice that could be given only by someone who hadn't been there herself.

I did come up with a plan of sorts. I had never yet gotten a full-fledged attack other than at night, after several hours of sleep. My "plan" was simply never to allow myself more than an hour or two of sleep at any one time. Somehow, I would keep myself awake during the nights (or what I thought were the nights) and take catnaps during the day to make up for them. I would do my napping sitting up too; no lying down . . . just in case.

Which meant I should have gotten up right then, like it or not, because I was growing sleepy, but when I tried, I was swamped by a tremendous billow of nausea and dizziness as my head came up, and I fell heavily back. A minute or two of lying there without moving and the worst of it passed, but I needed to wait awhile before trying that again. I'd allow myself twenty minutes—what I guessed were twenty minutes—and give it another shot. But better not close my eyes, though.

I blinked hard a couple of times to clear my vision and looked around me. As I'd told the GlobalSeas people, the first item of business was to get your mind productively engaged . . . and that meant reconnaissance. Study your surroundings, see what you were up against. And one could get a head start on that even from a supine position. So what, exactly, were my circumstances?

The tent, with smooth, almost straight-up-and-down nylon walls and a rubberized polyester floor, was about twelve by twelve, and a little over six feet high along its center ridge. The cot I was lying on had been set across the center line, but up against the back, as far as possible from the entrance. The light, harsh but not bright—something like thirty watts was my guess—came from a naked bulb, not inside the tent, but outside, on the other side of a small mesh triangle under the peak that was probably there for air circulation.

The cot was two feet wide, with a thin, new-seeming cotton-felt, gray plaid mattress. I lifted a corner of the mattress and saw that it lay on a taut canvas support attached to the metal frame by a series of sturdy, oval metal loops, like the links of a chain. The frame had three sets of tubular legs, the U-shaped, full-span kind that wouldn't damage a tent floor, one at each end and a double one supporting the middle. My cuffed right wrist was chained to the right-hand corner of the frame near the head of the bed, my right ankle to the lower right-hand corner near the foot. No sheets, no pillow, but there were a couple of folded blankets on the floor underneath.

The other items in the tent, besides the hassock-sized, hassock-shaped, lidded portable toilet, were a plastic kitchen garbage pail, six one-gallon plastic jugs of water, a one-liter plastic jug of the kind of milk that doesn't need refrigeration, and two grocery cartons, one without its lid, one with. I could see what look like packaged snack foods inside the open one. The closed one had a bag of tortilla chips on top of it. Nearby lay two plastic-wrapped rolls of paper towels, one with a dent where Gullveig had slipped on it.

Okay, fine; all the comforts of home. Now what were the chances of my getting myself out of there? My first attempt had been well short of a rousing success, but I wasn't through trying. First, a look at my restraints. I lifted my manacled right hand to my face to have a better look at the handcuffs. They were a sturdy, standard-issue set, each of the two cuffs made of a pair of curved arms hinged together, one ridged, one hollowed, with the ridged one sliding into the hollow one and ratcheting into place as it went. One of the pair was clamped tightly around my right wrist, and the other was clamped on the last link of the chain that led to the bed, where the other end was padlocked to the frame. The cuffs could be moved in only one direction—closed. This I brilliantly proved to myself by unintentionally clicking them a notch tighter. Not enough to cut off my circulation, but enough to make the sharp double-rim pinch. Ouch. I wouldn't be making that mistake again.

I wondered at first if it was going to be possible to break the cuffs apart by twisting my body round and round until the linkage between them snapped, but no, I soon saw that they were connected by two heavy metal links that rotated freely around each other. Clever, these handcuff manufacturers.

As for the loop of chain around my ankle, I spent a good ten minutes trying to work it over my heel, but all I accomplished was skinning the painful Achilles-tendon area at the back of the ankle and wearing a hole in my sock.

With a sigh, I quit fooling with the cuffs and the locks. I was enough of a realist to know that there was only one way to get out of them, and that was by getting hold of the key—an improbable prospect, but something to think about.

I'd been shifting around on the cot while examining the restraints, and I was ready to try standing again. Merely sitting up brought on a wave of vertigo, but not as bad as what I'd felt before. Worse was an overall feeling of lethargy and weakness. Caused by the dregs of whatever they'd shot into me, I supposed, and then, the beating I'd taken hadn't done me any good either. In addition, except for that brief burst of energy that carried me a whole dozen feet, right up to the wall—*smack!*—facing the tent entrance, I'd been slumped and inactive on the cot and, before that, in the coffin, for maybe fifteen or twenty hours, all told.

I wrote myself a mental reminder: Keeping in shape physically was going to be as important as staying mentally alert. You never, *never* knew when an opportunity to escape was going to come up—a mistake on their part, a miscalculation, a momentary letting down of their guard. Who knew how long I'd be here if I had to wait out the negotiations? It had taken fifty-nine days the last time. And a lot of things could go wrong during negotiations. There was no guarantee that I'd get out of this alive, let alone sane. So if my chance did come up, I wanted to be ready to take it, but if I let myself go to seed, I'd turn sluggish and dull. That meant I'd have to work out an exercise schedule and stick to it—sit-ups, push-ups, stretches, resistance training, running in place. All of that could be done in the tent, even with the chains.

It would be tricky to set up a regular routine without having a watch to keep track of the time, but there was a way around that. I knew that, given my druthers, I ate a big breakfast and a big dinner and skipped lunch because I didn't get hungry at midday. Thus, assuming that the food cartons meant that I was on a feed-myself-when-I-felt-like-it schedule, I'd exercise every second time I felt hungry, before sitting down to eat; that would do for a rough once-a-day strategy. It would also be a means of keeping track of the passage of time.

The exercise plan bucked me up; it meant that I was beginning to take some responsibility for control of my own life; well, to give it some thought, anyway. Gingerly I pushed myself all the way up onto my feet, relieved to see that the dizziness had mostly passed. I ironed out various bodily kinks with a few knee bends and slow stretches, then returned to my reconnaissance.

The chain from my wrist to the cot was about eight feet long, but the one on my ankle was only three. That allowed me, with a few contortions, to reach a maximum of seven feet from the cot, leaving me a couple of feet short of the entrance. That was why I'd been ordered to leave everything where it was; so that I wouldn't be able to set myself up to surprise anyone showing up there. But even if I did move it, so what? I couldn't see how merely getting within reach of someone was likely to do me much good while I was trussed up like this. I'd have to come up with something better.

I shambled the couple of steps to the cartons—*clank, clank*; I felt like Marley's ghost—and went through them, clumsily arranging the chains so they didn't pull at me. The first box was loaded with packaged food, as I'd thought: eight small bags of flavored potato chips; two boxes of wheat crackers and another of chicken-flavored crackers; packages of fig bars; peanuts; trail mix; energy bars; breakfast bars; beef jerky; single-serving, eat-from-the-box containers of dry cereal—Weetabix, the British version of shredded wheat—tapioca; vanilla pudding; dehydrated soup; "snack packs" of tuna paste and crackers, chicken paste and crackers, and cheese and crackers; peanut butter; blackberry jam; and a heap of resealable bags of pretzels, raisins, dates, molasses-coated popcorn, and mixed dried fruits. There were two dozen single-serving soft plastic bottles of various juice drinks as well. Maybe a week's supply of food altogether. Nothing that would create any garbage besides the packaging materials. All in all, a fast-food junkie's idea of health food and a whole lot more appetizing than my Turkish diet had been. I wasn't hungry, but I opened up one of the packages of fig bars to chew on while I investigated the second carton.

This one held supplies. There were plastic-coated cardboard cups, bowls, and eating utensils, a wrapped bar of Camay soap, and two rolls of toilet paper, but not just any toilet paper—these were from England: "Aqua-Pure garden-scented soft toilet rolls, specially formulated for chemical toilets. Positively will not chafe or block waste valves."

Excellent. I'd hate having my waste valves blocked. It felt good to smile. Whatever I'd been expecting, it didn't include garden-scented toilet paper. Some consideration for my comfort had gone into this.

No, that wasn't accurate. It had been Baldursson they'd been expecting, not me. Which brought up the question of the GlobalSeas CEO again. There was no way to tell what his condition was. According to the witnesses, he'd been wounded, perhaps seriously. For all I knew, he was dead. Or in another location. Or, for that matter, in the next room, in a nice little tent of his own, with his own supply of garden-scented toilet paper.

My best guess: Baldur Baldursson was dead, fatally shot during the shootout. And that meant—if they had truly let Lori go—that I was now their one and only meal ticket. I shook my head to try to make myself stop thinking about whether or not they'd released her or not—what good did it do?—but of course I couldn't help it. It was a worry that hadn't been out of my mind for one second since I'd first awakened on the cot. I had to figure out a way to find out for sure. That was something else I would work on. What could I come up with to trade for confirmation of her freedom?

I uncapped one of the water jugs and lifted it to my mouth, then changed my mind, unwrapped a paper cup, and poured the water into it. *Stay civilized. You have cups; use them.* Sipping and munching, hunched on the edge of the cot, I thought about my situation. They'd chosen the supplies carefully, with more than convenience in mind. Unless I was missing something, there was nothing that could be turned into a weapon. Maybe some trained Special Forces type could fashion something deadly from one of the plastic-coated paper "sporks"—those combination utensils that try to function as both a spoon and a fork but don't do too well at either (the bowl's too shallow for soup, the tines are too short for meat)—but I sure couldn't come up with anything. And there weren't any other utensils. No knives, no forks, no can opener. The chicken and tuna containers were plastic, with pull-off plastic lids. The peanut butter and jelly were in plastic squeeze-containers, and the rest of the packaging was all paper. Perhaps you could make a dagger from a plastic tuna fish lid? Better yet, mold a fake Glock 9-mm out of a couple of packages of fig bars held together with molasses?

The tent itself didn't offer much in the way of escape possibilities either. Fabric and rubber flooring. The entrance had an internal mesh curtain that had been tied to one side. The covering flap itself was secured by a plastic zipper. I could see that it had originally had a pull on either side, but the one that opened it from the inside had been removed. I couldn't see any way of getting the flap open from in here; not without making any noise, at any rate. And with the supporting poles and cables outside, there was nothing but fabric within, nothing to fashion into a weapon.

There was the metal bed frame—a piece of it could serve as a club or a spear or a knife—but trying to twist or bend or pull the steel to pieces without alerting the guards would be impossible. Probably impossible even *with* alerting the guards. The metal links that held the canvas mattress support? No, they were as thick as the links on the chains. What about the metal eyelets that prevented the canvas from tearing? Could I get them off? Possibly, but on closer examination they turned out to be plastic, and even if they'd been metal, what exactly would I have done with them?

The plastic pull handle on the chemical toilet was a possibility, but I knew I was kidding myself. There were at least three of them out there, and I knew they had guns. I was a reasonably fit thirty-seven-year-old, but thirty-seven was thirty-seven, and I was tied to a bed, with only one usable arm and leg. If I thought I was going to take out three armed people with a plastic toilet handle, I was dreaming. Any escape plans would have to be put on hold until I learned more about their ways and about the entire setup here.

Finishing the fig bars, I tossed the wrapper into the garbage pail, refilled the cup with water, and continued to explore. I was feeling a bit more chipper. As these things went, it really wasn't bad. If I refused to let it get to me, there was no reason—no *tangible* reason—I couldn't stick it out here until something developed, one way or another. The tent was big, with room enough to stand up straight along the whole length of the center ridge. Not the kind of place I'd choose to live in, but spacious enough. And if my catnap idea failed and I did suffer nighttime panic attacks, which my gut was already telling me I would, well, too bad—that was just the way it would have to be. But I'd keep them to myself. No more "shows" for the VBJ. Besides (I tried to convince myself), when the panic attacks hit they would give me a fair chance to try out Zeta's "self-limiting" mantra and her advice on focusing on the feelings. It couldn't hurt to try, and maybe (but I didn't think so) they might help. One way or another, I told myself, I'd tough it out. One day, one night, at a time.

Of course, it was one thing to be stoic about it now, when I was rational and tranquil. When the attacks came, it would be a different thing. In any case, it did no good to obsess about them now. According to Zeta, no one had ever died from a panic attack, and, for the moment, I was willing to make myself believe it.

I wished, though, that she'd been more definitive about whether anyone had ever gone stark, raving mad from one.

When it came to my physical safety, I couldn't see much reason for serious worry, at least for a while, other than the enjoyment Stig obviously got out of beating on me. What

I'd said to Ellert about Baldursson was even truer for me: There was no percentage in killing me. With me dead—assuming Baldursson was no longer alive—they'd have no chips to play. The game would be over and they would have lost. But it also worked the other way around. If they lost—if, say, the police began to get close—then I became a liability; they were safer with me dead.

When you're a lone, isolated captive, it gets hard to be certain of anything, but I really believed it wouldn't come to that. The Odysseus Institute would surely come through with the money for my ransom. When I'd been asked the question on the telephone, I'd answered, "Yes" without stopping to think about it. But now that I did, I knew that good old Wally would come through for me with flying colors.

After all, he could never stand the marketing fallout that would come from one of his own people getting himself abducted on the job and murdered.

And with Julian Minor doing the negotiating, I was in good hands, none better. Julian had a perfect record. In more than twenty kidnap cases, he had never once lost a hostage. Unfortunately for me, however, part of his competence lay in his maddeningly deliberate approach. Julian was not the man you wanted when you were in a hurry. If I remembered right, he had never taken less than a week to wrap up a kidnap situation, and five or six weeks was more like it. Could I last five weeks, chained up and confined like this, without coming out at the other end, drooling and bug-eyed? Could I last five days? It looked as if I was going to find out.

"Bryan Bennett."

It was Gullveig's voice. She had unzipped the top of the entry flap and was looking in at me.

"Yes?"

"I have good news for you. It's been decided. You can have your pills."

My knee joints seemed to come unhinged. I sat heavily on the cot. "Thank you," I said thickly. I was close to weeping. The intensity of the relief shocked me. I realized that I hadn't let myself absorb until this moment how filled with dread I was over the prospect of an attack, of multiple attacks. I'd been pushing it below the surface of my mind and lying to myself with that catnap nonsense. How long could that have worked before I fell wholly asleep? One night? Two, maybe? Ridiculous. But now, with no groveling or begging from me (and that, I knew to my deep shame, would have been only a matter of time), I would have those inestimably precious little orange ovals.

"But only one a day, one at a time," Gullveig said. "We hand it to you, and we watch you swallow it. We don't want you saving them up. When do you take it? Morning? Night?"

"I—" With an effort I checked myself; I'd been going to plead for two. "Night," I said. That was the crucial time; that was when my guard was down and the always-prowling, always-probing beast inside my head was most likely to find me.

"All right, we'll come by with one later."

"When?"

"In three or four hours. Six o'clock." The flap closed, and I heard the whisper of the zipper and then the swish of her socks on the floor as she shuffled away.

Oho, another little bonus. She'd slipped up there at the end. Watch or no watch, I now had at least a rough idea of the time: mid-afternoon. One more little tie to outside reality, one less uncertainty to leave me unanchored. I let my head sink back on the cot and closed my eyes. I was insanely, ridiculously grateful but tried not to show it or even to feel it. I knew all about the Stockholm syndrome, and I wasn't about to fall in love with my captors because they showed me a kindness.

Certainly not on the first day.

Chapter 23

They didn't come back with the pills. Not in three hours, not in four hours, not in ten hours. They didn't come back at all that day. I wasn't as dismayed by this as you might expect, because I'd done some thinking after Gullveig left, and among the things I'd reluctantly concluded was that they wouldn't follow through. In fact, I'd have been surprised if they had.

Experienced kidnappers—Asian or Latin American drug lords, say, or Mexican or South American kidnap rings (never before, to my knowledge, had the phrase been used for environmental activists in Iceland)—understand that the first few days of captivity are crucial to establishing the captive's docility and cooperation. And one of the ways to establish these is to waste no time demoralizing him. And one of the many ways to demoralize him is to get his hopes up, then dash them. Then do it again. And again. That, I thought, was what this pill thing was about. My pathetic attempt at escape had marked me as "difficult," and they were now in the process of showing me the error of my ways.

All things considered, I had little to complain about. There were means of demoralization that were far more drastic: torture, sensory deprivation, starvation, constant loud noise (usually, for reasons that made perfect sense to me, rock music). I was grateful that these people weren't taking any of those paths; not yet, anyway. But it looked as if I were back to tackling the damn panic attacks on my own.

After Gullveig left, I went back to reconnoitering. And I hatched a few fantastic new escape plans (*escape fantasies* would be closer to the truth), I planned how I would respond to a thousand different situations that might arise, and I busied myself leaving clues for the police to find afterward: leaving my fingerprints all over the place, getting tent material under my fingernails, and going through three of the plastic-covered spork handles to press my initials into the rubber flooring. *BB*, it turns out, is a particularly unsuitable set of initials for this purpose. Except for those two vertical lines, it's nothing but curves.

I also had another meal. What I seemed to be hungry for was breakfast—maybe a couple of boxes of the Weetabix with milk and dried fruit—but I figured it was evening or late afternoon, not morning, and I knew it was best to keep as near to my normal daily regimen as I could. Best, too, to eat in an enlightened fashion, course by course. It was too easy to slip into random grazing, grabbing whatever appealed at the moment (such as Weetabix). Therefore, having seated myself on the edge of the cot and using the closed lid of the chemical toilet as a table, I repasted on hors d'oeuvres (cheese and crackers), appetizer (dried lima bean soup diluted with water from one of the jugs, drunk cold from a cup), entrée (two packets of beef jerky), and dessert (dried mixed fruit). The beverage *au choix* was apple juice, drunk from a carton with the straw that came with it.

The ambience wasn't all it might have been, but the meal

was substantial enough and not all that bad. I could live with this. The food lifted my spirits enough so that I banged on the toilet lid with my fist and yelled, *"Mes compliments au chef!"* through the tent walls. There was no reply, and my little excursion into hilarity quickly subsided. Night was surely coming on. Panic time.

One bright spot shortly thereafter was the realization that I could tell day from night. The tent fabric was opaque, but a little light managed to filter in around the edges of the flap that covered the window, which was directly in line with the outside window. At some point the light had gone from the gray-blue color of daylight to the yellow-white of incandescent-bulb lighting.

This discovery was heartening, but the moment I realized that night had come I began imagining that I could feel the damn panic attack building, waiting for me to let down my guard and fall asleep. I recited poetry to myself, and I made up songs and limericks. I'd been refused a pen or pencil (I would have made a deck of playing cards from the cereal cartons) so I read aloud whatever I could find in English: fig bar ingredients ("Organic barley flour, organic sugar, organic fig paste"), Ivory soap wrappers ("It Floats! 99 $^{44}/_{100}$% Pure!"), toilet waste-disposal instructions (you don't want to know).

And for a while it worked. But deep into what I thought was the middle of the night, I was sitting on the edge of the cot, hunched and miserable, still fighting off sleep, when a sudden jerk of my chin made me realize I was losing the battle. I stood up and walked in place and did knee bends and stretches. I dug my fingernails into my palms and bit my cheeks and my already painful lip. But it was only a question of time.

Usually, panic attacks would hit me without warning. One second I'd be peacefully sleeping, and the next I'd be sitting up rigidly, eyes popping, raving and panting. But once in a while, instead I'd be nudged awake with the illusion that some tiny creature—a mouse, a little bird, maybe even an insect—was inside my skull, gently tugging at the seams of my mind, and that the stitches were beginning, one by one, to come undone. That's the way it happened this time. It wasn't really that awful a feeling in itself, but it was an infallible indication that an attack was on its way. A Xanax could head it off at the start, so that it didn't develop into a full-fledged attack, but I didn't have a Xanax, and I was determined not to amuse them by pleading for one. I know I should have sat up (when had I lain down?) and tried to ward it off somehow, but it was too late; all I could do was curl up on the cot with a whimper and shut my eyes and wait for it.

And then there it was. I was a terrified five-year-old, strangling in my horrible dungeon-cave, the cold, gritty metal of the neck clamp choking off my air. I felt the wretched dankness, smelled the foul bucket in the corner, but as always this nightmare world, convincing as it was, lasted only a second or two, falling to pieces when I reached up to claw at the collar and found nothing there. I knew at once where I was and who I was and how old I was.

But by then—also, as always—it didn't make any difference. Did the fact that I found myself actually a captive again, chained up in a tent, make it worse than it would have been at home? Not really. A panic attack, once begun, runs on its own steam, as independent of reality as it is of whatever might have brought it on, and there is no reasoning it away or willing it away. As Zeta had explained, once it starts, the all-emotion, zero-intellect limbic system is running the show, and it's too late for the sane, sensible cortex to get in on the act.

I believed it, but believing it didn't make any difference either. I was in its grip and there was no way out. In seconds, I was on my feet beside the cot, panting and crazy, and as absolutely certain as always that there was no way back to sanity. But eventually Zeta's endorphins kicked in and did their job, the amygdala and the hippocampus slunk grumbling back to their primitive cave, and I settled back on the cot, spent and sweating, but back in my real world, such as it was. I sighed with relief. Being the chained-up prisoner of a crazy eco-terrorist group was a walk in the park compared to living out my life in the hellish place I'd just been.

My last thoughts, before I drifted off, were good ones. I was pleased—and a little surprised, if you want the truth—at having actually found the resolve to keep the whole episode to myself instead of giving in to the need to bawl and moan and all the dismal, showy rest of it. Was it possible that trying to focus on the feelings, rather than running from them or simply giving in to them, had actually helped? Maybe so. And something else, another first: I didn't feel sorry for myself—well, only a little—instead, I was *angry* with myself, ticked off at being such easy, pusillanimous, self-pitying prey to things that weren't real. Zeta had given me some tools to fight them, and by God, I would use them. *Implosion therapy, here I come.*

As if I had any choice.

ONCE a panic attack had worn itself out, I would generally plummet into sleep the way a stone drops into a well. It was no different in the tent, even chained to the cot. I slept like a corpse, so that it was only reluctantly that I floundered to the realization that someone was pulling on my ankle. I hadn't heard anybody come in.

"What, what do you want?" I mumbled irritably into the thin mattress. I tried to jerk my foot away.

"Come on, hurry up, stand up."

"I don't . . . what's—?"

There were two of them again, Gullveig and Stig, and

between them they pulled me roughly to my feet, snagging the handcuff on the corner of the bed frame and scraping my wrist, drawing blood. Even then I was only half-awake.

"Ow. What time is it, anyway?"

"Shut up. Get on the floor. On your stomach."

When I was too slow to suit them, Stig shoved me down by the back of my neck. Once I was sprawled on the floor they lifted the mattress and looked under it, then began to pat me down.

I was more annoyed than frightened. "What are you looking for? Where do you suppose I'd get any—?"

Stig grabbed me by the jaw—fingers and thumb squeezing my cheeks—to pull my head around. "I'm not going to tell you again. Keep your mouth shut and stay down." For emphasis he squeezed harder, putting a twist into it and bearing down from the shoulder.

I couldn't help my eyes tearing up at the pain, but that's all the satisfaction I was going to give him. "To hell with you," I mumbled, to get in the last word. But I stayed down.

They poked in the cartons and the garbage pail, and even lifted the lid of the toilet to look inside. After a while, without saying anything more, they left. I stood up, got one of the blankets to cover myself with—even getting a simple blanket spread out over me was a hassle with the damn chains—and went back to sleep, grumbling to myself.

They hadn't even mentioned the Xanax. "Who cares, I don't give a damn," I flung after them in a last game mutter. I almost believed it too.

I had the impression I'd slept for no more than another few minutes before they were tugging at me again. This time it was my shoulder.

"Wake up. We need to move you. You have to get ready." It was my buddy Stig.

I shook off the hand and pushed myself up to a sitting position with my legs on the floor. My mind seemed more rested now, so maybe it had been longer than a few minutes. "Why? What's happened?"

"Get yourself ready, pig. I'm not going to tell you again."

I almost laughed. "Ready? What am I supposed to do to get ready?"

"Put on your shoes. Put on your coat." He pointed to where they'd been brought back and thrown on the floor. "Use the toilet. You're not going to get another chance for a long time."

I shook the handcuff chain. "What about this? How am I supposed to go anywhere chained to a bed? How am I supposed to get into a coat chained to a bed?"

"All right, then, forget the coat." He motioned to Gullveig to pick it up.

"Where are we going? Are the police—?"

My shoulder was gripped again and twisted hard. This guy was definitely starting to get on my nerves. "What is it with you?" he snarled. "Can't you just do what you're told without arguing for once? I don't have time for this. If you give us trouble, I'll kill you myself, I swear to God. I'm already sick of you."

BUT ten minutes came and went, and no one came back. An hour went by, maybe more, with nothing happening except some occasional rustling or quiet laughter or bits of unintelligible conversation from the other side of the tent wall. Two hours. "What the hell is going on?" I yelled. "Are we going someplace or aren't we?"

But that was just to let off steam. This was just another

part of the demoralization process, calculated to intimidate me and knock down whatever illusions of self-determination I might still hold. They wanted me to realize, not only intellectually, but at gut level, that I was totally dependent on their whims—and, just as important, to make me understand that they *were* whims, capricious and arbitrary. They could decide to let me have the pills, and they could un-decide to let me have the pills, they could interrupt my sleep whenever they felt like it, and they could alert me to changes and crises that would never materialize. And they were under no obligation to give reasons or even to have reasons for any of it.

After another hour, Gullveig came in and collected the shoes. No explanation.

Anytime they felt like it, I was to understand, they could decide to beat me, or starve me, or take away my toilet and make me defecate on the floor. They were gods, and I got nothing, good or bad, except as they cared to dispense. And with no one to talk to but them, and no information coming in from the outside, my apprehensions and self-doubts would naturally chip away at my resolve and firmness of mind and make me more easily controlled.

That was the theory. I didn't think that either Stig or Gullveig had the sophistication to do this on their own, which meant that the other one, the man who'd stopped Stig from pounding my face to jelly, was calling the shots, all right. Either he was the man in charge and the other two were hirelings, or—and this was a new thought—*he* was the hireling, and he had been hired to *direct* the whole operation.

And I knew of only one person in the world who that was likely to be: the shadowy, half-mythical figure known as Paris.

Was it possible?

Chapter 24

They were sitting in Detective Chief Inspector Ellert Ragnarsson's unadorned, 1960s-style office with its stained acoustic-tile ceiling and fusty tobacco odor, over a tray that held breakfast cookies with coffee for Lori and Ellert and tea for Julian. It was nine o'clock in the morning, and they had met to discuss the telephone call that Julian had gotten half an hour ago, shortly after *Morgunblaðið*, carrying the ad, had hit the streets.

Julian had already told them about his brief conversation with a female caller from the VBJ, in which the $850,000 offer had been refused, as expected, and in which Julian had demanded the answers to three proof-of-life questions (gotten earlier from Lori) before he proceeded any further. The kidnapper, Julian said, had hung up on him, which had frightened Lori, but Julian assured her that this was standard operating procedure and nothing to worry about. He expected another call, probably not until the next day, in which at least some of the answers would be provided, and they would move on to the next step in the bargaining process. This was simply the way it worked, and it was for the best, he had assured her.

"I know that," she said uneasily. "It's just that . . ." And as unexpectedly as before, hot tears had filled her eyes and spilled down her cheeks. She groped in her bag for a tissue and wiped them angrily away. "It's so hard to sit and wait, to leave everything up to them, to be doing *nothing*."

"Not quite nothing," Ragnarsson said. "I've had my people out in the coffeehouses, talking to our informants—the coffeehouses, that's where information is to be found in Iceland—and I'm reasonably sure we know who the people are who are holding your husband—and Baldursson, if he's still alive."

"Well, who?" Julian asked, when Ragnarsson just sat there looking pleased with himself.

Ragnarsson put down the pipe and clasped his hands on the desk. "We believe there are three of them: Magnus Halldórsson, a one-time radical professor at the university; Stig Trygvasson, one of his students; and a young woman, Dagnyár Eyjólfsdóttir, who goes by the name of Gullveig. All have been active in the VBJ from the beginning."

"That's quick work," Julian said. "Congratulations."

Ragnarsson accepted the compliment with a nod. "And now we're out talking to relatives and associates of these three, in hopes of turning up a lead as to where they might be holding Bryan." He turned to Lori, who was silently chewing at her lower lip. "Is there something you want to say?"

"I guess so, yes," she said hesitantly. "It's only . . . well, Bryan once told me that most of the hostage deaths that do occur happen not while they're being held, but in shootouts with the police. That scares me. I mean, if you do find out where they are, and . . . and . . ."

He smiled his reassurance. "Don't worry, we would not

go in with guns blazing, if that what worries you. We are not cowboys. If we should discover where they are, the first person I would call would be Julian. I would be inclined to follow his lead at that point."

"And so would I," Lori said, clearly relieved, reaching for her cup. "Whatever Julian says has my approval."

"Oh, that's fine for the two of you," Julian said, "but to whom do I pass the buck?"

They all smiled, but then the frown was creasing her forehead again. "Inspector . . . Ellert . . . those three people you mentioned—they're all Icelanders?"

"All Icelanders," Ragnarsson agreed.

"Then there have to be more than three of them. The man who talked with me and asked about Bryan spoke perfect English, American English, without any accent at all."

"Lori, we all learn English in school, at the same time we learn Icelandic and Danish," the chief inspector said kindly. "Most of us don't have accents."

"Oh, I'm pretty sure I can tell the difference."

He smiled. "Oh? And what if you didn't already know I was an Icelander? Let's say you spoke to me on the phone, in English. Could you tell I wasn't an American?"

"Definitely."

"Definitely," Julian chimed in.

"Mmp," said Ragnarsson. Jamming the pipe back into his mouth, he went to work tamping down the tobacco.

"Sorry," Lori said, with her own charming smile. "But it is true, Ellert. And the other ones—the three that actually kidnapped us—they all had accents like yours. Only that one didn't."

It was Minor who responded. "So you're saying there was an American with them?"

"Yes. Well, maybe a Canadian. And he . . . I had the impression he was the one in authority."

"And you told me he knew who Bryan was, isn't that so?"

"That's right."

"Ah."

"What are you thinking, Julian?" Ragnarsson asked, putting a wooden match to the tobacco and sucking in to get it going.

"What I'm thinking is that this has been rather a strange case from the beginning, with many unusual elements. And I'm thinking that if we put it all together, it suggests that we are now dealing with a very seasoned, knowledgeable craftsman, indeed."

"Craftsman?" said a scowling Ragnarsson, from within billows of fragrant smoke. "Are we back to this professional kidnapper idea of yours, then?"

Julian nodded the way a professor does when a student comes up with the right answer after sufficient prodding. "Have either of you ever heard of a man called Paris?"

"No," said Ragnarsson.

"I don't think so," said Lori.

"Then perhaps I'd better tell you a little about him," Julian said.

Chapter 25

Throughout the rest of that day my "orientation" continued. I was told I was about to be drugged again and loaded into the trunk of a car that would be shipped to Germany. It didn't happen. I was told, with considerable jubilation, that the ransom had been agreed to and I was about to be released. It didn't happen. "There may be trouble," they explained, this time with ominous overtones. "They say they don't have the money. You better hope they find it. The deadline's today." At one point the entrance flap was tied out of the way and I was blindfolded with an elastic bandage and told to sit on the cot facing the opening for "observation." That lasted about an hour, perhaps two. Whether anybody had observed me I had no way of knowing.

"All right, can I take it off now?" I'd called when I couldn't sit still any longer.

There was no reply.

"To hell with you, I'm taking it off," I declared. When I tore it off, I found myself alone in the tent, the entrance flap closed. A little later, Gullveig came in to get the bandage. No explanation, no lecture, no comment at all.

Through it all, I wouldn't give them the satisfaction of complaining. I simply did what I was told without resistance or protest. This was what I'd expected, and simply knowing what they were trying to do gave me an edge most prisoners didn't have. My passivity went deeper than that, though. As my time in the tent passed, I'd fallen more and more deeply into a listless but not unpleasant apathy, so much so that I'd begun to wonder if my food had been drugged. I resolved to stay away from containers that didn't have tamperproof seals. No more peanut butter, no more blackberry jam. The peanut butter would be sorely missed; I'd had it on white bread for breakfast, along with a container of applesauce and a box of the Weetabix.

Or maybe, all things considered, I was better off staying drugged, if drugged I was. I wasn't unhappy—well, I wasn't happy, but I wasn't devastated, either, not the way I'd always imagined I would be if this ever happened to me again. And my mind seemed all right. I could think lucidly enough. I understood my situation perfectly. I just didn't care. I felt removed from myself, observing my own feelings and activities without living them, like a curious but dispassionate researcher observing a white rat in a maze. *Isn't this an interesting reaction? Isn't that an interesting response?*

This is classic isolation-cell-prisoner behavior: the perception that you're not *you* anymore, and don't really have much in common with the body that's sharing your quarters. To counteract it, I knew that I ought to be following the advice I'd given the trainees: keep my mind active; devise more clues to give the police afterward; plan escapes; and, most important, establish some control over my circumstances. But that, it seemed to me, could wait. I was tired and traumatized, and I could afford to relax, to float, for one more day.

But there was one piece of my own counsel that I made myself follow, and that was to begin an exercise program. As planned, I waited until I began to feel hungry. At that point I dragged myself up off the cot, then got down on the floor beside it, arranged the chains so they didn't interfere, and went through two dozen push-ups and twenty sit-ups. I was puffing a little by the last few sit-ups, but I felt good anyway, my muscles agreeably achy. Then I ran in place, counting off eight hundred steps by twos, the equivalent of half a mile, rattling the damn shackles even more than necessary, so they'd know I was taking care of myself and not sitting around moping.

Once done, I flopped back onto the cot, out of breath and surprisingly exhausted. At home I was a jogger, generally going three miles without getting this fatigued. My appetite was gone too. The chains had made running much harder. Not only were they heavy and clumsy, but they'd chafed my ankle, even through my socks and pant leg. And I'd worked up a sweat, so that every crease and hollow of my body felt greasy. Keeping myself and my clothes clean was going to be a chore, and not just on account of the chain. There was soap, yes, but no basin, no warm water. Just the gallon jugs. And paper towels. There was no toothbrush, no toothpaste, no razor.

If my estimate of the time was correct, it was now Saturday evening, the end of my second full day of captivity. It had been almost three full days since I'd last shaved, on Thursday morning. Or washed anything but my hands or brushed my teeth or changed my underwear or seen myself in a mirror. When I ran my hand over my face, my cheek had a startlingly unfamiliar feel to it, not only bristly, but hard and scaly, as if I were touching the skin of a stranger. Suddenly curious to see myself, I shambled over to the toilet, raised the lid, and, kneeling, leaned over to look for my reflection in the chemical-blue water in the bowl.

It was clearer than I expected, and worse. "Oh Lord," I said aloud, appalled.

I looked like a hundred men I'd seen in pictures; the shocking photographs that the Red Brigades or the Red Army Faction or Shining Path would release after a kidnapping, the one in which the cowed, stunned prisoner would have some Marxist slogan in his hands or hung around his neck. I was gaunt and sunken-eyed, with wild hair, and lips that looked black in the reflection. My cheeks were deeply shadowed with stubble that seemed to run almost up to my eyes. The split in my lip was crusted, and the grimy collar of my shirt spotted with blood. I looked like a demented old street bum. And I hadn't been here two full days yet.

You're filthy, I said to myself. *You must smell. And you're on your knees looking at your face in a toilet bowl—off of which you then intend to eat.*

I stared at the reflection for a long time, settling things in my mind. I wasn't going to let this happen to me. This was it; this would be my low point, right here, on my knees in front of the toilet bowl. Dinner would be put off. I would wash myself and at least some of my clothing right now, I would start using one of the cartons as a lap table and stop eating off the toilet lid. I would begin ordering my life and regaining control of it.

As a start, against their explicit orders, I moved something in the tent. I shoved the toilet two feet farther from the cot, where the chemical smell would bother me less. My first small show of defiance.

Then I got to my feet and went hunting for the Camay.

LATER that night, I was still feeling my oats. This time I didn't try to keep myself awake to avoid a panic attack. If it came, it came. *Bring it on.*

Chapter 26

It came. Somewhere in the middle of the night I found myself sitting straight up clawing breathlessly at the non-existent metal collar around my neck. But for once in my life I was armed and ready. Before I'd gone to sleep, I'd repeated Zeta's counsel several times to make it stick in my mind.

"You don't fight it, you don't try to avoid it or moderate it with pills, or relaxation techniques, or slow breathing, or anything else. You face it down, once and for all. In fact, you purposely make it as bad as you can for as long as you can, so you can prove to yourself that you can do it."

Well, I can't claim that I had the guts to try that last part—I mean, it's plenty bad enough without me doing anything to make it worse, but I did honestly do my best not to just cover my head with my arms, draw up my knees, and mewl pitifully while it took me over, but instead to look it right in the eye: the hyperventilation, the racing heart, the awful, free-floating, unfocused terror, the certainty that I had gone over the edge and fallen into madness for good this time, and all the rest of it. I identified them, and I named them, and I told them to their faces they weren't even real. I almost believed it myself.

And damn if it didn't help. I can't claim I came out of it the winner. But I felt a lot like that kid who has finally found the guts to stand up to the schoolyard bully and tell him to take his best shot: bruised and bloody and thinking maybe that it hadn't been such a hot idea, but—what do you know?—still standing.

Progress.

With the garbage pail to use as a basin, washing up the previous evening had been cumbersome but not that difficult. To do it thoroughly required a lot of time and a few interesting contortions, but that was all to the good; regular, time-consuming, mildly demanding chores would help break the day into manageable segments.

The process had worn me out, though, so I waited till morning to work on my clothes and found that it proved even more awkward. Drying them was the problem. The only things I could get myself completely free of, and therefore drape over something while they dried, were my socks. Shirt, pants, and underwear could be gotten off only as far as the chains that connected me to the cot. So I was standing there, barefoot and bare-chested, with my wet socks hanging from the bed frame, futilely trying to spread out my washed and wrung-out shirt and pants somehow, when the entry flap was pulled open.

I'd kept my shorts on because I didn't want to be caught naked if they chose to come in; they had enough of an upper hand as it was. Still, being in my three-day-old underwear didn't help much, especially with a wet shirt dangling from one wrist and my wet pants dragging on the floor, so when I turned toward the entrance I felt at a distinct disadvantage.

The newcomer was the third member of the group, the man I'd come to think of as the mastermind, the man that might, or might not, be the notorious Paris. Once again, aside from the ski mask, he was dressed in ordinary street clothes, a dark blue sweater over a light blue shirt, and what appeared to be the same corduroy pants he'd had on the other day. I'd yet to see the others in anything but head-to-toe black.

"Laundry day, I see."

"Yes. Am I going to be able to get rid of this water somewhere?"

"Of course. I'll have it taken care of for you." Behind the politeness I sensed something fierce, a suppressed intensity. Anger? Anticipation? Of what?

"Thank you," I said. "I could also use some more paper towels."

"I'll see what I can do. It's nice to see you again."

"Also some— See me *again*?"

"Well, it was a long time ago. It'll come to you." Seen through the mask's mouth opening, his smile was all teeth: a grimace. "Sit down, will you?"

"I'd rather stand." Almost naked and standing was better than almost naked and sitting, especially since I was a couple of inches taller than he was.

"I'd rather you sat."

I hesitated. I was playing a delicate game here. I was stronger now. I'd no longer bow to every command; I would sometimes resist. But it was tricky. Annoying them was a dangerous proposition, and there was no point in doing it unless the benefits outweighed the risks. The idea wasn't to make me obstinate in their eyes, but only to make me an independent being with demands of my own to be considered. There would be times and issues that would call for an aggressive approach on my part, but they had to be carefully chosen.

Whether or not I sat down on the cot, I decided, wasn't one of them. I sat.

He looked down at me, his wrists loosely crossed in front of his waist, trying to seem very relaxed, but I wasn't buying it. He was wound up tight, all right. Something was on his mind.

"So how're you being treated? All right?"

"Pretty much. I haven't been beaten up for two whole days now."

"You haven't tried to escape for two whole days now."

A reasonable point, I thought. "Are you in charge here?"

"Why?"

"I'd like to know about my wife. Baldursson too."

"Baldursson isn't your concern. And your wife is perfectly fine. We released her, exactly as I promised."

"How do I know that?" Lori's security was one of those issues I damn well intended to be aggressive on.

He let a beat go by. "Because, Bryan, *I* keep my word when I give it."

I looked at him curiously, although of course the blank, ugly hood told me nothing. But that slight emphasis on the "I" put a curious personal cast on the statement. What was he saying, that I *didn't* keep my word? It puzzled me, but I didn't pursue it.

There were a few moments of uneasy silence, and then his shoulders rose and fell: a deep breath. "Your wife and your associates are naturally concerned about you, Bryan. They've asked for some proof that we have you and that you're alive and well. It's a reasonable request, and I'd like to reassure them. I'm sure you would too. There's no need to worry them needlessly."

"What you mean is, you need to prove I'm alive because you know they're not going to pay for a dead hostage." Unless I was way off base, he had just given me the opening

I needed to find out for sure about Lori; the *quid* for his *quo*. I tried not to show my excitement.

From behind the hood came a thin, fake laugh. "Obviously, I'd better not forget who I'm talking to. Let's not argue, then. You know all about these things, my friend. It's done all the time: proof of life. It's advantageous to all, so how about just getting it over with? I'll ask you a few questions they've suggested. First: You keep a ceramic object on the desk in your den at home. What is it?"

I said nothing. It was correct, all right. There was a cookie jar from Disney World with a cartoon of Pluto the dog on it, in which I kept Shep's treats.

"You need to think about that? All right, here's number two: Which side of the bed do you sleep on? And finally— which Mexican restaurant—"

"No."

"No? What does that mean, no?"

"I'm not giving you anything until I know you've kept your part of the bargain. I want proof that my wife is free and that she's all right."

"Well, who do you think we got these questions from?"

"Other people, people I work with, might know—"

"Oh, come now. Which side of the bed you sleep on?"

"Look, even if they did come from my wife, that doesn't prove she's free, does it? Or that she's alive *now*?"

He gave a phony sigh, as if gravely disillusioned.

"I'm hurt that you don't trust me, Bryan."

And why the hell would I trust you? "It's not a question of trust," I said. "I need confirmation, that's all."

"In other words, what you're telling me is, *you're* demanding proof of life?"

"Yes."

His laugh, an incredulous one, seemed a little closer to genuine this time. "I'm sorry to spoil your fun, Bryan, but let me point out that that isn't the way it works." He used both hands to take in the tent, the chains. "You're not in much of a position to make demands."

"I am if you want me to give you what you need for proof of life—which you'll have to have if you're going to get anything for me. I'll trade you, proof for proof. That's the deal." I waited, then went on. "Unless I'm mistaken, you know all about these things, my friend," I said, pushing it a little. "You want something, you give something. That's the way it works."

"Oh, so that's the way it's going to be." He came closer, sat on the square lid of the portable toilet with his knees perhaps three feet from mine and seemed to study me. "There are other forms of proof of life," he said at last. "Do you think your wife would recognize your ear?"

"Hard to say."

"Your finger, then. The one on your left hand there, for example—with the wedding band still on it."

I shrugged. "Even if it was recognized, it wouldn't be proof that I was still alive. You can get fingers and ears just as easily from the dead. More easily."

I knew that the man sitting across from me on the toilet lid was as cognizant as I was of such things, but I thought it best to make sure we understood each other.

"That's true, Bryan. But all the same, in the past I've found they do eventually serve to persuade. Sometimes it takes a second finger, or even a third, but in the end they seem to do the trick. I may be forgetting something, but I don't recall it ever having taken more than three. I suppose you could spare three of your fingers, but why would you want to put us all through the unpleasantness?"

I shook my head. "It wouldn't convince Julian Minor. It wouldn't convince my wife."

"Actually, I was thinking more along the lines of convincing *you*," he said pleasantly. I had the impression that he was becoming more at his ease. The game playing was entertaining him.

I couldn't help laughing, but it didn't last very long. I'd been holding my ground so far by keeping out of my mind, or at any rate out of the foreground of my mind, the realities of my situation. I too was acting as if we were simply playing an elaborate game, the complex rules of which I and my opponent both knew. As far as it went, that much was true, but when the talk turned to severed appendages, somehow the fun went out of it.

Now, I knew that the probability of losing a finger or any attachment was low. Statistically speaking, mutilation of this kind, while frequently threatened, was seldom resorted to—only about one percent of the time, as far as our records showed. I also knew, however, that, statistically speaking, the probability of drowning in San Francisco Bay was similarly low, because only one percent of the water was deeper than five feet. Statistics were unreliable guides for individual behavior.

I was starting to feel some qualms now, no denying it.

And now there was a new worry gnawing at me. Why was he so resistant to the idea of proof-of-life from Lori? Could it be that they hadn't . . . that she was . . . I didn't let myself think it. Strange: Getting information about her welfare had been my top priority since I'd gotten here, but I'd never let myself really believe that she was anything but all right. It was reassurance I'd wanted, that's all. Confirmation. But now . . .

"Look," I said. "Obviously, it's up to you. But I'll tell you this: Unless I'm satisfied that she's okay, you get no cooperation at all out of me. None, no matter what you do."

"Is that right?" he said dryly. "And is that all it will take? No other little thing I can do for you?"

"You can let me have a razor and a toothbrush. And a comb."

He didn't move, but merely studied me hard, turned suddenly, and without another word to me, opened the flap and left, zipping it up behind him.

I had no idea if I'd won that exchange or lost it.

Chapter 27 _____

A couple of hours later, after I'd wriggled back into my clammy but relatively fresh-smelling clothes and had some breakfast (not eaten from the toilet lid, but from a makeshift cardboard tray held on my lap), Stig and Gullveig came in to put me through the search-and-ransack routine again. Apparently, it was going to be a daily practice. While I was on my stomach on the floor, I asked politely if I might have a pen or a pencil. I was bothered more than I'd expected by not being able to write; that hadn't been a problem when I was five. But they didn't bother to reply.

Again, I need hardly say, they left without discovering anything. But I discovered something.

When they'd flipped over the mattress on the cot, I realized something that I'd noticed before, but that somehow hadn't registered as important: It was a *folding* cot. It folded in the middle. Now I lifted the mattress off again to have a closer look. I'd like to have tried actually folding and lifting it to see how cumbersome it was, but I was afraid they'd hear me and come in. So I made some rough-and-ready measurements, using my foot (eleven inches, toe to heel) as a ruler. Folded, it would be about thirty-eight inches by thirty-one, and about eight inches thick. When I hefted it, I came to the same conclusion I'd reached earlier: It weighed about thirty pounds.

I could get my arms around the thing and *carry* it! Sure, I'd be weighted down by it and helpless to defend myself and hobbled by the chains, but if there came a time when no one was in the guard chair for a minute, or if the guard fell asleep—and assuming I didn't trip over my own feet again—I could make it from the tent to the window in one or two seconds with the cot hugged to my chest. Once there, the cot would actually be an asset, adding both momentum and protection against the breaking glass when I went through it. And once outside, while running would no longer be an option, making noise would. Surely, the crash of glass and the clang when the cot hit the ground and the hullabaloo that I would provide with my lungs would bring out people from the nearby apartments, whatever time it was, and once that happened . . .

But for it to happen I had to know what was going on at the guard station. So over the next couple of hours I used my pinky and the handle of a plastic-coated spork, first to open up a space of an inch or so in one corner of the mesh window, and then to push the corresponding corner of the outside flap a little out of the way. Under ordinary circumstances, it would have been a two-minute job, but under ordinary circumstances you don't have to surreptitiously drag a metal cot around with you. And you don't have to avoid making any noise while you work.

But it got done, to my great satisfaction—not only because I'd made progress (possibly delusional) toward escape, but because, by moving the bed, I'd once again defied their instructions to leave everything in its place. Anything that didn't fit their mandates, no matter how trivial, was manna to my starving soul, a much-needed reassurance that I was still at least a little in charge of myself.

When I got hungry for the second time that day, at what I judged to be about six o'clock, I stuck to my earlier resolution and got going on my exercise routine. I was only a hundred steps into running in place when the sweat started popping out, so I stopped. It had taken me hours to wash and dry my clothes this morning, and I wasn't ready to go through it again tomorrow. But I also didn't want to turn back into the grubby guy I'd seen in the toilet-bowl reflection. So, before getting back to the workout I stripped down to my shorts again. I probably should have taken those off too, but even in these conditions—especially in these conditions—standards of modesty needed to be maintained.

I had finished running in place and doing push-ups and sit-ups and was sitting on the floor, swimming in perspiration, huffing and puffing, but feeling pretty good about myself, when the tent flap was zipped open, and in came Mr. Mastermind again.

I almost laughed at the absurdity of it. How come every time this guy walked in I was in my underwear? I pushed myself to my feet.

He got right down to business. "All right, Bryan, I'm here to confirm that your wife is safe. She was released unharmed one hour after we had possession of you."

That wasn't nearly good enough. "How do I know—?"

"Here." He put a newspaper in front of my face. *Morgunblaðið*, the banner said.

I shook my head. "I can't read Icel—"

He double-tapped a two-column photograph at the bottom, and there was Lori coming down the steps of what I supposed was the police station, with Ellert on one side and a uniformed officer on the other. It was nighttime, and she was looking down, so her face wasn't all that clear, but it was Lori, all right, and although she looked harried and concerned—who wouldn't?—I could see that she was okay. Neither of the cops was steering her by the elbow; she was taking the concrete steps on her own.

Ever since I'd first heard that the VBJ had her, I'd had a strange, sick feeling; the illusion that the floor beneath me was continually falling away, that either I was leaving the earth, or the earth was leaving me. But now the hard floor beneath the tent came back up to meet my feet, stable and secure. It was done. But my knees were momentarily undone by a crushing wave of relief. I sat down on the edge of the cot.

"Thank you," I breathed. I suppose I might have asked why I hadn't been shown this before, but I knew the answer—because leaving me in the dark about Lori was one more way to keep me unglued. Or was there more to it than that? Had this guy withheld the information because he was out ahead of me? Had he anticipated my reaction to his proof-of-life questions and kept something in reserve to trade for the answers? Could he be *that* savvy?

Could he really be, in other words, the mysterious Paris? Maybe so, I was starting to think.

I realized with a start that he had been staring intently at me for several seconds. He waited until my eyes met his. "You still don't know who I am, do you?" he asked.

"No."

"You have no idea."

"No.

"Don't you want to know?"

"Not really."

"You're lying."

He was getting antsier, more excited. Some impulse told me I'd be better off standing, and I got up again. "Rules of the game," I said. "My chances of getting out of here alive are better if I don't see anybody's face."

"You think so? Then let me give you something to worry about." To my surprise he snatched the mask from his head.

I peered at his tense, unremarkable face for a moment, then shook my head. "I'm guessing you're the one they call Paris."

"Yes." The word was as much question as assent, as if he were prompting me to add something. "And that's it?" he said, when I shook my head, looking puzzled. "You expect me to believe you have no idea who I am?"

"I just said—you're Paris . . . aren't you? You're a professional kidnapper. You—"

The thin-lipped mouth firmed. "You know me better than that, Bryan. We're old friends."

I studied him hard, then shook his head. "You've got me mixed up with someone else. I never saw you before in my life."

"Don't lie to me." He was whispering now, a hoarse, harsh whisper, "What's the point of that? You remember me, all right. I'm warning you, you're just making it worse for yourself in the end."

"Look, Paris—whoever you are—I'm telling you—"

"Shut up, you goddamn . . ." He was openly angry now. Discs of color had popped out at the sides of his throat. "Don't you tell me—" He caught himself, pulled the ski mask back over his head, turned on his heel, and stalked furiously out, slapping at the entrance flap when it caught against his shoulder.

"Hey," I called. "What about that razor?"

Chapter 28

Advantage, Bennett. Of course I knew who the guy was. His name was George Henry Camano, and while not exactly an old friend, he was an old acquaintance. I think it had begun to dawn on me with his repeated insinuations about my lying, and then, once I saw his face, that settled it. In fact, he had changed very little since my brief association with him. Until this moment, it would never have crossed my mind that the hapless George Camano I'd known and the famous, elusive Paris could conceivably be the same man. Well, people did learn from their mistakes, after all; they grew, they changed, and Camano had had a dozen years to do plenty of each.

The last time I'd seen him had been back in September of 1998, that most climactic month of my adult life, in which I'd reached both the high-water mark of my brief career as a negotiator and, with the catastrophic shootout deaths of the Houghey twins, the low point that had ended it.

The high-water mark had involved the man who'd just stormed out.

George Camano—he had yet to metamorphose into "Paris"—had been part of the gang of three men and one woman in Los Angeles who had abducted Leslie Goldwin, the fifteen-year-old grandson of Linda Smith Rutledge, the president of Le Sport Cosmetics. Camano, a one-time political science instructor at a junior college in Santa Monica, had been the leader. He and another member of the foursome had waited for the kid in the parking garage under the company's boutique on La Cienega Boulevard, where he parked his bike. They bundled him into the trunk of a waiting car and followed up with a demand for three million dollars. Two days later they made telephone contact with the Goldwin family, who then called me in to negotiate on their behalf.

It was Camano who did most of the talking for them, and over the course of two week's telephone-jockeying, the ransom had been brought down to $1.25 million. But it had been dangerous, touchy work. The kidnappers were flaky and unstable, sometimes high-handed and confident, sometimes on the ragged edge. I thought that some of them might be on drugs. They changed their demands without warning, reneged on their commitments, argued among themselves even while on the phone with me, and made wild threats and then withdrew them, always with the prospect of death hanging over the boy. On the very second day of contact, Camano had stated that the family would receive one finger a day until the ransom was paid.

"If it takes longer than ten days, we'll come up with something else," he had said coldly. "Take long enough, and you'll have all of him back for free." Fortunately, it was one of the threats he didn't live up to. In the end, it turned out that Leslie had been slapped around a few times, and he had been sedated most of the time, but nothing worse.

By the sixth day the police, with whom I'd been working closely, had determined where the boy was being held: a rented duplex on Normandie Avenue near Santa Monica Boulevard. Worried about Leslie's continuing safety, the captain in charge of the operation was in favor of a raid. He wanted to send in a tactical team to surround the building and force the kidnappers' hands. The deputy chief of operations for the West Bureau, who was overseeing the case, tentatively agreed.

But I was afraid that if they spotted the police, the delicate give-and-take I'd achieved with them would be tipped, and they might kill the boy. I had another plan: Hold off one more day to let the family pay the ransom. In the meantime, inasmuch as they had identified the two cars the kidnappers were using, the police would plant homing devices and bugs on both vehicles. After the gang picked up the ransom, even if they split up into two cars, it would be possible to follow them.

I offered my plan in the deputy chief's office on Venice Boulevard, with the captain present. The chief, an unlikely cop with a doctorate in public administration, had reservations. "I thought you didn't believe in lying to them," he'd said.

"I don't—not if they could come back and hurt the Goldwin boy or anyone else," I had replied. "But here we break faith *after* the fact, once we already have Leslie. Anyway, what would we be lying about? We tell them we'll follow their instructions on the ransom—and we do. What else is going on, what happens next, we're not required to tell them."

"But it's still breaking faith with them. You're not leveling with them. The result is the same."

"I guess it is."

"So what happened to all this bullcrap about trust that you've been feeding us?"

"It still stands. What I said was that the kidnappers have to trust me for me to be effective. They have to believe I respect them as people and sympathize with their position. That's not the same thing as saying I actually do. These are bad people. That's a scared, friendless fifteen-year-old kid they're terrorizing in there. I *don't* respect them, and I don't sympathize with their position. I'm just good at pretending."

The chief was shaking his head. "So all this leveling with them, all this trust-building . . . it's just a tool? There's nothing wrong with lying to these people as long as you can get away with it? Is that the way it works? Is that the way you negotiator-types see it?"

No, not by a long shot, it wasn't. Many—maybe most—of my colleagues would have problems with what I was suggesting. Some would call it an unacceptable violation of trust or impartiality. But then, none of my colleagues had quite the hands-on experience with kidnapping and captivity that I had. I had never claimed to be impartial. I despised the people who would do this, and I would do whatever I could, short of jeopardizing the innocent, to see them put away.

"No," I said, "just me."

He stood, walked to the double window, and stood looking down on the steady traffic of Venice Boulevard. "Look," I said, "I have a single, number-one goal: getting Leslie out of there in one piece without anybody getting hurt—especially cops or innocent civilians. But I have secondary goals too—getting the ransom money back and locking up these creeps. Trust is a tool to accomplish those goals. In this case, not leveling with them is a tool too."

A slow smile spread across the chief's face. "Son of a

gun," he said to the captain. "You know, I'm starting to like this guy."

My plan won out. The next day, after I asked for and got a final proof-of-life indication to make sure the boy was still all right, a not unusual wild-goose chase ensued. Per Camano's instructions, $1.25 million in used twenty- and fifty-dollar bills was bundled into five closed, unwrapped grocery cartons and placed in the trunk of my car. As directed, I then drove to a bar on Slauson Avenue and went to the pay phone. As soon as I got there, a call came in directing me to another public telephone, this one at the Burbank airport. From there I was sent back across Los Angeles to a parking lot at the far end of Huntington State Beach in Orange County, where I was to await yet another call. When it came, I was told to remove the parcels from my own car and place them in a green Plymouth family van parked near the telephone booth. The keys would be found taped to the underside of the rear license plate.

Finally, I was to drive the Plymouth back to Los Angeles to the Fern Dell parking area in Griffith Park, leave the van there, walk down Fern Dell Drive to the corner of Western and Franklin Avenues, and hop on the first southbound bus that came along on Western, getting off anytime after Sunset Boulevard. From there I was on my own, free to find my way back to Huntington Beach to pick up my car. Leslie Goldwin would be released, Camano promised, when the ransom money was safely in their possession.

As indeed, he was. The boy soon wandered, mumbling and dazed, into a carpet store in Santa Monica, thinking it was a police station. The four members of the gang, having meticulously taken all the right precautions—excepting a meticulous examination of the two cars in which they were traveling—were arrested at a date stand near Indio before the day was out. All but $800 of the $1.25 million was recovered as well. They had stopped on a whim to buy cowboy hats and boots in Palm Springs. The clerk recalled afterward that they'd made him nervous because they couldn't stop laughing. He'd thought they were high—which they were, but not on drugs.

When they were tried, one of the four turned state's evidence against the others and was given a suspended sentence and put on probation. The rest all went to prison, with Camano getting the longest term. For me, it was the sweetest possible ending, and I took real pride in my part: Leslie Goldwin was back home; nobody had been hurt, let alone killed; the ransom, except for that $800, had been recovered; and the kidnappers got what was coming to them.

Months later, at the end of the trial, Camano had spotted me in the courtroom. It was the first time we'd met face-to-face.

"You son of a bitch, I trusted you!" he snarled at me as he was being taken out.

"I guess next time you'll know better," I had replied.

At the time it had seemed like a good answer. Now I wasn't so sure.

Chapter 29

"I don't have a lot of free time right now, Professor Parkington," Teddy said when Zeta cornered him by the psychology faculty mail slots in the giant Rubik's Cube that was Guthrie Hall. It had been two days since she'd asked for his research assistance, and she had finally taken matters into her own hands and gone looking for him.

"I don't think this will take very much of your time," Zeta said. "And it *is* important."

"Well, actually, I already—"

"Come into my office for a minute, will you?"

Teddy rolled his eyes a little when he thought Zeta wasn't watching (she was), searching for sympathy from the faculty secretary (there wasn't any), and even said, "Sheesh!" under his breath, but he clumped resignedly behind her down the corridor to the cluttered lair of an office that was her due as an emeritus.

"Now, then," she said, plumping down behind her desk and indicating the lone visitor's chair. "Sit."

Teddy looked at the two blue-bound volumes of the *Journal of Experimental Psychology* on the seat. "Where should I put these?"

She gave him an ambiguous wave. "Anyplace you want."

Why her off-campus office should be as neat as a monk's cell, while the office here in the department had never been anything but a shambles, was something that she found interesting, but not enough to devote any serious thought to.

Teddy put the tomes on the floor and looked at her, radiating reluctance. Zeta knew what his problem was. For one thing, Teddy was not happy in his work. He had been brought on as a graduate research assistant for a joint psychology-anthropology project studying the reasons for turd-throwing in monkeys, but this year's cutbacks had eliminated the study, and he was now functioning twenty hours a week as a general research dogsbody, available to one and all. For another, as an emeritus professor, Zeta would have no say in whether his assistantship would be renewed the following year, so any effort he spent in pleasing her was a waste of his time, as he saw it.

"I need you to do some research for me. I want any newspaper references you can find from 1978—better check plus or minus a couple of years too—that relate to the kidnapping of a child named Bryan Bennett in Istanbul. His father's company was called Driscoll Construction Enterprises." She wrote it out for him as she spoke. "Bryan Bennett. Driscoll Construction Enterprises. Istanbul. 1978."

He looked at the paper and shrugged.

"And I need a couple of journals." These she'd already written out, and she handed the slip to him now. "*Psychiatric Annals*, volume 25, number 12, December 1995, and *American Psychologist*, volume 58, number 11, November 2003."

Another look, another world-weary shrug.

She eyed him. "Is there a problem here, Teddy?"

"Professor Parkington, with all due respect, you could do this yourself in about twenty minutes."

"Computers and I don't get along very well. We have issues."

"There's nothing to it. You just enter the terms in a couple of search engines. You use the university code—"

Zeta held up her hand. "Please. I'm a psychologist. I know how the mind works. There is only so much space in the brain, Teddy. The number of neurons is finite, and at my age mine are already filled to the brim. If I add inconsequential items like input parameters for search engines, then other things will have to go to make room, and I can't take the chance of losing something I really need."

He looked uncertainly at her. "You're . . . are you joking?"

"Do I look as if I'm joking? Now be a good boy and get to work."

Chapter 30

I knew that I was bound to pay for irritating Camano the way I just had, but, boy, it had felt great. In a way, though, I was almost sorry for him. I mean, imagine: years and years of stewing about how I misled and lied to him and ruined his life, of fantasizing about someday getting even with me. And then, out of nowhere, an astonishing stroke of luck drops me into his lap. His moment of retribution, of sweet revenge, of triumph has finally arrived. He snatches off his mask . . . and I don't even remember the guy! Understandably, it had provoked the hell out of him, which had done my morale a world of good.

Having said that, I thought it might be a good idea to "remember" him the next time we met.

AS the evening wore on, I didn't make any effort to force myself to stay awake. The experiences of the last two nights had given me some sense that, against all expectations, I might at long last be making some headway against the attacks. (Nice to think that something good might actually come out of all this.) And so, if anything, I was eager to see how I handled the next one.

Well, maybe *eager* isn't the right word. Let's say *curious*.

IT didn't take long to find out. At some point in the night I woke up, choking and terrified, fingers clawing at the collar around my neck that wasn't there. As always, the illusion held for just a second or two; as always, for another couple of seconds, there was relief at realizing that it wasn't really there and that I wasn't really back in my dungeon cave; and then—as always—the paralyzing, all-consuming fury of a panic attack had me by the throat more tightly than any collar could, blotting everything else out and curling me into a panting, fetal ball on the cot.

I tried my best to fight back. Against every instinct, I made myself concentrate on what I was feeling, I kept up a steady drone of "self-limiting"—and found little relief. It wasn't working. It was as bad as ever. Had I made no progress at all?

I was probably fifteen excruciating minutes into it when I realized that something *was* different. Yes, I was endlessly suspended just off that cliff edge; yes, my heart felt as if it had knocked its way out of my chest and was bouncing around on the floor; yes, those wobbly wheels in my head were spinning loose and flying away, and yet . . . It took me a while to figure out what the difference was. It was this: At some level I knew that this unbearable state *would* end, that I wasn't locked into it forever. It was as if there were a gauzy, shimmering curtain that had never been there before, on the other side of which, dimly perceived, was the "other" world, the *real* world. And this frenzied, delirious world that I was in was the imposter, a temporary state that I would soon emerge from . . . as I'd always done before.

And that, believe me, changed everything: I wasn't going crazy; I wasn't dying; I was having a panic attack: a short-term, *self-limiting* panic attack. It made all the difference in the world. I fought back with renewed energy and could practically feel my enemy give way, bit by bit. Now, suddenly, a panic attack wasn't so different from a headache or an upset stomach: wretched while it lasted, but bound to go away in time. I could feel the rigid tendons in my neck loosen, feel my heart slow down and climb back into my chest where it belonged, feel myself able to stop panting and take a deep, full, wonderful breath.

Had I actually beaten this thing that had dogged me so long and given me so much misery? Could it be as easy as that—three nights of "exposure therapy"? Hope engulfed me like a warm, velvety bath, so much so that even my current situation didn't seem quite as awful as it had been, and I turned on my side to settle myself into sleep.

BUT for once, the expected après-panic coma didn't arrive, headed off by the abrupt, highly unwelcome comprehension that I was in a lot more trouble than I'd thought. I'd suddenly remembered a report I'd read a couple of years earlier.

Lyle Harvey, a psychologist colleague at Odysseus, had done a psychological profile of Paris based on the various dribs and drabs of information that were known, or thought to be known, about him. The man we called Paris, Lyle had surmised, was a single, white male in his thirties or forties, who'd had a troubled childhood, who possessed a certain ingratiating charm, who had a grandiose sense of self-worth, who was reasonably well educated, etc., etc.—in other words, your everyday psychopath/sociopath/serial killer. Unfortunately for me in particular, however, there was more.

Paris also showed evidence of borderline paranoia, which meant, as Lyle explained to me over coffee after I'd read his profile, that Paris tended to filter every event, every encounter, through a lens that imbued it with significance for him and him alone. Not quite the aliens-are-sending-me-coded-messages-on-the-backs-of-Wheaties-boxes kind of paranoia, but close enough. He found cause for grievance where there was none, and magnified his fertile sense of injustice where there was. And he had no inhibitions about settling accounts. At least two of the five murders he was known to have committed had been prompted by personal grievances, real or imagined; not, as Lyle had smilingly pointed out, that it made much difference to the victims one way or the other. Oh yes, and Paris was also an exception to those statistics that said mutilation was often threatened but rarely resorted to. This was a guy who followed through on his threats.

So how could I have failed to remember all this until after I'd added yet another grievance against me, as if the old one wasn't already enough to get me killed and dismembered (hopefully in that order)? All I can say is that it had taken me this long to really get it through my skull that the beef-headed Camano from so long ago and the "brilliant" Paris I'd been reading about for years really were one and the same.

There was something else that came back to me only now. "I trusted you" had been his last words to me at the trial, but not his last gesture. As they prodded him toward the exit, he had raised his arm, straightened it, and leveled his right forefinger at me. No, not with the traditionally raised thumb to emulate the cocked hammer of a revolver, but with clear enough meaning all the same.

I'll get you for this.

Jesus. Well, I sure wasn't going to sit around waiting for him to kill me in what he had implied to be a particularly unpleasant way ("you're just making it worse for yourself in the end"). I had to find a way to get myself out of there, and I had no time to waste in doing it. I had to . . . but now sleep caught up to me. My eyelids slipped down again.

Chapter 31

An electrifying flashback popped them open a minute later. *Camano had failed to zip up the entrance flap!* He'd batted fussily at it when it had gotten in his way as he'd stomped out, and he'd just kept on going. The flap had fallen back into place, and that had been it. No *zzzzzziiippp* had followed, then or later, and no one else had come in since then. So, unless somebody had checked while I was asleep, it was open right now. And yes, I could see even from the cot that the zipper hadn't been pulled around. With my heart pounding once more, but for a very different reason, I sat up, taking care not to clink the chains. I considered trying to get to my little peephole in the mesh window to see what was going on at the guard station, but I didn't want to chance alerting the guard with any unnecessary noise.

Besides, I knew that it didn't make any difference whether he or she was asleep or awake or in the chair or out of it: I was going to make my move now, tonight. I had to; what were the chances of them ever leaving the tent unzipped again?

I removed the blankets from the cot, but left the mattress—additional protection against the glass—and, with excruciating care, folded the cot up, holding my breath most of the time and going stone-still whenever there was the tiniest clink of chain or creak of metal. It took a long time, during every second of which I expected someone to look in to see what was going on. But that didn't happen. With my ears on high alert, the only sound I heard from outside was the occasional slither of a turning magazine page. That and the occasional clearing of a throat, a man's throat. Stig? Yes, when I listened harder I recognized his voice. So it was him in the chair. Gullveig or Camano would have been my preference, but it was what it was. Stig would have to do.

I hefted the cot one way and then another to come up with the most secure grip, and settled on wrapping my arms around it, clasping my hands, and hugging it to my chest. That would expose my forearms to the shattering glass, so I stuffed some paper towels inside my sleeves for padding. I supposed more padding would have been a good idea, but I was afraid to use up any more time than absolutely required. No one had checked on me for hours. How much longer could it be before one of them decided I was due for some hassling?

Getting the cot noiselessly into my arms was tricky, and shuffling in tiny steps toward the entry without clanking was even trickier. I curled the chains around my fists to take up the slack, but not enough (I hoped) to trip me up. Even so, in negotiating around one of the cartons I caught the leg chain and created a distinct *clink*. I did the best I could to cover it by coughing, then clearing my own throat, then emitting what I hoped were the grunty, snorty noises a sleeper makes when he turns over in the middle of the night and rearranges himself.

There was a piercing, pregnant silence from the guard station for several seconds—I imagined Stig, head alertly up, listening keenly—and I set myself to throw my body at him, metal cot foremost, the instant I saw the flap begin to lift. But it didn't lift, and eventually there was the sound of a page turning again. I waited another second, then took a dozen more baby steps to cover the final foot and a half to the entry. Because the window and the guard chair were off to the left of the tent, and not directly in front of the tent opening, I shuffled off a few more feet to the right so that I could break out of the tent on the diagonal, and not have to manage a right-angle turn after I got through the opening.

The cot was starting to get uncomfortably heavy, so I lowered myself to a squatting position to let my thighs take the weight and give my arms a rest for a minute. The whole while I was down, my ears strained to pick up any sounds. I knew a window was open because I heard an owl hoot, and in the distance the same steady traffic I'd heard before. But from indoors, nothing. It was, in fact, so preternaturally, pregnantly quiet that I began to wonder if they were just playing along; if they were on to me and there was a welcoming committee waiting out there. I suppose I could have shuffled over to the peephole I'd made in the mesh window, but it would have taken minutes for me to wobble my way there and back. Besides, I was afraid that my luck at keeping the noise down wouldn't hold—that I'd stumble over something or catch one of the chains again.

So this was it; time to go. I outlined my route in my mind: Two running steps would get me out of the tent, with three more to go to reach the window. Where exactly Stig was sitting I didn't know. If he was more than two or three feet from the window, my guess was that I'd be through it before he could stop me. But if he was closer, he'd have to be dealt with. If he was to its left, I'd try to clip him with the left side of the bed frame as I went by; if to the right, then with the right side of the frame. And if he were sitting right in front of the window, blocking my way? Then he was coming with me.

I stood up, bent down enough to make it through the five-foot-tall entry, reminded myself to watch out for the strip of fabric across the bottom of the opening . . . and charged out into the room.

The window was indeed open a few inches at the top, as before. The up-from-the bottom shade covered the lower three-quarters of the window, as before. Out the top I could see the spindly tree branches, as before. It was dark, but in the gleam of a street lamp I could see a sleety rain falling. The chair had been placed a few inches to the left of the window. In it was Stig, minus the hood and fittingly rat-faced, with the open magazine on the arm of the desk. At the moment I burst into the room he was checking his wrist-watch, but when this clanking, shrieking apparition (me) erupted from the tent and bore down on him, his face came up, openmouthed.

There was an instant's paralysis, and then he tried to jump to his feet, but the lap desk on the chair got in his way and sat him down again. By that time I was on him and, following the plan, I swung the left side of the metal bed frame at him, catching him in the forehead with a solid, immensely satisfying *thunk* that sent both Stig and the chair over sideways and out of the way. Without breaking my stride—or rather, my lunge—I lifted the cot to shield my face and rocketed myself at the window.

Through it I went in an explosion of glass, taking the crackling window shade with me and grateful for its protection. As I smashed through, I caught a glimpse of the terrain I was heading for out of the corner of my eye. I'd hoped that the existence of the tree signified a planting border around the building, and that a supple, squashy, thornless bush—

AARON ELKINS

rhododendron or box elder would have been nice—would be there to break my fall. Or at least that I'd land on soil and not on concrete. But no such luck. There was a five- or six-foot border in front of the building, all right, but it was gravel. Better than concrete, but not what I'd had in mind. Also, I had assumed the window was about four feet off the ground. Six was more like it.

I tried to keep the cot in front of me as a shock absorber, but somehow I got spun around and came down flat on my back—hard—with the damn cot landing heavily on my chest and the icy rain spattering my face. I think it was the weight of the cot, and not the fall itself, that knocked the wind out of me, but whatever it was, it scotched my plan to start yelling. Instead, I was busy gasping and flopping around, trying get my lungs going again.

It took a good twenty seconds to get enough air back into me to attempt to get to my knees—I still couldn't speak, let alone shout—and by that time, here they all came, running hard through the sleet, without their hoods: Camano, Stig, and a pudding-faced young woman who had to be Gullveig. I looked wildly around. Surely someone must have heard the commotion, but, no, even in those few apartments that were lit, the windows remained vacant. Somehow I made it to my feet and steeled myself to face them, wrapping the chains more securely around my fists to use as weapons.

I didn't have a chance.

Still gasping and convulsed, I was roughly forced down onto my face. I did what I could to struggle, but a second later, there was that now-familiar sharp jab in the hip. When I twisted my head, I could see Stig bent over me, and I managed to swing backhanded at his arm. It knocked the hypodermic out of his hand and out of me, but too late. I could feel the fluid burning into me. My head was already swimming.

Ah, God.

258

Chapter 32

I came awake to find myself, as so often before, tearing with both hands at the metal collar encircling my neck. But this time . . . this time it didn't melt away. The metal was *real*—cold and gritty against my fingers. Without knowing it, I'd already torn a couple of nails scrabbling at the thing.

It was pitch black; I could see nothing, not even my own arms, but I knew I was no longer in the tent. The air was cold, dank, flinty . . . a *cave*? As the coming panic swelled and coiled inside me, I searched with my fingers, trying to make sense of things. Attached to the collar was a *chain*. Shaking, I jumped up and followed the links hand over hand over a rough, stony floor, my blood turning more into icy sludge with every step. Five steps in all, to where the chain was hooked through a ring bolt embedded in the rock wall. On its own, a moan began to build up steam in my chest, but as I crossed over the border from sanity to craziness it morphed into a hooting, strangled laugh, the *hoo-hoo-hoo* of a matted-bearded lunatic who had been locked up in some dark cellar for decades. I heard it—I hated it—but I couldn't do anything about it.

It seemed to go on for a long time, that stupid, chimplike hooting, and then, suddenly, I was in the grip of a panic attack like nothing I'd ever been through before. The mother of all panic attacks. I couldn't even begin to describe it. I wouldn't *want* to begin to describe it. My "victory" of the previous night was a bad joke. My memory of the attack is fuzzy now, thank God, but I know that I gibbered and whinnied and rolled around on the floor, and *hoo-hoo-hoo*ed, and that at one point I was on my knees, banging my bloodied head against the wall, trying to blot myself into oblivion—to kill myself—so I wouldn't be around when my head exploded and my heart shredded.

But eventually a new thought, a *coherent* thought, broke through: This had been going on for however long—twenty minutes, thirty minutes—and here I still was. It hadn't killed me. My head hadn't exploded. My heart hadn't burst out of my chest. The worst possible thing I could imagine, the thing that had tracked and terrified me for decades, that I was more afraid of than anything else in the world, had actually *happened* to me—not just in my mind, but *really*— and I'd outlasted the damn thing.

This wasn't just Zeta's self-limiting phenomenon; I hadn't merely outlasted it, I'd gotten the better of it, because I knew now that it didn't have the terrifying power it had pretended to have. What was it Zeta had said about overcoming a fear of elevators? *You grit your teeth and get on one and ride it up and down and up and down until you're over it, and by the time you get out you might be sweating, but you've pretty much got it licked.* Well, what do you know, it was true, not that I could take the credit for it. After all, I hadn't volunteered for the experience, and the truth was that I hadn't even really believed in it. But that didn't seem to make any difference. Damned if it didn't work anyway. It was like physicist Niels Bohr's apocryphal reply to the visitor who asked him whether he truly believed the horseshoe nailed over his door brought him luck: "Of course I don't, but I'm told it works even if you don't believe it."

However it worked, I knew that I'd just had my last panic attack, doozy that it was. Over the next couple of minutes I routed the remnants of the now-retreating tumult out of my head altogether. I don't know how else to put it other than that I simply set my jaw and willed it gone. And it went. I'd made it back into the real world, and I wasn't ever again setting foot in that other one.

There was just this one little problem: The real world now looked suspiciously like the one I'd just scrambled out of. I was alone in a dank, pitch-black cave, chained by a rusty metal collar around my neck to a ring bolt sunk in the rock.

And I actually, unbelievably, told myself a lame little joke: "All you need to make this complete," I said, "is an iron mask."

I snickered, I sighed, and I fell into the usual post-panic-attack swoon.

THE next time I woke up, the blackness was no longer absolute. I was looking at a lichen-crusted rock wall glistening with moisture, with some thin frost or snow in some of the deeper crevices. So I was really in a cave. And the collar was real too, sitting heavily on the base of my neck. I closed my eyes for a few seconds and somewhat fearfully did one of those self-assessment things but, to my enormous relief, there was absolutely no sense of panic there. Well, nothing worse than anybody would feel: not exactly on top of the world, but a long, long way from the horror of all-out panic. A metal collar around the neck, it turns out, is nowhere near as fearful as the fear of a metal collar around the neck.

I hurt in a lot of places: my split upper lip, my wrists and forearms—which had some blood-crusted scrapes and cuts on them from going through the window—and my ribs, front and back, which had taken a terrific knock when I hit the ground. And I'd bruised my forehead banging it against the walls during the night. I was also cold, but not freezing; they had put me back in my parka and gotten my shoes back on. All in all, I could have been in a lot worse shape.

I found that I was lying on the gray plaid mattress that had been on the cot and was now laid directly on the floor of the cave. Except for the cot, the other supplies and materials that I'd had before seemed to be here as well; even the toilet, I was relieved to see. The tubelike cave was about eight-feet high and twelve-feet wide, and the pallid light came from a grated opening to the outside, about forty feet upslope from where I was. I couldn't tell whether the grate was locked or not, but even if it was, it was only chest-high, with plenty of room to clamber over it. Getting to it would be the problem.

Which reminded me that a closer look at my constraints was in order. My fingers quickly told me that the collar around my neck was a hinged affair made of two arched pieces. Where the two ends came together they overlapped, and a hole in the end of the upper segment fitted securely over a U-shaped bar welded to the other, much the way a hasp lock fitted together. It was through the opening in the U that the rusting chain was threaded, its final link padlocked so it couldn't fit back through. The oversized link at the other end of the chain was in the form of a ring bolt that had been embedded in the rock wall. The whole thing was about ten feet long. They sure seemed to have access to a lot of chains, these people.

I went to the ring bolt and tugged on it, of course, jerking it every which way, but it didn't give a millimeter. I suppose it might have been possible to chip away at the rock surrounding its base if I'd had something to chip with, but the only possibilities were those paper sporks, and I doubted that they were up to it. There were loads of hand-axe-sized rocks on the floor that might have been used for the job—or as weapons—if I could get to them, but the area within my reach had been swept clean.

The cave stretched out behind me, sloping downward for another thirty feet before the darkness swallowed it up. A few yards into it was a moldering skeleton that I'd first taken for that of a human being but soon realized that it wasn't. (The horns were my first clue.) Probably a goat, I thought; perhaps the former occupant of my collar. Of my captors there was no sign, but I knew that they were nearby, because I had hazy memories of their coming in with flashlights to look at me while I was sleeping, and of the gate clanging open and shut. They'd been in sweaters or fleeces, not coats, so I knew that they'd set up shop nearby.

I opened a plastic bottle of cranberry juice and flopped down on the mattress to do a little cogitating. With each passing minute I was more sure that the panic attacks were over and done with, and that was a wonderful thought.

Which is not to say that I had nothing to fear. Not only did Camano have it in for me from the beginning, but now I'd gotten a look, a good look, at the faces of the other two.

No question about it now. I'd have to be killed.

Chapter 33

"He'll have to be killed," Stig declared. "He saw our faces."

"If you'd been wearing your hood the way you were supposed to . . ." Camano grumbled.

"He saw Gullveig's face too."

"Well, I couldn't very well run out into the courtyard wearing a hood, could I?" she spat back.

"Whatever the reason," Stig said. "We can't let him loose. Once the news about Baldur Baldursson's death gets out, the police—"

"Another event for which we have you to thank," Gullveig said bitterly. She had been showing more and more signs of displeasure with Stig recently. Camano doubted that they were still sleeping together. "All the same, Stig is right, Paris, you know he is. He'll have to be killed."

Camano was so disgusted with the two of them he could hardly bring himself to reply. The longer this mess went on, the more screwed up it got. And now he was reduced to freezing in this damp, moldering, falling-down, two-room hut with its single worthless, stinking stove (was that evil-smelling stuff peat? Coal?) in the company of these two cretins.

The place belonged to an ancient great-uncle of Gull-veig's who had built it in 1938 as the guard shack and ticket booth for "Vatnajökull Cave, Iceland's second-longest lava tube." This was the attraction that was to make the family's fortune when the coming tourist boom arrived as a result of the decision by the Cunard cruise line in 1938 to make Iceland a port of call on its transatlantic cruises.

Unfortunately, it didn't happen that way. German U-boats put an end to the North Atlantic pleasure-cruise business for more than seven years, and by the time the war was over, the busybody geologists and spelunkers had demoted Vat-najökull to Iceland's eleventh-longest lava tube, a designation that failed to draw any tourist hordes. The shack had been abandoned for going on seven decades now, and the cave next to it had been forgotten years ago as well. And the rock-strewn, six-mile-long track that led to the place, more imaginary than real to begin with, was now mostly a memory.

That was the good part—unless you already knew about that track and were specifically hunting for it, you'd never find it, and if you didn't find it, you weren't going to find the shack and the cave either. Then too, the cave itself could practically have been designed to hold a prisoner; great-uncle Snaevar had thoughtfully embedded twin ring bolts in the walls, originally for the chain that would hold the surging crowds back, but equally good for keeping a captive in one place without the need for constant guarding.

All the same, these very advantages were a source of personal concern. In a city, if one had to, one could disap-pear in two minutes. Just walk out into the street, turn the nearest corner, and fade into the crowds. But here!—with no people and no other buildings, there was nothing to fade into. There weren't even any trees. A police helicopter would spot you in no time. Besides, the city-bred Camano was simply out of his element when he was in the country, and he knew it; especially godforsaken country like this. The jumbled, brown moonscape of lava outcroppings and jagged boulders that surrounded the shack and went bleakly on for miles in every direction made him uncertain, threw him off balance.

That was why he had vetoed the idea of using it in the first place, when Gullveig, Stig, and Magnus had been all for it. But now things had changed, and they were lucky to have the place.

"Yes, all right, he'll have to be killed," he finally agreed, as if he hadn't decided on it the minute he'd heard that Bryan was in Reykjavik. "But not yet. We need him alive until this is wrapped up."

"Why?" asked Stig.

"In case there are more proof-of-life questions," Gullveig said knowledgeably.

"Exactly, Gullveig."

"When, then?" persisted Stig.

"Tomorrow, I think. I want to close down negotiations then, anyway. This is getting too damn ridiculous."

Stig nodded, satisfied. "I want to do it myself. I owe him."

Camano raised an eyebrow at him. *Not the way I do, you don't.* "We'll see," he said.

Chapter 34

It took me twenty minutes or so of tossing things around in my mind to conclude that I probably wasn't in any immediate danger; not tonight, anyway. Camano was knowledgeable enough to want me available in case more proof of my being alive was required before any money changed hands. And Julian, a stickler when it came to such things, was knowledgeable enough to demand it. Besides, the fact that they'd supplied me with a parka, shoes, blankets, and food had to mean that they preferred that I keep body and soul together for at least a little while. (Didn't it?)

But how long was a while? If I really intended to get out of here alive, I needed to get going on a plan now.

Okay. Plan.

Huddled over lunch (cheese, chicken-flavored crackers, beef jerky, and mixed nuts) with my coat zipped up and a blanket draped over my shoulders, I managed to come up with one. Not so much a plan, really, as a set of assumptions, based on the inferences and observations I'd gleaned over the last few days, on which a plan of sorts could be constructed.

Item: Getting out of here depended on getting the key to one of the two padlocks on the chain. This was surely the most firmly based of the assumptions.

Item: Camano would have the key on him. This was the flimsiest assumption, based on an equally shaky inference: On the first day of my captivity, when Gullveig had needed the key for my handcuffs, she'd asked Stig for it and his reply had been, "He keeps it. I'll get it from him." Well, who else could *he* be but Camano? And didn't *keeps it* imply that he kept it, not in a drawer somewhere, but on his person? And if he had the key then, wasn't it probable that he had it now? (I know, I know, I said it was shaky, didn't I?)

Item: Paris's sizeable ego had taken a huge hit when I'd ruined his Big Moment by professing to have no recollection of George Henry Camano.

Item: Because this had to be driving the man nuts, at some point before they did me in he would want to confront me with his identity and with the fact that, in the end, it was he who had bested me. But . . .

Item: There was palpable enmity and an underpinning of rivalry between Camano and Stig. Therefore, considering Camano's giant-size ego, he would be loath to have Stig hear about his bumbling past. Which meant that he had to keep it from Gullveig as well. Which meant . . .

Item: When he did come, he would come alone. It would be me, Camano, and the key, and that would be when I'd have to act. Or never.

I needed a weapon.

Chapter 35

On-scene witness interrogation of Svanhildur Hreinsdottir, recorded and transcribed by Constable Jónmundur Petersson, 0400, 04 April 2010.

Q. *Will you state your name and address?*

A: *My name is Svanhildur Hreinsdottir, and I live right here, at Digranesvegur 44, apartment 66 D.*

Q: *And about what time did you witness the incident you are about to describe?*

A: *Maybe an hour and a half ago.*

Q: *That would be about 2:30 a.m.?*

A: *About.*

Q: *Please tell me in your own words what you saw.*

A: *I was watching television—I don't sleep too well, and I was watching a program about lions on National Geographic, and I was just thinking about making myself a—"*

Q: *And you heard something?*

A: *Yes, I heard this tremendous crash, so I ran to the window, that window right there, and I saw that one of the ground-floor windows in D block was broken and there was a man lying on the ground in front of it, trying to get up, and he was holding something heavy, some kind of big box or crate in his arms, so I thought, well, he must be a burglar trying to get away. And sure enough, in a minute a bunch of people came running out—*

Q: *How many people?*

A: *Three, I think. Yes, three. And they just picked him up and took him back inside. And that was all.*

Q: *Would you be able to describe any of the three people?*

A: *Oh, no, it was dark.*

Q: *Could you tell if they were men or women?*

A: *(Shakes head.)*

Q: *Could you hear anything they were saying?*

A: *No, I didn't want to open my window.*

Q: *What about the man with the package in his arms? Could you tell what he looked like?*

A: *(Shakes head.) Well, he was a man, but don't ask me how I know. You can just tell.*

Q: *But you didn't dial 112 at that time?*

A: *No, because when they took him back I saw that he wasn't exactly walking straight, if you know what I mean, so I thought, well, I bet he wasn't a thief at all, he was just drunk and he fell through the window by accident. But then when they went back inside, the first thing they did*

> *was put some kind of big canvas up over the*
> *window so you couldn't see in. But there were*
> *shadows on it, on the canvas, and I could see*
> *that they were running around—there was a lot*
> *of activity, you know? For about half an hour,*
> *and then suddenly it was all quiet, as if they all*
> *left. Well, the whole thing struck me as kind of*
> *funny by then, and that's when I called 112. I*
> *hope I didn't bother you for nothing.*

Q: *No, ma'am, you did the right thing. Thank you*
   very much.

END OF TRANSCRIPT

Seated in the visitor's chair, Detective Sergeant Tinna Gudmundsdóttir waited politely, hands folded in her lap, until the detective chief inspector lifted his head, signifying that he'd finished the slim case file. "This happened more than sixteen hours ago," he said. "What has taken so long to inform me?"

"Unfortunately, I didn't see the report until four this afternoon, but, naturally, as soon as I read it I thought of Bryan Bennett."

"I understand. And so you went out to look for yourself?"

"Yes, sir. I've just come back from there. It's one of those new building complexes in Kópavegur, mostly still unoccupied—a perfect place to hold someone. And there's no doubt that that's where they had him. A tent set up in the middle of the living room, a cot, even a *BB* pressed into the rubber flooring. Also various—"

Ellert scowled. "A beebee?"

"His initials. Bryan Bennett."

"Ah."

"I tried to find out to whom it was rented, but the manager was away in—"

"Never mind about that right now. Put Halli on all that." He was leaning back in his chair, tranquilly puffing on the calabash, but his mind was spinning ideas. "They need to find someplace else in a great hurry," he said, thinking aloud. "They don't have time to go looking for another apartment to rent; they'll have to use someplace that's already available to them—but someplace well suited to hold a captive in secrecy." He lifted a shaggy eyebrow at her. "Does anything come to mind?"

Tinna looked at him. "You think . . . ?"

"I think. Can you leave in thirty minutes?"

"You want me to come with you?"

"I want you, I want Brynjar, I want Björn, I want Klemenz. Gummi too. If they're off duty, bring them in. Two cars. No, better make that three."

"WELL, well, well." With a shake of her head, Professor Emeritus Zeta Parkington gathered together the journals and printouts that Teddy had found for her and laid them aside. Her guesses about Bryan's condition had been confirmed. The young man was in for a few shockers when they next got together.

Good thing he was having himself a nice, relaxing week in Iceland right now.

Chapter 36

The temperature in the cave must have been near constant, but I got colder as the day wore on and the dampness and the chill worked their way into my bones. I spent most of the time squatting or lying on the mattress with my coat collar turned up, my hands in my pockets, and both blankets snugged around me. No sign of Camano, but Gullveig and Stig came for the usual jailhouse shakedown, during which I asked them for gloves. To my surprise, Gullveig came back a little later and tossed an old pair of mittens to me.

"I see no reason for unnecessary suffering," she said when I expressed my gratitude. Since Stig hadn't come with her, I assumed he was of a different opinion.

For the rest of the day, I was left to my own devices, which was all right with me, because I had work to do. Not long after dark the crunching of footsteps and the beam of a flashlight alerted me that someone was coming.

Be Camano, I urged.

And it was; the flashlight's jiggling beam illuminated his face briefly as he fumbled with the gate catch. *It had worked! He was here—and he was alone!* A combination of exhilaration and apprehension flared up in me like a match. I tore off the mittens, flung aside the blankets, and threw myself onto the mattress, curled up on my side and facing the entrance. I lowered my eyelids until my eyes were slits. Through a curtain of quavering eyelashes I watched him approach. It took all my willpower to keep still.

He stopped ten feet away and ran the beam over me. "Bennett."

I didn't respond.

"Bennett!"

I didn't respond.

"Bennett, I know you're not sleeping."

Nothing from me.

He hesitated and came closer. It seemed impossible for me to tense up any more, but I managed. I imagined I could hear my nerves twanging like piano wire.

He used a foot to nudge me in the ankle. I uttered a grunting noise or two, figuring it would be more convincing than complete silence. He did it again, in the hip this time, and closer to a kick. I made few more grunts and weakly, irritatedly flapped an arm at him. I realized with a little shock that I was imitating my father's reaction to attempts to rouse him from the semiconscious aftermath of one of his binges.

I could tell that Camano was now uncertain. He came a little closer and bent slightly down, shining the light directly into my face. I closed my eyes all the way.

"Bennett?"

I waited for the next kick, and the instant it came, my right arm, the upper one, swept out in an arc and encircled his legs behind the knees while my left hand grabbed his right ankle. A hard shove on the ankle, a simultaneous pull against the back of his knees with all my body weight behind it, and the knees buckled, the flashlight went flying, and he toppled over onto his back, scattering soup packets and juice cartons. I scrambled to my own knees and got hold of his shoulder as he began to struggle up. Although the flashlight had ended up pointing away from us, it provided enough reflected light for me to see the rapid progression of expressions that crossed his face, one after the other, in the space of two seconds: surprise, incredulity, anger.

He squirmed up and went for my eyes with his thumbs, but I twisted my face away, and he got his hands around my neck instead and squeezed. We were staring into each other's eyes, our faces only a few inches apart. I pressed the point of the weapon I had fashioned into the hollow at the base of his throat. Camano went stone still. His fingers eased up a little, but didn't come away from my neck.

"What the hell is that supposed to be?" he croaked.

"What does it feel like?" I said. I rotated the handle a bit so that he could see a little of it from the corner of his eye.

What I hoped it looked like, of course, was a knife. What it *was* was the hollow plastic flush lever from the toilet, into the narrow cavity of which I'd jammed the handle of a spork, first breaking off the two outside tines and leaving only the central one, which was intended to have the feel of a knifepoint.

Apparently it did. His fingers loosened a little more.

"Take your hands off my neck."

He hesitated, deciding. I took a chance and pressed the point a little harder into the yielding skin. Fortunately, it yielded more than the plastic-coated paper point, but not by much. Any more pressure on the point, and it would fold right up, but Camano folded first. He let go of my neck, otherwise keeping very still.

"Now lie down and turn over onto your side, facing away from me."

As he did, I kept the tine pressed against his neck from behind. "Now reach into whatever pocket you have it in and give me the key to the padlock."

"I don't keep it on me. Do you think I'm that stupid? I wouldn't—"

I pressed the spork a tiny bit harder into his throat—I didn't dare really lean into it because that lone, pathetic little tine was already bending. A spork, I was finding, wasn't any better at killing someone than at eating soup. "Don't make me kill you. If I have to, I will."

"All right, all right, hold it. Let me sit up. It'll make it easier."

"No."

He muttered a curse, pulled a key ring with one lone key on it from his hip pocket, and held it up.

I snatched it from his hand and took a step back, out of his line of vision. "Move, turn, and so help me God, I'll kill you right now," I said.

With my eyes never leaving him, it took me a while to find the key slot in the padlock, but eventually I did. Once I'd gotten it off, the arms of the collar spread open easily, and I took it off with a heartfelt sigh.

"All right, you can sit up now, but keep your back to me." I quickly slipped the collar around his neck, locked it to the chain, stepped back out of reach, and relaxed enough to rub the sore places on my neck. Then I picked up the flashlight. "Go ahead, you can get up now."

He got to his feet and faced me. Anger twisted his mouth like a knife scar. "I'll kill you for this, Bennett. You're going to die for this."

I tossed the key fifteen feet or so deeper into the cave. "That's for when they come to find you. If they come to find you. See you around, Camano." I found one of the mittens, picked it up, and started hunting for the other one.

He squeezed out a laugh. "Where do you think you're going to go? We're twenty miles from Reykjavik. We're twenty miles from anything. It's pitch dark. There's nothing out there but lava flow. No roads, no nothing. You'll freeze to death long before daylight, if you don't trip over a rock and break your head open first."

"I'll chance it." The truth was, my planning had taken me only as far as the cave opening. I was still working on part two.

"My people will see you. You're dead meat."

"I thought it was pitch dark." I was still hunting for the other mitten.

"All I have to do is yell and it's all over."

"Then why don't you?"

We both knew why he didn't. The lichen-covered walls of the cave swallowed up sound like acoustic foam.

"I'll kill you for this," he said again. "You can't get away."

"You'll enjoy the cuisine," I said. "I particularly recommend the chicken paste and crackers. The blackberry juice makes an excellent accompaniment, pleasingly tart, but not overly precocious." I gave up on the second mitten. "Well—"

"Sonofabitch," he said, and then, suddenly, he looked as if he'd taken a punch under the ribs. "*Sonofabitch!* You called me Camano! You . . . you knew who I was all along!"

"I wondered when you were going to notice," I said. I know, I should have been out of there by then, not standing around conversing with him, but revenge is indeed sweet and, to my shame (but not that much), I was soaking it up.

He stared. "You . . . you lied to me . . . *again!*"

"Looks like it. I guess you're just a slow learner. So long, George. I'll see that somebody comes for you."

As I turned to leave I realized I still had my nifty spork

combat knife in one hand. I tossed it to him. "Here, this came in pretty handy for me. Maybe you can use it too." I was discovering a new level of meanness in myself. It felt wonderful too.

It fell at his feet. When he saw what it was made of, he was apparently too enraged to speak, but he swelled up like a puffer fish—I swear, his eyeballs actually bulged—his head went back, he shook his fists, he opened his mouth, and he let out the most rabid, raging, animallike bellow of fury and impotence I'd ever heard come from a human throat. It beat my trifling panic whimpers by a mile.

"I'm sorry you're taking it like that, George," I said.

Walking to the entrance, I held the flashlight low and kept it pointing at the floor. A few steps shy of the gate, I turned it off altogether. It would have been prudent to stand there for a few minutes, letting my eyes adjust to the darkness before stepping out, but more than anything else I wanted out of that cave, and the instant I got the latch open I stepped eagerly out into the night . . .

Chapter 37

. . . $\mathbf{A}$nd was startled by a blinding barrage of light. All I could do was flinch away from it and throw my arm up over my eyes. Good God, what—

"Get him!" someone said harshly, and I was wrenched away, stumbling and still blinded, into the darkness on the other side of the lights. The hope drained out of me, and the resistance as well. I was as emptied as a collapsed balloon. There would be no more opportunities.

"I'm very glad to see you again, Bryan," said a quiet voice. "You're looking well, considering."

It took a second for the ball to drop. *"Ellert?"*

"Indeed, Ellert. Are you all right?"

I was so stunned that the best I could do was nod, openmouthed.

"Where are they, Bryan? Are they in the cave?"

"I don't believe it," I mumbled, staring stupidly at him. "How did you . . . how did you . . . ?"

He shook me by the shoulder. "Bryan! Are they in the cave?"

"He's . . . he's, um, yes, he's in the, the cave. Paris."

"Ah, so it *is* the famous Paris."

"Yes, Paris," I said, blinking, as both my vision and my command of speech returned. "But you don't have to worry about him. He's chained to the wall. The others, I don't know. They're around here somewhere. There are two of them—"

"They must be in the shack," he said. "We saw a light, but it went out as we approached." He nodded to a female sergeant standing beside him, who said something in Icelandic to another cop.

Following Ellert's gaze I saw that there was an old plank cabin a few yards from the cave entrance, unlit except for the brilliant bank of lights trained on it. The lights, I saw now, were the headlights and spotlights from three lined-up police cars. Ellert and I were standing behind the cars, along with four or five uniformed officers, with everyone's eyes focused on the silent shack.

The cop came back with a bullhorn for Ellert, who flicked it on and brought it up to his mouth.

"Ellert," I said, "things are likely to go better if you can do this without the bullhorn. We're not that far away from the cabin. They can hear you without it."

If he had a turf-conscious bone in his body, I hadn't been made aware of it yet. He nodded and put it down on the hood of the nearest car.

"And if you can call them by name, that'd be good too. Their names are—"

"Stig Trygvasson and Dagnyár Eyjólfsdóttir, otherwise known as Gullveig Válisdóttir."

I shook my head. "How did you find that out?"

"Dedicated police work, what else? There was also a third one, a professor, Magnus Haldórsson. But we found his body yesterday. Along with Baldursson's. Both apparently killed in the shootout."

"Oh. So Baldursson *is* dead. I thought so."

"And now," Ellert said, "we'd better get on with it." He cupped his hands around his mouth and shouted a rather long message in Icelandic toward the cabin, but there was only silence in response.

I took advantage of the wait to ask a question. "How the heck did you manage to find this place? And don't just say 'dedicated police work.'"

"But that's what it was. Once we learned the names of the VBJ members, we went out and talked to every relative and friend we could find, in hopes of learning where they had you. This cave belongs to the woman's uncle, and when we heard about it, it was the first place we looked, but it was deserted. So was every other potential hideout we looked at. However, after you raised that fuss at the apartment complex in Kópavegur last night—"

"You know about that too?"

He smiled. "You made it hard to miss. A man jumping out of a window—*through* a window—at two o'clock in the morning, attached to a bed, is likely to arouse the interest of the neighbors and result in a police report. It was soon clear that the man in question was you, and that you were no longer on the premises. Where would they have taken you—assuming they weren't annoyed enough to kill you? Well, the cave once again became the most likely place . . . and here we are."

"They're not answering, Chief Inspector," one of the officers said.

"Let's give them another chance." This time he tried in

English. "Stig, Gullveig, we know who you are. There is no way for you to escape. Come out of the building with your hands held up high. You have my word that you won't be—"

The cabin door was suddenly wrenched open. Framed in the doorway, pinned like a butterfly by the glare, Stig stood, squinting and agitated, with Gullveig in front of him. His left arm was clamped around her neck, and his right hand held a pistol to her temple: the quintessential hostage scene. Gullveig, head down and hands at her sides, looked even more than usual as if she were made of wood.

"I have a gun!" Stig yelled, briefly brandishing it before sticking it back in Gullveig's ear.

"We have five guns," Ellert replied calmly, "and every one of them is bigger than yours. What's more, we can see you, and you can't see us."

"If you think I won't kill her, you're wrong!"

"If you do, your brains will be all over the floor one second later. We have a sharpshooter trained on you right now."

I looked around. If there was a sharpshooter, he was remarkably well hidden. Ellert was a convincing liar.

"Where do you think this can go, Stig?" Ellert asked. He had a way of sounding quiet and calm even when he was shouting. "What can the end be? We can't simply walk away and let you leave, you know that." He had a good style, I thought. He'd make a good negotiator. "So simply release her, throw the gun down, and walk out. Slowly, hands up where we can see them. You have my promise that you won't be harmed."

"I'm warning you, I'm willing to give my life for what I believe, and I'll take her with me if I have to." Stig's voice was strong, but quivering with emotion. Christ, he's made up his mind to die, I thought; to martyr himself, as he probably saw it. He was working up his nerve to go through with it, and maybe to kill Gullveig as well.

"Ellert, can I help?" I said, when he raised his hands to his mouth for another shout.

He lowered his hands. "You're the expert."

What he expected was advice, but I had a nasty feeling that time was running out. I stepped briskly forward, shaking off his restraining hand, into the light. If Stig was surprised to see me free, he didn't show it. As for Gullveig, her eyes never came up from the ground in front of her.

"Stig," I called. "I know what you're thinking."

"You can't begin to comprehend what I'm thinking."

"You've already killed Baldur, there's no hope for you—"

"And don't think I'm not ready to kill you too, you goddamn parasite. Just keep talking."

"—but what happened to Baldur . . . that was a crime of passion. Unpremeditated. You didn't intend to do it. There are mitigating circumstances."

"You mean I'll only get ten years instead of twenty? I'd rather end it here and now."

It occurred to me that the last time I'd tried negotiating a real-time hostage situation two children had died. Despite the cold, sweat rolled down my sides and beaded up on my forehead and scalp. Lord, I didn't want any more dead bodies on my shoulders. I tried to keep my voice steady and not to speed up, but I could hear the words coming out in a rush.

"Stig, if you make them kill you now, that's the end of it; your side of things will never be heard. But if you come out of there, there'll be a trial. You'll have a chance to tell your story, to express your views in public. There'll be press coverage, tremendous coverage. You'll get TV interviews, newspaper interviews. All you want."

His lip curled. "Oh, sure," he said sarcastically, but then

his face showed some indecision. "Is that true, what he says?" He directed the question not to me, but to where he thought the police were. A good sign, I thought. He was looking for a way out, after all.

"Oh yes," Ellert replied serenely. "Very true, entirely true."

Stig came to a decision. He straightened up from where he had been hunched behind Gullveig, took his arm from around her neck, and threw the gun on the floor behind him.

You know those movies where the girl wallops the guy and decks him with one punch? Ridiculous, right? I mean, have you ever seen that happen in real life? Well, I'm here to tell you that it does happen in real life. The gun was still clattering on the wooden planks when Gullveig spun around, hauled back one strapping arm, and let him have it right in the chops. Stig's head wobbled, his eyes rolled up, and down he went, as boneless as a half-empty sack of flour.

I'm telling you, it gave me a warm, fuzzy feeling all over.

Chapter 38

Two Weeks Later

"Do you know who Elizabeth Loftus is?" Zeta asked me.

"Sure. Psychologist. Did some great work debunking the repressed-memory baloney a few years back. Used to be here at the U. She's down in California now, isn't she?"

"Yes, UC-Irvine. Are you familiar with her lost-in-the-mall experiments?"

"Mm, I don't think so, no."

"One tall brewed coffee, one café latte grande, no foam."

The call came from the barista behind the counter. We were in the University Way Starbucks, to which we'd walked from Zeta's office, where I'd told her what had happened in Iceland, and what the happy aftermath had been: Not only had there been no panic attacks since that night in the cave, but I had tried—and succeeded!—flying home without the aid of chemical assistance. Almost as gratifying, the scent of manure from farms on my way to work no longer got my adrenaline pumping, and I had eaten (and tolerated, if not quite enjoyed) a banana muffin one morning the previous week. As to cockroaches, I had yet to cross paths with one, but I was confident of a happy result.

In other words, as far as I could tell, I was liberated—not only from the wretched panic attacks, but from the whole devil's brew of unpleasantries that went along with them.

"Bryan, my boy, I'm absolutely delighted for you," she'd said. "I don't believe I've ever come across a case like this, even in the literature."

"Feel free to write it up," I said airily. "I have no objection to being a poster boy for flooding therapy. I endorse it whole-heartedly. Hey, you think there could be any money in it for me?"

She didn't crack a smile. "With your permission," she said soberly, "I *would* like to write it up." She paused. "But not for that reason."

"Not for what reason?"

"Not because of what you've been telling me."

I was puzzled. "Well, what then?"

"Let's go get a cup of coffee" had been her answer, and so here we were.

I went to the counter and came back with my latte and Zeta's coffee. "Okay, what about Loftus and her lost-in-the-mall experiments?"

"Well, there's been quite a string of them now, but let me give you the one that started it, the classic example."

A teenage boy named Chris, she said, had been given descriptions of four events in which he'd been involved as a child. All had been written by older relatives. Chris was told to write about all of these events for several consecutive days, offering whatever additional details he could remember as time went on. If he couldn't recall any, he was told to say so. What he didn't know was that one of the four "events" had never happened. It described an occasion when Chris, then five, had supposedly gotten lost at a shopping mall and had been found by a stranger who had reunited him with his family.

Over time, Chris "remembered" more and more about the incident. He'd wandered off to "look at the toy store, the Kay-Bee Toys." When he'd realized he was lost, his first thought had been "Uh-oh, I'm in trouble now." Before long he was "really scared." "I thought I was never going to see my family again." The helpful stranger who'd rescued him was recalled in detail: an old man, bald and bespectacled, and wearing a blue flannel shirt.

Chris was then told that one of the four memories was false; could he guess which one? He chose one of the real ones. When told that being lost in the mall was the false one, he had to be convinced before he finally accepted it. Since then, the fake-memory implantation method had been used in dozens of controlled experiments. Not everyone falls for the fake story, but plenty do.

I had listened both politely and attentively, and now I was waiting for the punch line, but Zeta only looked at me, her lips pursed.

"Okay," I said. "That's interesting, but why exactly am I being told this?"

"Bryan," she said soberly, "what if I told you that your memory of being kidnapped—the abduction, the fifty-eight days, the whole thing—is a false memory?"

I just stared at her. "Zeta . . ." was all I could get out for a few seconds. On the one hand, I could see she wasn't kidding, but on the other, I didn't see how she could be serious. "Zeta, I'm sorry, but that's ridiculous. I *know* it happened. Hell, my parents went into hock to pay off their share of my ransom. It ruined their lives."

"They did pay off part of the ransom, Bryan, but it wasn't for you."

"Wasn't for *me*?" I shook my head, as confused as I'd ever been in my life. "Zeta, you are really losing me here. . . ."

"I could use some more coffee," she said, standing up. "How about you, Bryan? I'll get it."

"No. Yes, please." I appreciated the minute or two she wanted to give me to myself, and indeed, I needed it. She hadn't told me much, but what she had was surpassingly weird.

I sat there staring at the tabletop trying to make sense of what she'd said. *No, how could it be? I remembered so clearly—*

She returned with black coffees for us both this time. "All right. You told me your parents never spoke directly to you about it afterward, but that you couldn't help overhearing their exchanges, right?"

"Yes, but if you're telling me it was a case of a six-year-old kid's misunderstanding of grown-up conversation forget it. They were talking about the kidnapping and all the money they'd had to come up with for the ransom, all right: whispers, arguments, recriminations—it ruined their marriage, ruined their lives."

"I don't doubt it. But it wasn't your kidnapping they were talking about, and not your ransom."

"This is supposed to be an explanation?"

"I don't seem to be doing a very good job of it, do I? All right, read this."

She undid the clips on her old-fashioned patent-leather clasp purse, took out a folded sheet of paper, and spread it open. On it was a poorly photocopied article from a newspaper or a magazine. "This is from *Hürriyet*, the English-language Istanbul newspaper. November 18, 1978. Read it."

I was apprehensive. Wherever this was going, I didn't like it "Do I really want to?"

"Read."

I took it from her and smoothed it out on the table.

ANOTHER ISTANBUL KIDNAPPING

November 18. The young American son of a Driscoll Construction Enterprises manager was abducted yesterday afternoon from a children's playground near the Pera Palace. Witnesses say the seven-year-old was—

"They've already got it wrong," I sneered. "I was five."
Don't ask me what point I was trying to make.

"Keep reading," Zeta said placidly.

—was abducted by four armed men and taken away in a gray Skoda sedan. Yavuz Cahit, a private Driscoll security guard, was shot three times as he tried to prevent the crime. As of this morning, he was in the intensive care ward at Taksim İlk Yardım Emergency Hospital, in serious but stable condition. The boy's younger brother, a five-year-old, was shot in the foot during the melee. He was treated at the hospital and released this morning. No word has yet been heard from the kidnappers. Police are pursuing several leads.

"No," I said. "They've gotten everything mixed up. Nobody got *shot* in the foot. And I *did* get kidnapped. Richard was the one they left behind in the playground."

She was slowly shaking her head. "No, Bryan. T̶
the way it was. I had the police in Istanbul c̶
records. It was your brother, Richard, who ̶

"But . . . but it's so clear in my mind . . . being put in the truck with a load of manure . . . living in that miserable dungeon . . . being beaten when I . . ."

The gray head continued to rock back and forth, wise and kindly. "No. What you remember is your parents talking about it. You assumed they were talking about you."

"No! Come on, Zeta. That's—hey, what about my little toe? Did I *assume* I didn't have it anymore?"

"No, you were shot in the foot during Richard's kidnapping," she said patiently, using her forefinger to tap the relevant place in the article.

"But . . ." It took me a moment to get my thoughts in order. "Look, there's a big difference here. This is nothing like that experiment. In that one, somebody explicitly made up a story to fool the kid with. His own relative told him it really happened. Well, surely nobody ever told me any made-up story about—"

"No, you made it up yourself. Look, those months during and after the kidnapping were a time of terrific stress for you and your family. Kids' antennae are very receptive to that kind of thing. You would have sensed the tension, felt the discord, known something was very wrong. You'd have heard the whispers: dribs and drabs about kidnappers, ransom, captivity. It was all beyond your six-year-old grasp, so your mind filled in the gaps for you to make it comprehensible."

I considered this. And rejected it. "Aw, no—"

"Bryan, according to the police records from 1978, the ransom—for Richard, not you—was asked for and was eventually paid. No toes were involved."

I was massaging my temples, trying to get my head around this. I still couldn't believe it. "But I'm telling you, I can see it all right now, as clearly as I can see you. It's not ~ome vague, dreamlike recollection, it's been burned into my mind. I can *see* those black hoods they wore, I can see—"

"Yes, just as Chris could see the blue flannel shirt and the glasses of the man who never was. No, Bryan, you were never kidnapped. It didn't happen."

"But—"

"And your brother, Richard, didn't die of polio. He never fully recovered from his imprisonment. He never even came home. He died in the hospital, two months after he was released."

"But I remember the polio epidemic—"

"There was a polio outbreak in Istanbul in 1978, yes, and you used it fill in one more gap. The hospital records show his cause of death as—and I quote: 'multiple respiratory and digestive infections and inflammations resulting from weakened immune system due to his two-month captivity in harsh circumstances.' I have the death report in my office. I'll give it to you."

Well, I couldn't see how I could argue with that, or with the police report. Reluctantly, I was coming around to believing her. (Odd, that one should be so unwilling to let go of the most terrible experience of one's life.) "Wow," I said softly. I had my cup in my hand, but I'd forgotten it was there.

Zeta was peering at me with a mix of personal and professional interest. "What's worrying you, Bryan? What are you thinking?"

"I'm thinking about Lori, actually, about what she's going to say when I tell her that all those panic attacks I woke her up with over all those years, all those stupid phobias that have narrowed her life as much as mine, all those trips we didn't go on because of me . . . it was all because of something that never happened—something I made up. That's what's worrying me. I mean . . . what's she going to *say*?"

She considered the question. "I'd be worried too," she said.

LORI was, if anything, more confounded than I was, but she took it better, and by the time I finished talking and we finished hugging, she was laughing.

"It was bad enough we could never go anywhere together because of what happened to you, and now I find out it never even happened? You owe me big-time, lover! World, here we come—Paris, London, Tokyo . . ."

COMING SOON

From Edgar® Award–winning author

Aaron Elkins

SKULL DUGGERY

Gideon Oliver and his wife are on vacation in Mexico when a local police chief requests his assistance on a case. Starting with a mummified corpse and a skeletal examination, Gideon soon discovers that two bodies have been misidentified, and their deaths could be related. Finding the connection between them will prove more dangerous than he could possibly imagine—and place him into the crosshairs of the killer he's hunting.

penguin.com

M435T0309

From the Edgar® Award-Winning Author of *Little Tiny Teeth*

AARON ELKINS

UNEASY RELATIONS

Buried ceremoniously, high in a cave on the Rock of Gibraltar, lies the skeleton of a human woman, clutching the skeleton of a part-Neanderthal child, who is quickly dubbed Gibraltar Boy by the world's press. Fascinated, Professor Gideon Oliver jumps at the chance to visit the site. But two deaths, possibly murders, have rocked Gibraltar. As Oliver tries to piece things together, he's about to fall for some deadly tricks. After all, unlike the Gibraltar Boy, he's only human.

penguin.com

M673T0310

Also from the Edgar® Award–winning author

Aaron Elkins

LITTLE TINY TEETH

Sailing the Amazon with a group of botanists, "Skeleton Detective" Gideon Oliver is on his dream vacation. But it turns nightmarish when fierce headhunters narrowly miss killing the group leader, and then a deranged passenger kills a botanist and flees. Long-past enmities and resentments—and new ones as well—might explain things. When a fresh skeleton turns up in the river, Gideon is sure that, in this jungle full of predators, humans may be the deadliest of all.

M434T0309

Don't miss any of the
Professor Gideon Oliver novels, with
"a likable, down-to-earth, cerebral sleuth"
(*Chicago Tribune*).

From Edgar® Award–winning author
Aaron Elkins

"Aaron Elkins is a gifted storyteller."
—*Midwest Book Review*

"Elkins has established himself
as a master craftsman."
—*Booklist*

SKULL DUGGERY

UNEASY RELATIONS

LITTLE TINY TEETH

UNNATURAL SELECTION

WHERE THERE'S A WILL

GOOD BLOOD

M432AS0310